THE SUMMER OF EVERYTHING

THE SEASONS OF BELLE SERIES: BOOK 1

MICHELLE MONTEBELLO

The Summer of Everything
Copyright © 2022 by Michelle Montebello
All rights reserved.

This book is a work of fiction. Any references to real events, real people, and real places are used fictitiously. Other names, characters, places, and incidents are products of the author's imagination and any resemblance to persons living or dead, actual events, organisations or places is entirely coincidental.

No part of this book may be reproduced in any form or by any electronic or mechanical means, including information storage and retrieval systems, without written permission from the author, except for the use of brief quotations in a book review.

Michelle Montebello is an Australian author and British English spelling is used in this novel.

ISBN: 978-0-6452296-3-9

Editing by Lynne Stringer and Marcia Batton
Cover Design by Kris Dallas Design

 Created with Vellum

For Eve and Connor,
You turn the bleakest days into sunshine.

And for Brett,
For all the seasons.

BLURB

For twenty years, Belle Hamilton has waited patiently for her partner Ben to propose. When he drops a spectacular bombshell on their relationship, everything she holds dear crumbles.

With her life in tatters, she packs her bags and heads to Europe, finding her way to the cobbled streets of Rome.

There she develops an unexpected relationship with Italian bartender Andre, while discovering that happiness can be found, and dreams can come true, if she follows her heart.

But it's not all smooth sailing for these start-crossed lovers. Past hurts and cultural expectations are a stubborn foe, and what always seemed so perfect between them may prove to be their ultimate undoing.

'Tis moonlight, summer moonlight,
All soft and still and fair,
The solemn hour of midnight,
Breathes sweet thoughts everywhere.
~ Emily Bronte

ONE

There was something about the seasons that Belle had always loved. As she paused at a city street crossing, afternoon peak hour heaving around her, she wondered what it was. Perhaps it was the transition of summer into autumn, resplendent hot days bowing to crisp burgundy mornings. Or perhaps it was the glittering beauty of winter, with its frost-bitten trees gently stirring with spring's rebirth.

Maybe it was the season's unyielding ways, infallible like the tide, morphing and circling with steadfast predictability, whilst at the same time being entirely unpredictable. Her relationship with Ben came to mind, and the way their years together spun in that same unyielding way. He was everything to her, every season—the thunderstorms and snow, the blue skies and autumn colours. The person who was there for her at the end of every day.

And yet, even now, after twenty years, when there was little left to discover about each other, he could still surprise her. Like the way he'd asked her out to dinner on a Wednesday night at his favourite restaurant when he should have been working late and she should have been at home cooking. That was Ben. Always two steps ahead, quicker than a heartbeat. He knew how to ruffle their sedate life, keep it ticking over. Although she had to admit, this time it felt different. This wasn't just an impulsive mid-week date night at Tetsuya's that he'd arranged. Ben had something on his mind.

She crossed the street, heading for the restaurant, horns blaring amidst a tidal wave of pedestrians. Ben had been acting peculiar for weeks now, leaving an odd energy in the air. At times he was preoccupied, at others he showered her with unusual amounts of affection, as though he were anxious and exuberant in equal measure. She'd even spied the robin egg blue Tiffany box at the back of their closet, beneath his ski gear, where she almost never looked but had happened to be rifling around when searching for an old photo album. She hadn't opened the box though, had just felt the glorious weight of it in her hand, wondering what bejewelled treasure lay within its satin interior.

An engagement ring perhaps.

She allowed herself an indulgent smile as she walked, the bottoms of her shoes squelching in a film of sugar and juice from the café she worked at. The big proposal. Could it be? Twenty years together was a significant amount of time, and it wasn't unreasonable to assume an engagement ring was hiding in their closet.

'It's only taken him twenty years. Better late than never, I suppose,' her best friend Riley had said, when Belle had confided in her. The fact that she'd uttered those words at all imparted further belief that it must be true. Although if Belle were completely honest, Ben was running slightly behind schedule.

By eighteen years.

Her only niggle was that she wished she'd had time to

run home and change. Her hands were still sticky from working the coffee machine all day and her café uniform was spotted with grease and sauce. A proposal deserved a beautiful dress, a face of dewy makeup, or at the very least, clean hands. But Ben had sprung this on her merely hours before, and she hadn't brought a change of clothes with her.

The restaurant was a block ahead, Tetsuya's on Kent Street, a favourite of Ben's, and eye-wateringly expensive. Her paltry waitress's salary wouldn't even cover the appetisers, and she always felt guilty eating there when she knew she couldn't hope to pay the bill. That, and all the other places Ben loved to go, never failed to remind her of her meagre earnings compared to his solicitor's salary. If he became junior partner soon, the gap between their wages would grow exponentially, and she would also be reminded of that other thing. That she'd yet to follow her dreams of becoming a chef because starting a family with Ben had always seemed imminent and all else was put on hold in anticipation.

Belle reached Tetsuya's and paused before the glass front doors to straighten her brown braids and dust off her clothes again. She checked her reflection in the glass, her petite frame and blue eyes staring back at her. Dining at Tetsuya's in her café uniform, with messy braids and squelching shoes was not what she'd had in mind for his proposal, and she cursed Ben again for giving her such little notice. Still, it was obvious he'd been nervous, the meeting a whim.

She pushed through the doors and was greeted by the maître d'. 'Hello. I'm meeting my partner this evening. The booking is under Ben.'

The maître d' cleared his throat pointedly, assessing her clothes. He glanced at his booking screen with a raised eyebrow, then looked up with a perfunctory smile. 'Benjamin Turner? He's already here. Right this way.'

She followed him through the restaurant, past tables of diners who gave her outfit a double-take, all the way to a table at the back. Despite the appalled stares at her clothes, her stomach cartwheeled at the thought of what was to come.

Years of being patient, of watching others tie the knot sooner, of feeling that slippery slope towards forty become slipperier without marriage or children, had finally come to this. She might not have been wearing the most glamourous outfit, but if she could count on anything, it was Ben's love for her. He adored her quirkiness, her casualness, and her braids. He loved that she preferred sneakers to heels and a quiet night at home instead of a noisy bar. While Ben was ambitious and focused, Belle was relaxed, with a gentle disposition. It had always created the perfect balance.

As they approached Ben's table, he rose to greet her, kissing her cheek. The maître d' slid out a chair for her and when she and Ben were both seated, he laid down menus, then scuttled back to the front of the restaurant.

Ben gave her a tentative smile, his hands fidgeting on the table. There were two empty glasses of scotch in front of him already. God, he *was* nervous. Butterflies flitted around her stomach, her throat dry.

'How are you?' he asked, glancing over her outfit. 'You came in your work clothes. I thought you'd go home and change first.'

Belle cringed. 'You hardly gave me time. I finished work at six. I had to rush straight over here.'

'It's just a waitressing job. Surely you could have asked to leave early.'

She ignored the slight as she picked up the menu. He

wanted the night to be perfect and she understood that, even if she had to tolerate the occasional jibe about her job. Sometimes he forgot that she'd put all her dreams on hold for their future, to be home in the evenings to cook and keep house while he concentrated on making junior partner. If she were a chef, she'd work sixteen-hour days with rarely a day off and they'd hardly see each other, let alone be able to start a family. But she was the first to admit they'd become stuck in a holding pattern. Her dreams were shelved and yet somehow having children had become just as elusive.

A waiter arrived to take their drinks order and as she watched Ben order a third scotch and a glass of wine for her, she had no regrets. He was her first love, her only love— there had never been anyone else in her life. High school sweethearts, best friends forever, soul mates. She loved his ocean blue eyes, the way his brilliant mind worked, his soft brown hair that was always tousled after a day in court, like he'd run his hands through it a thousand times. Her heart soared at the prospect that the little blue Tiffany box could be tucked away in his pocket at that very moment.

She flipped open the menu, wondering when he planned to ask. Before dinner? Afterwards? Would he get down on one knee? Her mind could hardly latch onto a single thought with the anticipation. 'What's the special occasion?'

Their drinks arrived and Ben quickly gulped back half of the scotch, setting his glass down on the table. 'I just thought dinner with you would be nice.'

'But we never eat out on a Wednesday night.' She raised an eyebrow at him.

He leant forward and reached for her hand, which she gave him. He rubbed his thumb fondly over her fingers. 'See, that's the thing, Belle. Why haven't we done more of this? On a Monday, on a Wednesday, whenever. Haven't you noticed that we never seem to go out anymore? And if we do, it's always planned. We haven't been spontaneous in years.'

Belle set down the menu and considered his words. He had a point. They hadn't been impulsive in a long time. Their social life was carefully crafted around his career and her shifts at the café. If she were perfectly honest, she preferred staying at home anyway, experimenting in the kitchen with new recipes, having him taste for her, feeling especially proud when he loved the dishes she made. She enjoyed eating at restaurants occasionally for the learning and inspiration it brought, but her own kitchen was where she loved to be most.

'I just feel like the spice has gone from our lives, you know?' he said.

She tried not to let his words sting, focusing instead on how they could make things better. 'Okay, so how do we fix that?'

He smiled sheepishly. 'Well, that's why I asked you here tonight. Because I have something important to tell you.'

'You do?' This was it; he was going to ask her. How long had she waited for this moment?

'You know I love you more than anything, right?'

'Yes.'

'And since high school, it's only ever been you.'

'Of course,' she whispered. 'You're the love of my life too.'

'Well...' He took a deep breath. 'I've met someone else.'

Belle wasn't sure she'd heard correctly. She almost asked him to repeat the words, but a strange ringing had started in her ears and extended to her brain, so she could no longer focus on anything. The room began to spin, and her seat felt like it had fallen through a hole in the floor, and she was tumbling fast.

'Belle, did you hear me?' Ben's voice came from far away.

She shook her head, trying to blink away the moment, but no matter how hard she tried, Ben was still there, staring at her, an incomprehensible confession laid out before them. 'I'm sorry, you what?'

'I've met someone else.'

She glanced down at her hand in Ben's, his thumb still caressing her fingers, hands that knew her body, that had held her, loved her, and dried her tears. She swallowed, but it was painful to get past the lump in her throat. 'You've met someone else? What does that mean?'

He dropped his gaze, staring at his scotch. 'It means I met a girl. Someone I like.'

Belle fought for words, but they stuck to the roof of her mouth like peanut butter. 'A girl. When? How?'

He ran his free hand through his hair and shrugged. 'I don't know. It just happened.'

'How does *that* just happen?'

He glanced up again and met her eyes. 'I didn't mean it to. I wasn't out looking for her. We just met and we clicked.'

Belle wrenched her hand away as if she'd been burned. She leaned back in her chair, still trying to process his revelation. This wasn't a proposal. This was the world being tipped on its side. 'Who is she?'

'Her name's Olivia. I met her through work. She's a solicitor too, at my firm. We spend a lot of time together and it developed into more.' He watched her warily as she sat staring at him, dumbfounded. 'I'm so sorry, Belle.'

'But...' She had a million questions, none that she could

put into logical sequence. She was reeling too much to know where to start. 'I don't understand. Developed into what?'

'I have feelings for her,' Ben clarified. 'We get along well. She's fun and spontaneous, exactly what's been missing from our relationship.'

'If you wanted *fun*, you could have just asked me,' she retorted.

He flinched but didn't reply.

'What's happened between the two of you? Have you been out together? Kissed? Have you had sex?'

He let out a breath, not meeting her eyes.

'Oh, God.' She clutched her stomach. She was about to throw up. 'You haven't, have you?'

Ben's shoulders slumped as he finally looked at her. 'I could lie and tell you no.'

Belle felt the moment her heart cracked in two, like a physical wound. She looked around the room, certain everyone was watching her, laughing at her pain.

Ben sat back in his chair; guilt etched into his expression. 'I didn't mean for this to happen. I've been struggling with us for a while. I just didn't know how to tell you.'

'But you could have,' she said, tears threatening at the corners of her eyes. 'You could have sat me down and told me you were unhappy, and we could have fixed this.'

'I know. But I thought it would pass. Then I met Olivia and I realised just how unhappy I was. By then, it was too late. I didn't want to stop seeing her.'

The waiter arrived to take their order, but one look at their solemn faces and he cleared his throat. 'Shall I give you another few minutes?'

'Please,' Ben said.

The waiter left and Ben returned his eyes to Belle's, searching them. 'Are you okay?'

'Do I look okay?' she snapped.

'I didn't mean to hurt you.'

'Are you having a mid-life crisis?' she asked a little too loudly, causing several tables to glance their way.

Ben's face turned crimson. 'Will you keep your voice down? And no, I'm not having a mid-life crisis. I'm only thirty-eight.'

'And I'm thirty-five. I should be having children, not being cheated on by my partner.'

He sighed and had the good grace to look as miserable as she felt.

'I thought you were going to propose,' she said.

His expression tightened with confusion. 'Propose?'

'I found a Tiffany box behind your ski clothes, up on the top shelf of the closet. I didn't look inside it. I assumed it was an engagement ring.'

'Oh, Belle.' He closed his eyes, reaching for her hand again, but she didn't give it to him. 'That wasn't for you and it's not an engagement ring. It's a diamond bracelet for Olivia. I saw it when I was walking past Tiffany's and I... well, I bought it for her. I haven't given it to her yet. I felt guilty about it, so I thought I'd hold off until you and me... until we...' He pulled his hand back off the table and slumped further down into his chair. 'This is bad. I'm so sorry. You were never meant to find that.'

How had it come to this? How had she missed the signs? All those late nights he'd spent at the office while she was at home cooking. Had he been with Olivia all those times? Had he been wining and dining her, taking her to hotels so they could sleep together? Or had their lust become a reality in Belle's bed? Her vision swam with the thought of them tainting her sheets.

'Did you still want to order dinner?' Ben asked.

She almost laughed at him. 'You can't be serious. I'm not even sure why you brought me here. Couldn't you have told me you were cheating on me in privacy? Did I need to be humiliated in public?'

He winced. 'I figured you'd be less inclined to throw something at me if we were here.'

'Jerk!'

'I deserve that.'

She stood abruptly, surprising herself and almost knocking her chair over. 'I'm leaving.'

He nodded forlornly. 'Okay.'

'Are you coming?'

He glanced up at her. 'What do you mean?'

'Are you coming home so we can talk about this?'

'Belle, I...' He cringed. 'I don't want to go home. I want to sell our place.'

As if his confessions hadn't caused enough pain, the blade plunged deeper inside her. 'Sell our place? What are you talking about? We love that house.'

'It doesn't feel right to keep it if we're not together anymore.'

'Not together?' She shook her head, confounded. 'But we haven't even talked about this. You've dumped it all on me now and I'm supposed to be okay with it? Don't I get a say in our relationship? If I even want to sell the house?'

'What's there to say, Belle?' he said, looking pleadingly up at her. 'It's over.'

The ringing had returned to her ears, and she clutched the back of her chair as the room tilted again. She'd just managed to process his infidelity, and on some level, even wondered if they could move past it, but the word 'over' felt a hundred times more final than anything he'd said before it.

'I'm going to stay with Olivia for a few days, to give you space,' he said.

The flood of tears Belle had fought to keep at bay were straining against her eyelids. She didn't want space. She wanted Ben. She wanted all their days and months and years before this moment to come back so she could catalogue what went wrong and try to fix it. 'Won't you even come home tonight?'

'No,' he said, dropping his gaze to the last of his scotch in the glass. 'It's not a good idea. I don't want to confuse things.'

Although she wanted to wrap her arms around him and beg him to reconsider, to not throw away the last twenty years, she couldn't stand there any longer being silently judged by the other diners for wearing her food-splattered uniform. Ben, with his mind so clearly made up, wouldn't look at her.

She swallowed away the hurt, her heart shattering into a million tiny pieces right there in the restaurant, realising for the first time that while he was her one and only, she wasn't his. Not anymore. Ben had outgrown her. She turned swiftly and left the table, certain that he would call her back before she reached the front doors. That he'd cry out that he'd made a mistake, that he was a fool.

But he didn't. He let her go, and perhaps that hurt just as much as his infidelity.

He'd given up on them.

TWO

Belle let herself into their house an hour later. The hallway reverted to darkness as soon as she closed the door, and she could barely muster the energy to find the light switch.

She'd had to wait an hour for a bus home, and the tears had come as she'd queued in a line of commuters. She'd tried to cry silently into a disintegrating tissue, but at some point, her tears had transformed into noisy sobs that she couldn't mask, drawing the stares of people around her. By the time she'd stepped off the bus in Pyrmont, on the other side of the city, she was so mentally exhausted she could no longer think straight, trudging the block home and turning her key in the lock.

She dropped her bag onto the floor and kicked her sneakers off, but she didn't continue down the hall to the kitchen. She didn't turn the light on. She didn't scream or vent or throw a vase. She was numb, her limbs like lead as she slid down the hallway wall and crumpled onto the tiles.

All the questions she should have asked Ben rushed over her. Who was Olivia? What made her so special? And how could Belle be replaced so quickly? But had it been quick or had their affair been going on for much longer? Just how many months had Ben been cheating? Sharing their bed while he thought of another. It seemed that Belle had blinked, and the rug of her relationship had been pulled out from under her.

She knew what her mother would say. *Come home. We'll work this out together.* Or her father. *You always were a little out of his league.* Or Riley. *Good riddance to him!*

One thing she knew for certain was that she couldn't spend the rest of the night sitting on the floor of her hallway. And she couldn't stay in her house of lost dreams, surrounded by the detritus of her relationship. She had to leave, but to go where? Where could she outrun her pain?

She fumbled along the hallway floor for her bag, rummaged inside for her phone, and dialled Riley's number.

'Of course you can stay at mine,' Riley said without hesitation. 'Do I need to ask why?'

'No,' Belle said flatly.

'Did something happen with Ben?'

'I don't want to talk about it.'

Riley was silent. Belle held her breath, praying she wouldn't enquire further. She didn't have the strength to relay what she was still processing herself. 'Well, I'm out for the evening and I probably won't be back until tomorrow morning,' Riley said. 'Just ask Darius at reception to let you in. He has a master key. I'll call him now to let him know.'

Belle exhaled in gratitude. 'Thanks. Where are you?' Although she already knew the answer to that question.

'In an apartment on the North Shore with a very handsome police officer,' she said.

'On second thought, you don't need to tell me.' Belle wasn't sure she had the emotional fortitude for Riley's latest dalliance. She didn't want to know that the world outside still turned, while hers had come to a staggering halt. She didn't want to know of love or happiness, and she certainly didn't ever want to smile again. All she wanted to do was lie down, close her eyes, and wish the whole terrible nightmare away.

BEFORE SHE'D OPENED her eyes, Belle could smell the bitterness of coffee and the fat from bacon frying in a pan. It drifted in through her partially closed door, enticing her awake, reminding her of where she was. Not in her bed back at her lovely Victorian terrace in Pyrmont, with its pretty floral coverlet and comfortable cotton sheets. Not beside the man she loved and who was supposed to love her, the weight of his arm resting securely over her as he slept. No, she was in Riley's spare bedroom, with its unfamiliar eiderdown quilt and Egyptian sateen pillowcase that her head kept slipping off.

She rolled over, trying to fall back to sleep, but Ben's infidelity came surging again like a hurricane. He'd fallen for another woman—kissed her, touched her, severed a sacred bond. Just how unhappy had he been to fall into someone else's arms, an unhappiness he'd never hinted at before? It left her feeling cheated in more ways than just the affair. Cheated of the chance to right a wrong she hadn't known existed.

Belle would have remained in bed all day if she could have, but Riley's muttered expletives reached her ears, and when she heard a dish shatter on the tiles, she groaned and pushed the covers away. Slipping into the only pair of sensible pyjamas she could find in Riley's drawer, she padded out of the room. She'd left her house the night before still wearing her uniform, not even pausing to pack a bag with spare clothes and toiletries.

'Morning!' Riley was on all fours on the kitchen floor, scooping up shards of broken crockery.

Belle almost forgot her misery and broke into a confused smile. 'What are you doing?'

'I dropped a plate trying to cook breakfast.'

'You don't cook breakfast.'

'For you, I'm willing to make an exception.'

Belle stepped over Riley on the ground. 'Here, let me cook instead.'

'Thank you.' Riley stood with several large pieces of crockery in her hands. 'I have to leave for work soon.'

'It won't take a minute.' At the stove, Belle scrunched up her nose at a pan of charcoaled bacon and fried eggs that resembled rubber. 'Well, this is beyond edible.'

Riley opened the lid of the bin and tossed the broken pieces in, returning to the floor with the dustpan and broom to sweep up the rest. 'It's probably best you start again. I'm surprised I even knew how to turn the stove on.'

'There's hope for you in the kitchen yet.' The grief she felt over the loss of her relationship subsided a little as she lost herself in her other great love—the preparation of food. She collected bowls, a whisk, and a sharp knife, then hunted through Riley's fridge and pantry, searching for ingredients.

'Did you have any problem getting in last night?' Riley asked.

'No, Darius was lovely as usual. He let me straight in,' Belle replied. 'I hope you don't mind. I borrowed some pyjamas. I found a new toothbrush in your bathroom too.'

'They're *my* pyjamas?' Riley cringed at the pink flannel with piglets on them. 'I didn't know I had those.'

Belle chuckled. It was the only flannel pair she had

found amidst the red lace and black chemises. 'Would you like hotcakes with maple bacon or baked eggs with mushrooms and goat's cheese?'

'I wouldn't eat that goat's cheese.'

Belle glanced at the expiry date and gagged. 'It's six months old! I'll make hotcakes and bacon.' She retrieved the offending cheese and tossed it into the bin, followed by the charred remains in the pan. 'What time did you come in last night? I heard you creeping down the hall.'

'It was five this morning, actually. And I was quiet.' Riley poured the last of the broken crockery pieces into the bin, her eyebrow raised. 'You must have been wide awake.'

Belle shrugged as she laid rashers of bacon on a tray and slid it into the oven. 'Probably.'

'Want to talk about it?' Riley pulled coffee cups down from the cupboard.

Belle didn't want to. Talking about it made it real and she wasn't prepared to accept that Ben's betrayal hadn't been part of some strange nightmare.

'Let's start with coffee then,' Riley said. '*That* I can make.'

Belle smiled reluctantly. Yes, she needed coffee, something to push through the fog of exhaustion and disbelief. While Riley operated the coffee machine, she concentrated on combining milk and eggs in a bowl and whisking them, before sifting flour in. It was easy to forget her troubles when she had a whisk in her hand or a pan on the stove, when dough needed rolling or there was chocolate to temper. She found the ritual of slicing and baking, stirring, or frying a source of comfort, preferring it after a long day at work in the same way someone might prefer a stiff drink.

Cooking was like an obsession—she felt it in her bones. To realise now that she was thirty-five and had shelved her dream of becoming a chef for the fantasy of starting a family was like a kick to the stomach. Ben had never appreciated her sacrifices. He'd always thought her desire to cook was a bit silly.

'That's not a real career,' he'd once said to her. 'It's more like a hobby.'

Who did he think created those expensive dinners he ate at Tetsuya's? Someone just fluffing about in the kitchen? Like her father, if you didn't study law or something equally respectable, your dreams weren't worth his consideration.

'You're going to whisk right through my two-hundred-dollar mixing bowl if you're not careful,' Riley said, setting a coffee down in front of her.

Belle relaxed her arm. She hadn't realised she'd been taking her frustration out on the eggs. 'Sorry. I got carried away. Who buys a two-hundred-dollar mixing bowl, anyway?'

'Someone who never uses it.' Riley slid onto a bench stool to watch her. 'It's beside the point. Are you going to tell me what's going on?'

Belle sighed and closed her eyes, but when she opened them again, Riley was still watching her with expectation. She avoided her gaze, turning away to pull the tray of bacon out of the oven so she could brush maple syrup on the rashers. 'I'm fairly certain Ben and I are over.'

Riley, who'd been slouching, sat upright on the stool. 'Over? What do you mean?'

'He told me last night at dinner that he's met someone else.' They were words she'd never dreamt of uttering this time yesterday, words she never thought she'd utter in this lifetime, and yet there she was, saying them out loud in Riley's kitchen.

It was clear Riley was shocked, but to her credit, she

quickly fixed her face in an unsurprised look, as though she'd just been told it might rain later. 'That's what he said?'

'Yes. That he met a girl—a lawyer. Olivia. Apparently, she's lots of fun, the opposite of me.' Belle blinked rapidly, trying to stave off tears, as she returned the tray of bacon to the oven, then set a clean pan on the stove, turning the heat to medium.

'And what has he done with this girl?' Riley asked. 'A few dates. A kiss?'

'Everything,' Belle mumbled, adding butter to the pan, watching it sizzle.

Riley sat back in her chair; her lips pursed as though she'd tasted something sour. 'Well, I didn't think he had it in him.'

'That's extremely unhelpful,' Belle scolded, pouring a scoopful of pancake batter into the pan.

'So, what now? Is he going to pursue it with this... what's her name? Olivia.'

'It's serious with her. He told me we were over. He wants to sell the house.' Belle forced down the indignation of it again, concentrating instead on flipping the pancakes.

'Did he ever tell you he was unhappy?'

'Not until last night. Until it was too late, which is no good to me. What am I supposed to do now? I can't fix us; I can't glue us back together. I can't do anything because he left it until the damage was done, until he was already emotionally involved with someone else to tell me there was a problem.'

'That's why I don't do relationships. No good can come from them,' Riley said, sipping her coffee.

'Again, extremely unhelpful.'

'I'm just saying,' Riley said. 'You gave that jerk twenty years. And for what? You're right back where you started.'

Belle should have known better than to expect words of comfort from Riley. She was hardly measured when it came to men, bed-hopping from one to the next, enjoying fleeting one-night stands, then slinking away before they woke, refusing to take their calls.

For the first time, Belle admired her friend's stoic ability to keep her heart closed to love. She'd given everything she had to Ben—her heart, her loyalty, her love, and what had it amounted to? Riley was right—she was back where she started, a naïve sixteen-year-old girl with a pocketful of dreams and no idea how the world really worked.

'Have you heard from him since?' Riley asked.

Belle gave a helpless shrug. 'I texted him late last night, to ask him if it was really happening. He just replied, "yes, sorry".'

'Yes, sorry?' Riley scoffed and shook her head. 'He owes you a lot more than a "yes, sorry".'

With a stack of pancakes ready and the tray of maple bacon out of the oven, Belle served them breakfast and took up the seat beside Riley at the bench.

Riley shoved a forkful of pancakes into her mouth. 'I'm starving. That police officer wore me out.'

Belle grimaced. 'I'm trying to eat breakfast.' But she had little appetite anyway. She was simply going through the motions, like talking and breathing. Her one saving grace was that she had a day off from the café and wouldn't need to front customers with bloodshot eyes and a tired face.

As she picked at her food, listening to Riley gobble down hers, her eyes wandered to a stack of mail on the benchtop. Beside it was a printed copy of a flight itinerary. She didn't mean to snoop, but the date and destination caught her eye and she slid it towards her. 'What's this?'

'Hmm?' Riley was still shovelling pancakes into her mouth.

Belle held the itinerary up. 'Are you going somewhere?'

Riley glanced at it, then swallowed. 'Oh, that. Yeah. I'm thinking of taking a trip.'

'You're *thinking* about it? This flight leaves in six weeks.'

She waved a hand at it nonchalantly. 'I booked it on a whim, to London. It's nothing.'

'Nothing?' Belle placed her fork down and glanced over the itinerary again. 'This is a one-way ticket. There's no return flight. How long are you going for?' She felt a flutter of panic in her stomach.

'I don't know. A few weeks. A year. Maybe indefinitely.'

'Indefinitely?' She knew she was repeating Riley's words, but she was shocked, each revelation stunning her harder than the last. 'When were you going to tell me that you were leaving indefinitely?' Not only was she shocked, she was also hurt.

Riley shrugged. 'I would have, eventually. But to be fair, up until yesterday, you had Ben. I didn't think you would care.'

Belle's shoulders tensed. 'That's a terrible thing to say. I would always care if you packed up and left.'

'It's not a big deal,' Riley said. 'Like I said, I'm undecided about how long I'm going for.'

But it *was* a big deal. How long had she lived with her eyes closed? First, her boyfriend was keeping things from her, now her best friend. Had she been so oblivious to everything and everyone that life had marched on without her? 'Why are you leaving?'

Riley sighed and put down her fork. 'Because I'm tired of Sydney. Tired of my life. Tired of doing the same old thing and seeing the same old people. And yes, you're my best friend, but you've been occupied for the better part of twenty years. And I've always respected that. But at some point, I need to live my life too. I'm not living it right now. I'm just existing.'

'Well, take up a sport or a dance class with me. You don't have to move to London.'

'I need to do something different. I'm lonely, Belle. I just am.' She slid out of her seat and collected her plate and cup, walking to the sink and setting them in it. Her shoulders sagged, as though her larger-than-life existence had deflated like a balloon. Her back was still to Belle when she spoke again. 'If you need to, you can stay here until I leave. I'd be happy for the company.'

There was so much for Belle to wrap her head around that all she could muster was a grateful, 'Okay.'

'After I leave, and you sell your house, you can still stay. I'll have the lease transferred into your name.'

'I'd never be able to afford this place on my own.'

'You could advertise for a flatmate.' Riley turned and offered her a small smile.

'Maybe.' Belle tried to return it but found it difficult. How could she smile when nothing about the future seemed certain anymore?

THREE

Riley left for her job at the art gallery in Paddington shortly after breakfast and Belle, with little to distract her from the interminable hours ahead, decided she should go home to the Pyrmont terrace and pack a bag. She would need clothes and toiletries but mostly, she was hoping to catch Ben there. It was illogical to assume she would, given it was already midday and he'd be at work, but she'd grown desperate. She'd considered calling him—there was so much from their conversation the night before that was unfinished—but every time she picked up her phone, her fingers stalled on his number. What could she possibly ask him? *Have you changed your mind yet?* She knew what his answer would be. *No.*

Sleep deprived and teary, she showered and slipped back into her café uniform, then climbed into her car parked downstairs. She arrived in Pyrmont twenty minutes later and turned the car off in front of her house.

That lovely, renovated Victorian terrace, purchased ten years ago after she and Ben had fallen in love with it, stood before her, a beacon of everything she struggled to hold on to. Their future had been so certain back then. She remembered his smitten smile the day they'd inspected the house. He'd galloped up the narrow staircase to the second floor, stepping out onto the balcony and whooping with joy at the sliver of city skyline peeking through the trees. Despite the age and the cracked walls and the time and money they would need to pour into it, he'd declared there and then that they would make an offer, that they had to have it, no matter the cost. She'd been so proud of him, so giddy with love that her heart had almost burst. Their dream house for their dream future.

Oh, life had been full of promise back then. He hadn't cared that she'd worked in a café or that their life was sedate. He'd loved her more than anything in the world, content with what they'd had.

Belle had never suffered heartbreak before, this foreign, nauseating, blade-twisting emotion. Now, as she let herself into the house and walked into her cold, silent kitchen, she wanted nothing more than to throw herself to the floor and refuse to leave quietly. Equally, she wanted to run and hide from the whispers in the walls, from every happy memory she'd ever had in that beautiful house because it all felt tainted now.

It was almost midday and sunlight moved across the back door, spilling over the walls. She was right—he wasn't at home, and there was no opportunity to speak to him in person, so a phone call would have to suffice. She fished her phone out of her jacket pocket and found Ben's number in her recently dialled list. He was always at the top, the only person she ever rang, and she tapped his name to call him.

Ideally, he'd be at lunch and able to talk, but her hopes

were dashed when he answered sounding annoyed. 'What's wrong?' he snapped before she had a chance to say hello. 'I can't talk right now.'

Belle flinched. 'Hi.'

He paused and she knew he was running his hand guiltily through his hair. 'Sorry. Hi.'

'Are you at lunch?'

'No. I'm about to walk into court.'

'Oh. I just...' She had seconds before he hung up on her, but with a head full of clutter and not knowing where to start, she floundered.

'Is there a reason you called?'

'We need to talk.' The words burst out of her. 'It can't end like this.'

'You want to have this conversation now?' he hissed through clenched teeth. 'I'm about to cross-examine.'

'Not now, but later.'

'I said everything I needed to say last night.'

'But I miss you. I'm not ready for any of this. Can't we talk? Please. All I want to do is understand.' *And to change your mind. To beg you to come back to me.*

He sighed, exasperated. 'Fine. I'll call you later tonight.'

'Are you coming back here? I could wait around until this afternoon. We could talk properly.'

'You're at the house?'

'Yes.'

'I wasn't planning on it. I'm staying at Olivia's for a few days.'

'But Ben—'

'Look, I can't do this now,' he growled. 'I'll call you later.'

Before she could ask what time to expect his call, he'd

hung up on her. She stared at the phone, uncertain if she felt better or worse for speaking with him. She couldn't recall a time when he'd ever sounded so thoroughly irritated with her, a renewed reminder of how quickly their relationship had disintegrated. But she had their call later to look forward to, and next time she wouldn't be hindered by spontaneity.

She spent a few more minutes lingering in the sunlight until it moved on and she was cast back into the shadows, then she went to pack her bag. It was the first time she'd been inside their bedroom since Ben had delivered his staggering blow. The bed was still neatly made, for neither of them had slept in it the night before, and she noticed that several of Ben's belongings were missing—two pairs of shoes, his toiletries, some shirts, and business suits. He must have returned at some point to collect them.

The realisation was even more gut-wrenching when she went to the closet, flung open the doors and stood on tiptoes to reach behind his ski clothes. Sure enough, the Tiffany box was gone. He'd wasted no time gifting Olivia the diamond bracelet. Had she cried tears of joy when he'd slipped it onto her wrist, wrapping her arms around him, thinking smugly to herself, *you're mine now*? Did she wonder about Belle, the broken woman left behind?

Belle collapsed onto the bed, her chest heaving with sobs that came from way down in her soul. And although her eyes were too raw and swollen for more tears, they filled anyway, stinging her eyelids. She remained that way until the afternoon found her, curled up in a ball on the bed, crying, the room growing cold with the fading light.

An hour later, she forced herself up—defeated, deflated. It felt like someone else's hands collected her belongings and stuffed them into a bag for her. She hardly remembered the act of it, only that fifteen minutes later, she had a backpack full of things, her pillow under her arm and a heart so completely shattered she wasn't sure it would ever mend.

FOUR

Belle arrived back at Riley's later that afternoon. Riley was hosting an exhibition at the gallery and would be out until late, so to pass the time until Ben called, Belle found several empty drawers in the spare room and neatly pressed her clothes into them. Even with distraction the apartment was too silent.

Closer to dinnertime, she distracted herself in the kitchen, making a salad that she wouldn't eat, and checking her phone every few seconds for Ben's call. She wished she'd asked him what time she could expect it so she could mentally prepare herself. The wait was agonising.

By eight pm, she still hadn't heard from him, and the walls were closing in on her. She dropped him a text, asking if she should ring him instead. After no reply, she tried calling, only to be greeted by his voicemail. Nine o'clock became ten o'clock and by midnight, she safely reasoned that he wasn't going to call. That the twenty years they'd shared hadn't been worth his time.

She shouldn't have been surprised as she stared at her phone screen, which remained hurtfully blank, the minutes ticking past midnight. She'd felt him slipping away in that awkward, unpleasant phone call earlier that day when she'd begged him to talk to her and he'd reluctantly agreed, as though she were a persistent cough he couldn't shake. If there had been any doubt about how keen Ben was to end their relationship, there could be little of it now.

THE NEXT MORNING, Belle was back at the café. Even something as mundane as serving coffee and slices of cake provided a welcome distraction, relieved to put Ben and Olivia out of her mind for a few hours.

After work, she boarded a bus back to Riley's, but any hope of finding her friend there for company was quickly dashed when she was greeted by the silent apartment again. *Working late*, Riley texted her shortly after. *Don't wait up for me.*

Faced with the prospect of another night alone, Belle called her mother. It was something she'd been putting off, the act of telling people what Ben had done, which she felt reflected poorly on her rather than him. *The girl who couldn't keep her man happy. Twenty years and she couldn't tie him down.*

There was no getting out of it—she would have to tell her parents the news, particularly as Ben and her father were close. It was a relationship she had nurtured over the years, proud of the bond that had formed between them. Ben was like the son her father had never had, especially since she'd failed so miserably in following in her father's footsteps. When your boyfriend was a solicitor and your father a supreme court justice, it was hard to ignore the 'waitress' in the family.

At least her mother was happy to hear from her. 'I thought you'd fallen off the edge of the Earth,' she chided.

'Sorry. I've had a lot on.'

'I'm just about to put a roast in. Have you eaten yet?'

'No.'

'How quickly can you get here?' she asked. 'We could cook together.'

'For a roast, I can be there in fifteen minutes,' Belle said.

'And to see your mother, of course.'

She smiled. 'That too.'

Her mother hadn't asked if Ben was coming—it was common knowledge that he worked late—and Belle was thankful that she didn't have to explain the real reason yet. She showered the stickiness of the café away, dressed, then climbed into her car, driving the short distance to her parents' house.

Minutes later, she swung into the driveway and parked the car, staring at the house she'd grown up in. While her childhood had been a happy one, the relationship she shared with her father was fraught with difficulties. She couldn't say for certain why it was so, only that for as long as she could remember, he'd shown her little else but his perpetual disappointment in her. Maybe Edward had wanted a son. Or maybe, and she suspected it was the case, they were just too different. They rarely saw eye to eye, clashing on almost everything, her refusal to study law most of all. For that reason alone, the house had always felt suffocating as a child, and as soon as she'd come of age, she'd taken an almighty breath and a lease on a shoebox of an apartment, promptly packing her bags, and moving out.

She found her mother in the kitchen, checking the temperature on the oven. Grace Hamilton glanced up, smiled, and in two quick strides, her arms were around her daughter. 'Hello, my darling. I just put the roast in.'

Belle returned the embrace. 'It smells good already. Rosemary and garlic?'

'Just like you taught me. It's about the only thing I know how to make without burning.' She glanced at the bench. 'The vegetables, on the other hand, are a different matter.'

It was obvious Belle's cooking talent hadn't come from Grace's side of the family. She glanced at the mess on the bench, at chopping boards covered with vegetable peelings and an odd assortment of knives, as though Grace hadn't been able to decide which one performed the job best. 'What would you like me to do?'

'You could take over the vegetables. I always undercook them.'

'Are you sure you're not Riley's mother?' Belle said, dropping her bag onto a bench stool and washing her hands under the tap. 'She could burn water.'

Grace laughed. 'How is she?'

'Fine. You know, Riley is Riley.'

'Yes, I know.'

Belle picked up the chef's knife she'd bought her mother for Christmas several years ago. It was still stunningly sharp, having hardly been used, and Belle immediately relaxed into its weight, its handle becoming an extension of her arm. She began chopping the vegetables, letting her love for cooking fill the space left by Ben's betrayal. Her shoulders eased, and her mind went blank. Still, if she could count on anyone to notice the sadness in her soul, it was her mother.

Grace leant against the bench, her arms folded across her chest, watching her chop. 'Is everything okay, sweetheart?'

Belle paused her chopping and blinked back tears, surprised that she had any left, the potatoes on the bench becoming a watery blur.

'Darling,' Grace said, straightening, 'what's happened?'

Belle forced a smile as she glanced up. 'How could you tell there was something wrong?'

'Because you're my daughter. And your eyes never lie.' Grace stepped forward and brushed the hair back from Belle's face, cupping her chin in her hands. 'Tell me, what is it?'

Belle had hoped to eloquently relay it all, but it came pouring out in one big messy sob, as she put the knife down and her mother held her. She told her of Ben's invitation to dinner two nights before, the idea that he might propose, only to learn that he'd met someone else and that he was ending their twenty-year relationship.

Grace held her close, stroking her head and making soothing sounds as though Belle were a child again. When she spoke, her voice held the same surprise that Riley's had. 'He's met someone else? Who?'

'Her name is Olivia,' Belle said, pulling away and stemming her dripping nose with the sleeve of her jumper. 'She works in law too. He said he has feelings for her.'

Grace blinked, then shook her head. 'Well, I'm shocked. Did you have any idea? Was he acting strange?'

'Not at all,' Belle said. 'It was a complete surprise.'

'Oh, sweetheart.' Her mother rubbed her arm. 'Have you spoken to him since?'

'He promised that we'd talk last night, but he never called.'

Grace pursed her lips with disapproval. 'So that's it? What happens now?'

Belle returned her attention to the potatoes. Somehow,

the more she relived the nightmare, the more normal it became, and that was a frightening thought. 'He wants to sell the house.'

'*Sell the house?*' Grace looked even more astonished. 'Isn't it a little soon for that? You both love that house. And he's only just met this girl.'

'I'm not sure they've just met. It's been going on for a while.'

The front door opened and closed, and Grace sighed. 'Your father's home. He's going to take the news hard. You know how he feels about Ben.'

Belle did know, and it was the part she'd been dreading the most, explaining it to her father.

Footsteps preceded him down the hall, then Edward appeared in the kitchen. Despite his seventy years, he was still the imposing man Belle had always revered, age doing little to soften him. The only betrayal were the creases around his eyes, the drooping of his lids, and the slight shuffle in his gait, as though his body were no match for the sharpness of his mind.

'How was your day, love?' Grace asked, taking his laptop bag and suit jacket, as he shrugged out of it.

'Busy.' His eyes flickered to his wife, before settling warily on Belle. 'I didn't know you were visiting.'

'Hi, Dad,' Belle said, wiping her hands on a tea towel and walking towards him. He leant down so she could kiss his cheek. 'I came for dinner.'

He grumbled and she wasn't sure if he was happy or unimpressed about it.

'We won't be long,' Grace said. 'We're running a bit behind.'

'I'll get some work done in the office then.' He gave

them a brief smile, collected his laptop bag again, and left the kitchen.

Belle sighed, returning to the vegetables. She'd given up trying to decipher her father's complexities a long time ago. He was a clever man, respected for his brilliance in the courtroom, but at home, when it was just the three of them, he was a self-imposed outcast, choosing to disengage from them at every opportunity. He often had little to say, and praise was a rarity from him, not that Belle had given him many reasons to be proud. She was an underachiever and, as he liked to remind her, the only Hamilton in decades not to attend university. 'Why did I bother spending thousands of dollars on a prestigious school for you if you were just going to end up in a café?'

All his praise, it seemed, had been reserved for Ben's achievements—Ben passing the bar, Ben's consideration for junior partner, Ben winning that unwinnable case. In fact, the only thing Belle had ever done right was be with Ben. And now she'd failed at that too.

'We better get those vegetables in, or we'll be eating at midnight.' Grace touched her arm gently, bringing her back to the room.

Belle took an unsteady breath, feeling the weight of her inadequacy settle on her. It was exhausting being a constant disappointment, and she wondered again what her father's reaction would be when she confessed the news, a moment she was not looking forward to.

———

BY THE TIME they sat down to eat, Belle had worked her stomach into knots. She'd already carved the lamb, laid out honey-baked carrots and crunchy potatoes on a platter, made thick, glossy gravy, and had whipped up a side dish she'd been experimenting with over the past few weeks—sweet and savoury beets and onions.

'This is wonderful. I knew I invited you for a reason.' Her mother winked at her.

Belle broke into a smile, waiting for her father to share a compliment too, but all he said was, 'Do we have salt and pepper?'

'Right here.' Belle passed them to him.

They helped themselves to food, and Edward poured wine, then they ate in a silence that might have been awkward for some but was normal for their family.

'These beets are lovely,' Grace said after a while.

'I've been experimenting with them,' Belle explained. 'It took me a few attempts to get them right.'

'I just marvel how you can make something from nothing and have it turn out so perfectly. I must have missed that gene,' Grace said.

Belle noticed the strange look that passed between her mother and father before Grace cleared her throat and dropped her gaze to her plate. Belle swallowed a lump of meat, knowing that she'd have to get on with the business of telling her father about Ben before her nerve packed up and left. 'Dad, I want to talk to you.'

'Oh?' He helped himself to more lamb.

'Yes. It's about something that's happened recently that's come as a bit of a surprise.'

Edward set down the serving tongs and stared at her. 'Okay, out with it then.'

'It's to do with Ben.'

He paused, something flickering in his eyes before he reached for another spoonful of potatoes. 'If it's about that girl he's met, I already know.'

Belle straightened. 'What do you mean you already know?'

Edward shook his head as though it were nothing to get upset about. 'He dropped into my chambers last week and we had a chat about it. He explained it all.'

'Explained what?' Belle stared at him, trying to corral the questions that darted around her brain, but there were too many.

'That he's tried to make it work with you. He's tried and he's given up. You've grown into different people. These things happen.'

It was more than Ben had told her, and yet his audacity astounded her. He'd run the affair by Edward first, going behind her back and assuring her father was on side early, so that she wouldn't stand a chance. But what hurt most of all was that Edward was validating Ben's actions, agreeing with them. He was saying that what Ben did was *okay*.

'Edward, let me get this straight,' Grace intervened, placing her knife and fork down and leaning forward, 'Ben came to see you a week ago and told you he was with someone else and that he planned to end things with Belle.'

'That's right,' he said, eyes widening slightly, as though he realised he was on the receiving end of an attack about to be launched.

'He only told Belle last night. For a whole week you knew. Don't you think you should have mentioned it sooner?'

If Belle was hoping for remorse or sympathy, her father was the wrong man to expect it from. 'I didn't know he was going to wait a whole week before telling her. He simply came in to explain his side and that he was going to tell her everything. It wasn't my place to get involved. Is there any more gravy in the boat?'

Belle grimaced, the food she had forced down threatening to creep back up. Suddenly, she was on the outside looking in, as they sat around the table in some strange facsimile of family life. Winning her father's respect had always amounted to an uphill battle, but *this* was the ultimate betrayal from the two men in her life who she loved the most and who should have loved her.

While she sat speechless, Edward continued eating, seemingly oblivious to her hurt, or perhaps unmoved by it. 'The thing about Ben is that he's ambitious and driven. He has goals. Perhaps he should be around like-minded people.'

'Like-minded people?' Belle said. 'What are you even talking about? Has everyone gone mad?'

'I'm disappointed in you, Edward. Regardless of how much you like Ben, you should have come home and told me straight away,' Grace scolded.

Edward shook his head. 'What's done is done. At least it happened now before you started a family together.' He pointed his fork at Belle. 'That would have been worse.'

Grace placed her hand on Belle's and patted it gently. 'Maybe your father has a point. If Ben wasn't happy, it's best you know now.'

'That doesn't make it any easier.'

'Of course it doesn't,' Grace said quickly. 'But perhaps now you can concentrate on the things you've always wanted to do, like go to culinary school. And work in a commercial kitchen. There's nothing holding you back.'

Belle shrugged miserably. 'I'd have to start out as an apprentice. I'd be looking at three years of entry-level work at least. I'm not sure I can survive on that wage.'

'You're not going to work in a kitchen,' Edward announced sharply. 'You'll go to university and study something reputable. Hamiltons become lawyers. We don't become chefs and we don't work in cafés. Four generations of our family have attended university.'

'I don't want to study law,' Belle said firmly. 'I want to cook.'

'Then you really shouldn't wonder why your relationship fell apart,' he retorted.

The table fell silent. A look of finality appeared on Edward's face as though he was finished with the topic of Ben and culinary school. Belle had no stomach for it anymore either, as she pushed food around on her plate. They moved on to safer topics, like the weather, with voices so strained and polite it was torturous.

Afterwards, Belle helped her mother clean the dishes, then when she was ready to leave, she poked her head into her father's office and said goodbye.

Although he glanced up from his laptop screen, it was with a look of absentmindedness rather than concentration, and Belle knew it wasn't work he'd been thinking about. He offered her the glimmer of an apologetic smile, but mostly he just seemed tired. Tired of the same old arguments they seemed to constantly circle around.

'Have a think about university,' he said. 'I'd be happy to put in a word for you at UNSW. Even if you don't want to study law right now, something like commerce or social science might interest you.'

She knew this was his version of the olive branch, but even so, he wasn't listening. Her heart was in food, and that would never be good enough for a Hamilton. And he would never know just how much his words had stung that evening. 'Sure, Dad. I'll think about it.'

At the front door, her mother held her close. 'I know he can be difficult sometimes, but he means well.'

'When will I ever be enough?' Belle said into her mother's shoulder.

'Oh, stop that,' she chided, pulling back sharply to look at her. 'You *are* enough. He loves you very much. Don't ever forget that.'

Perhaps this was the first time Belle had truly seen the vulnerability in her mother's eyes, that blind faith she reserved solely for Edward. Grace was a determined woman, with a quiet strength that could eclipse the hardiest of souls, but somehow, when it came to Belle's father, she always seemed a lesser version of herself. That was how she looked now. Drenched in sadness for something Belle would never quite understand. She seemed to want to force the words into Belle, begging her to believe them. *He loves you very much. Don't ever forget that.*

'I know he does, Mum,' Belle said, and she did. 'He's just so hard on me, and right now, with everything going on, I'd hoped for a little sensitivity.'

'He is who he is, darling.'

Still, it didn't make Belle feel any better.

As they walked to her car, Grace's arm threaded through hers. 'What are you going to do about Ben?' she asked.

'I'm not sure there's anything I can do. He's made his mind up.'

'Are you still staying at the house?'

'I'm in Riley's spare bedroom. I've been avoiding the house.'

Grace nodded as they paused beside the driver's door. 'Stay here. Bring your things over. You can have your old bedroom back. And I'd love the company.' Her smile was so hopeful that Belle's heart broke. She could never move back there.

'I don't know, Mum. Everything's still so fresh. I haven't got my head around any of it. And I'm not sure I could tolerate Dad on top of everything else. Or that he could tolerate me.'

Grace smiled and pushed aside a piece of hair from Belle's face. 'Well, just think about it. You're always welcome.'

As Belle drove back to Riley's house, she thought about all that had transpired in the last two days. Ben had leapt into someone else's arms, Riley had announced she was leaving for London, and Belle was floundering, somewhere between hopelessness and homelessness. She had a home, of course, that lovely Victorian terrace in Pyrmont that had once held her most precious dreams in it, but was now like a crypt, and she had Riley's apartment, for the next six weeks anyway. Then she had her parents' house, with constant disappointment lurking in her father's gaze. None of those places felt like home though, and with her paltry wage from the café, moving to a new place would be expensive, unless she wanted to share with a stranger.

What this topsy-turvy new world had taught Belle was that her life had been dramatically reduced to just a few people. In all her time with Ben, she'd never maintained friendships other than Riley's, for every ounce of her energy she'd poured into him. She'd placed him high on a pedestal, above all else—friends and her dreams of becoming a chef. Now that he'd left her, she had little to fall back on. No circle of supportive females, no money in the bank, little of anything, really. Ben had taken more than just his love away. He'd inadvertently stripped her of independence. And she'd given him the means to do it.

FIVE

For the next month, Belle moved through a fog. She went to work, served coffee and food for eight hours, then landed back at Riley's apartment to sleep, but it all seemed distant and mechanical, like she was filling someone else's shoes. Ben, the person she'd spent years coming home to, had all but disappeared from her life, and it was as painful and bewildering as losing a limb.

The only reminders of her old life were the times she went back to the terrace to collect clothes or the mail, but on occasion, when she walked down the hall or into their bedroom, she would catch the perfumed scent of something heavy and overpowering, like musk or vanilla, and she'd realise that Olivia had been in her house. The thought that that woman could taint her home, the place she'd once shared so much joy with Ben, made her never want to go back there. Had they slept in her bed, made love in her shower? Had they laughed and talked of new dreams in her kitchen?

'The quicker you can sell that place, the easier it will be to move on,' Riley said one Saturday morning over coffee in her apartment, when Belle had told her that she'd smelt Olivia's perfume again. 'You don't need that constant reminder. They're just rubbing it in your face now.'

Belle had endured another fitful night of sleep, where the small hours had merged in a tangle with the dawn, and she'd woken with a heavy heart. They said the amount of time one mourned a breakup was equivalent to half the time spent in that relationship. Twenty years with Ben meant ten years of grieving. Once upon a time, she would have laughed at such a notion, but now, not knowing if she'd ever smile again, ten years didn't seem like such a stretch.

'You look like hell.' Riley was watching her over the rim of her cup. 'Want another coffee?'

Belle pushed her mug towards Riley. 'Yes, please. And thank you. I love being told I look like hell.'

'You know what I mean.' Riley smiled apologetically. 'I know you're not sleeping. I can hear you tossing and turning at night.'

'Sorry, I don't mean to keep you up.' Belle ran a hand through her dishevelled hair. 'There's so much going through my mind that when I close my eyes, my thoughts race. I can't switch them off.'

Riley refilled Belle's mug with coffee, then slid it towards her. Belle collected it with both hands and wrapped them tightly around it for warmth. The mornings were growing colder as autumn laid down its roots, the leaves outside turning crimson and gold. Belle had always loved the turn of the seasons, particularly summer into autumn, for the way the colours transformed the landscape, but she took little joy in it these days, noticing it only as an afterthought.

'Can you remind me when we need to move out of

here?' she asked, lifting the mug, and taking a cautious sip through the steam.

'I'm handing the keys back the morning I fly out, so the day before would be good. All my things will be in storage by then. Any luck with the house hunting?'

'I have a few more places to see today, but so far I haven't found anything promising. The share houses are either filthy, full of randy males, or they're miniature drug dens.'

Riley grimaced. 'Maybe you should talk to Ben. Tell him that you'll be staying at the house until it sells and that he needs to be mindful about bringing Olivia over. It's your place too. He can't expect you to be homeless.'

'Honestly, I'm not sure I could stay there. It would be too sad.' Belle smiled glumly. 'I still can't believe you're going away.'

'It's time. In fact, it's long overdue. I can't be here anymore. I can't keep doing the same old things.'

Belle watched her friend as she took a wistful sip of her coffee and set it back down on the bench. Riley was strikingly beautiful in a way that made men—and their wives—stop and stare, the kind of looks that halted conversations and quickened hearts. Yet, despite all the attention, the envious glances, Riley was lonely. It was almost a crime that she should be, given how attractive she was, but men were wary of loving her, and women were afraid to befriend her, and so it became a perpetual cycle of everyone holding her at arm's length. Her raven-haired, green-eyed beauty had made her an outcast.

Belle found Riley smiling at her and tilted her head to the side. 'What?'

'You should come with me.'

She spluttered into her coffee. 'To London?'

'Yes.'

She shook her head empathically. 'Oh, I couldn't.'

'Why?'

'Because I have a job and not a lot of money to travel right now.'

'Or are you staying in case Ben changes his mind?'

Belle scoffed, but she couldn't hide the way her cheeks flamed at the suggestion. It was true. Every minute of the day she checked her phone for contact from him. That was a lot of screen glances over the course of a month. She was embarrassed to say that if he'd wanted her back this very moment, she would have gone, no questions asked.

'He doesn't deserve you putting your life on hold for him again. He never deserved it in the first place, and yet you're still doing it.'

'That's not what I'm doing,' Belle argued, but the flame in her cheeks continued to betray her.

'Any day now, your house is going to have a for sale sign out the front. He's not coming back.'

Belle knew this. God, how she knew this, but some part of her couldn't let go. It was too soon and too raw to contemplate not having Ben in her life. 'I've just gone through a huge change,' she tried to explain. 'I'm not ready for another. I need to plant my feet somewhere for a while and breathe.'

Riley stared at her for a long time, then let out a sad sigh. 'Just don't plant yourself for too long, kid. Wallowing will only make you feel worse.'

Belle took a sip and nodded, setting the cup down again. 'I've been thinking about cooking, although I'm not sure where to start. I'm too old for an apprenticeship and too old to go back to school and study.'

'What about asking your café to move you to the kitchen? You could get experience there.'

'We serve pre-made sandwiches and Caesar salads. I'd hardly call that experience.'

'It's a start.'

It *was* a start, and she hated to sound ungrateful. She'd been sloshing about in her misery for weeks and despite her best efforts, had found it difficult to pull herself out of it. Nothing at the moment was good enough, not a share house or a job in the café's kitchen because all she wanted was her old life back, where her days turned with the comforting predictability she was used to. But those days were gone and there was no point pretending any different.

'I'll find a place to stay, then I'll talk to the café about moving me to the kitchen,' she said, forcing enthusiasm into her voice.

Riley smiled, pacified. 'That's my girl.' Her mobile phone rang on the bench between them, and she scooped it up, pressing it to her ear. 'Hello. Yes, Darius.' Her eyes narrowed and she glanced at Belle. 'Uh, okay. I guess he can.' She placed the phone back on the bench. 'Ben's downstairs.'

Belle started, almost knocking her coffee over. 'Ben? Here? Now?'

'Yes. Darius is sending him up.'

'What does he want?'

'How should I know?'

Belle groaned, rising from the stool. She knew she looked a wreck—pale skin, eyes dull with exhaustion. There was no time to change out of the tracksuit pants and over-sized jumper she'd thrown on when she'd woken, or the thick woollen socks that had a hole in one of the toes. They would have to do. A quick run of the toothbrush over her teeth and a hasty weave of her hair into a plait was all she had time for when the knock came at the door.

She walked out to the living room and found Ben waiting in the small entranceway next to Riley, both their hands jammed into their jeans' pockets, avoiding each other's eyes.

'Hey,' Belle said. Her breath caught in her chest as she stared at him, realising all over again how unbearable the last month without him had been, how much she'd missed him. She might have hated the sin, but she still loved the sinner. 'What are you doing here?'

'I uh... thought we could talk.' His gaze darted nervously towards Riley, who was drilling holes into him with her stare.

'Sure.' Belle's voice squeaked. 'Come in.'

Riley's nostrils flared as though she'd smelt something unpleasant. She snatched her handbag from the hall table and glanced at Belle. 'I have to open the gallery. I'll see you later.'

After Riley left and the door closed, Ben fixed wary eyes on her, as though she were a predator circling him.

She cleared her throat and beckoned towards the living room. 'Can I fix you something to eat? Waffles, a Spanish omelette?'

He smiled, visibly relaxing at the offer of food, two of his favourite dishes she'd cooked for him often. 'No, I'm fine, thanks.'

'I haven't seen you for so long,' she said, once they were seated on opposite sofas, facing each other. She hungrily drank him in, his perfectly symmetrical face and crystal blue eyes. He smelt of everything she'd missed, of freshness and cologne and mint, the kind of smells she'd fallen asleep to each night, as he lay next to her.

'Sorry I haven't been in touch to talk,' he said, with a sheepish look. 'It's just been crazy and well, I haven't known what to say to you exactly. I feel awful about the way I ended things. I mean, there's never a *good* way to end things, but I could have handled it better.'

He was rambling, but she was hardly taking the words in anyway. Having him this close to her after so long was torturous. She wanted to reach out and touch him, but she also knew that he was too distant now, no longer hers, and that perhaps her touch wouldn't be welcomed.

'How have you been?' he asked, linking then unlinking his fingers together, a nervous trait she'd always found endearing.

'How do you think I've been?'

He nodded as though that were a fair reply. 'You look well.'

Belle frowned.

'I mean, you know.' He dropped his gaze and shook his head.

'I miss you,' she said, the words tumbling out. 'I miss us, and I miss our home. I love Riley for letting me stay here but I want to be back in our house, with you.'

He gave her a sad smile. 'You know we can't do that.'

'Because you didn't give us a chance,' she said.

'Look, it wasn't my intention to go behind your back. I met Olivia and we clicked. What I feel for her is what I used to feel for you. You and I are more like friends now.'

His words cut deeply, and she flinched. The lawyer in him could be unthinkingly direct. 'We were in a twenty-year relationship, Ben. We weren't going to have fireworks every day. We had love and history and stability instead.'

'I'm sorry. I can't help how I feel.' He sighed. 'Look, I didn't come here to argue.'

'Then why did you come? To absolve yourself? Because it wasn't to make me feel better,' she said, finding strength in her voice. Challenging him felt good, like a release of all the pent-up hurt she'd been bottling inside.

'I came to talk to you about the house.'

'What about it?'

He leant forward on his knees. 'I've decided not to sell it.'

She narrowed her eyes at him. 'What do you mean you're not going to sell it?'

'I'm going to move into it.' He clapped his hands together. 'With Olivia.'

Belle felt like she'd been punched in the stomach.

'Did you hear what I said?' Ben asked.

'Yes, I heard what you said. Why would you move into *our* place with *her*?'

'Because I love that house. I worked hard to buy it and I don't want to sell it.'

'But that's our place. Yours and mine.'

He shrugged. 'Technically, it's my place. My name is on the contract and it's my money that's paid the mortgage all these years.'

His insinuation that he was the only one to love the house cut her deeply. She loved it too, and although he'd contributed financially to the mortgage, she'd contributed in other ways, by paying utilities and buying groceries. He also must have thought she was an idiot. He knew better than anyone that under the law he couldn't displace her so easily.

'Look, you don't have to move out yet,' he offered. 'You can start packing your things next week. That'll work for us.'

She straightened, lifting her chin. 'If you want to move back into the house, you're going to have to buy me out.'

He blinked, then an amused smile twisted his lips. 'Buy you out? Belle, come on. You didn't contribute anything to that mortgage. It was my money that paid for the house.'

'And it was my money and my support that meant we had a life there.' She fought the urge to give in. Once upon a time, she would have backed down and accepted her fate, and while she was loathed to squabble over money, she was too upset at his suggestion that for the past decade, she'd enjoyed a free ride. 'You might have paid for the house, but I contributed in other ways that mattered. I put my dreams on hold for us.'

'I never asked you to do that.'

'No, but you never encouraged me not to either. You were too self-indulgent. So you can't tell me I don't deserve anything from that house.'

He stared at her, looking bewildered. 'What do you want?'

'What's rightfully mine.'

He scoffed, then when he realised she wasn't joking, he frowned. 'Are you being serious?'

'Yes.'

'You haven't forgotten I'm a solicitor, right?'

'No. And have you forgotten who my father is? I might not be a solicitor, but I know my rights. Family Law, Ben. Our separation is considered the same as that of a married couple. I'm entitled to half that house. Or should I move back in and the three of us can live together?' She didn't bother reminding him that she was also entitled to a percentage of his superannuation as well as half of the home's contents. He knew the law; he was just trying to pull the wool over her eyes.

Ben let out an exasperated breath, clearly not having anticipated such shrewd resistance. 'For God's sake.'

She crossed her arms and pinned him with her gaze.

He relented begrudgingly. 'Fine. You're within your rights to lodge an application for property settlement and arrange an independent valuation of the house.'

'But that's a lengthy process.'

'It is.'

And therein lay the problem. She didn't have time. She needed money in her pocket before Riley left. 'I need something sooner than that. Can you make me a cash offer?'

He frowned. 'I can, but you're going to end up with substantially less. I don't have that kind of money lying around to buy you out. It's all tied up in the house.'

'What about your superannuation?'

His jaw twitched with irritation. 'What about it?'

Belle sighed. Her head thumped with an emotional hangover. 'Look, just make me an offer. And try not to insult me while you're doing it.'

Ben's nostrils flared. 'I'll crunch some numbers and get back to you. But it's not going to be a lot, so prepare yourself. I'm not a bank. What would you do with it anyway?'

His arrogance was infuriating, and she was overcome with the need to shock and hurt him, just as he'd done to her. 'I'm going to London.'

The words poured out, and there was no way to stuff them back into her mouth. Ben's eyes bulged, and while she secretly enjoyed his reaction, her heart thudded at what she'd just announced.

'London?' His forehead creased. 'Who with? For how long?'

'With Riley. Indefinitely.'

He was still seated on the sofa facing her, but his spine was rigid now, his expression confused. 'When were you going to tell me about that?'

'I wasn't,' she said.

He was obviously stunned that she could be capable of something so wildly adventurous as going overseas. He ran a hand through his hair, then down his face, rubbing his jaw. 'I just thought you could have told me. I mean, I would like to have known.'

'Why? What business is it of yours now?'

'I don't know. It just feels weird that you would do this without telling me.'

She almost laughed at his self-righteousness. How had she failed to notice it before?

'So you're going with Riley?' Ben asked, still looking whiplashed. 'Why would you go with *her*?'

'Because she's my friend.'

'She's also a...' He faltered but his meaning was clear.

'A what?' She would make him say it just to embarrass him.

'You know... she's a bit loose.' His face flushed and he looked down at his hands.

Belle shook her head and stood up. 'I have a lot to do. Was there anything else you wanted?'

He glanced up with surprise, then stood as well. 'I guess not. I just...' He swallowed as if unsure of himself suddenly. 'I guess I'll just call you when I've decided on an offer.'

'Sooner rather than later, please.' She saw him out, then returned to the sofa and sat down again, letting a burst of air escape her lungs. Her legs trembled as though she'd climbed a tremendous summit, somehow making it to the top and plunging a flag deep into the ground, victorious. What was most exhilarating, if not slightly terrifying, was the seed that had taken root in her mind. *I'm going to London. With Riley. Indefinitely.*

It had only ever been intended as a white lie, something

to jolt Ben, but could she do it? Could she be so impulsive? There was little keeping her there, not a relationship or a job she loved, and she was almost homeless anyway. But did she dare use what money Ben might give her for a trip overseas? Only moments ago, her life had been falling apart. Now it was falling into place, like water filling a dry stream. The only thing she wasn't sure she had was the courage to do it.

SIX

The following week Ben called to inform her that he'd transferred a sum of money into her bank account. When he told her the amount, her voice trembled with indignation. 'Thirty thousand dollars? That's paltry and you know it.'

'It's two thousand for each year we were in the house, and an extra ten because I'm feeling generous,' he said.

'I'm owed more than that. The house is worth over a million.'

He sighed with impatience. 'Just take the money, Belle. You need it now; you made that clear. If you fight me, I'll drag it out in court, and you'll get nothing for a long time.'

Her blood pressure rose with frustration. Thirty thousand was a fraction of what she was owed, and while common sense told her to seek legal advice, to ask her dad at least, time wasn't on her side. She could have kicked herself for not keeping her cards closer to her chest. It had been a rookie move to reveal to Ben that she'd been desperate for the money, and now he was exploiting it.

On the other hand, she couldn't deny that what he was

offering would still go a long way. It could help pay for culinary school or give her breathing space while she found a better paying job. Or... it could get her to London with some to spare.

She didn't mean to, but while she was on the phone with him, she accidentally slipped into a daydream, thinking of flights and foreign lands, and leaving all her troubles behind, while Ben complained in her ear about how he was thirty thousand dollars poorer.

'And you'll need to sign a waiver to say you won't come back for more after this payment. This is final. We cut all ties as of now.'

'Whatever,' she said. 'I won't be here anyway.'

The line fell silent while he digested her news all over again. 'You're actually going through with it then?'

'If you mean London, I think I am.'

'But why would you go? All that travelling and living out of a suitcase. That's not you, Belle. You like a quiet life, with everything clean and organised. Are you sure you've thought this through properly?'

She detected the note of insecurity in his voice, and it occurred to her that Ben wasn't concerned for her welfare or how she would cope living out of a suitcase. He couldn't fathom that she was leaving him behind. That for once, her decisions weren't central to his existence. How gratifying it must have felt for him, safe in the knowledge that she was still there, still holding a torch for him, while he wooed someone else. Her decision to leave had tripped him up, and she would be lying if she didn't derive some pleasure from that.

He moaned in her ear for a few minutes more before she feigned a burning casserole in the oven and ended the call. She wasn't going to enter a debate with him about her plans. Contrary to what he thought, she didn't owe him anything, and the one consolation to the collapse of her relationship was that she no longer had to run things past him. The last month had been the worst of her life, but she was slowly realising that she was her own person, no longer the shadow of someone outspoken and impressive, rather a woman who could make her own decisions.

It had been a long time, if ever, that she'd felt that way.

It was addictive.

No, more than that. It was liberating.

SHE DIDN'T TELL Riley straight away that she was considering joining her. If there was one thing Belle had mastered to a fine art, it was deliberation, to the point of procrastination. She had a rigid process for making decisions. She liked to sleep on them and spend considerable time turning every conceivable outcome over in her head until it ached. And although she'd enjoyed teasing Ben with the notion that she could just pack up and leave, whether she could deliver on it was another story.

But it was after one particularly difficult day when three shared apartments had fallen through and her job at the café was under threat due to new management that Belle realised the trip she'd spent the past week musing over was no longer a fanciful idea, but a potential lifeline. She would be homeless soon and possibly unemployed, and if she didn't want to be forced back to her parents' house, she would have to make a swift decision.

'Are you joking?' Riley declared over dinner one evening when Belle blurted it out.

'No, I'm seriously thinking about coming with you.'

Riley almost jumped out of her seat. She was sitting so precariously on the edge of it that Belle worried it would topple forward. 'But I...' She looked astonished. 'I don't even know what to say. I didn't realise you were considering it.'

'Well, Ben gave me some money from the house and the transaction has cleared. It's not enough to buy my own place. I could spend it on culinary school, but I'd still be homeless. Plus, the café might be putting people off, so I could be unemployed soon too. I'm not sure anything is keeping me here.'

'Not even Ben?' Riley asked, her excited look giving way to scepticism.

'The way he spoke to me last week, like I thoroughly irritated him...' She shook her head. 'No, not even Ben.'

Riley's face split into a wide grin. 'That's a good enough reason for me, kid.'

Her excitement was infectious, and Belle felt the first shivers of anticipation course through her. A speck of an idea had transformed into a plan. A big plan. She was going to London, and who knew when she would be back.

She hardly slept that night, knowing the conversation with her father the next morning would be infinitely trickier. A trip overseas had never been on the cards before and was yet another step away from law school. Nevertheless, she couldn't put off telling him, no matter how her stomach coiled at the thought.

Sunday arrived, and she drove over early to help her mother prepare brunch. She had composed an ambitious menu of wild mushroom bruschetta, apple pancakes, corn and zucchini fritters and a platter of fruit. There was coffee and freshly squeezed orange juice and a tray of cherry chocolate friands, all of it contrived in the hope of keeping Edward distracted while she delivered her news.

When they sat down to eat and he slipped away from their conversation by losing himself in the Sunday paper, she took the opportunity to raise it. 'I'm going to London.'

Her parents paused their eating. But while Grace's eyes lit with happiness, Edward's hand, the one turning the page, suspended in the air.

'London?' he repeated.

'Yes.' There, it was out, and she felt better already.

Until her father looked down his glasses at her with a confused look. 'What do you mean? For how long?'

She shuffled in her seat, hoping he would return to his newspaper soon. 'I haven't set a timeframe. My plans are open-ended.'

Her father was still staring at her as though she'd asked him for one of his kidneys. 'What in the devil are you going to London for?'

She took a deep breath, her palms saturated in sweat suddenly. 'Because there isn't much keeping me here right now. Olivia is moving into the house with Ben, Riley's leaving soon, and the café will be under new management. I may not even have a job in two weeks, let alone somewhere to live.'

He dismissed her announcement with a shake of his head, returning to his newspaper. 'You don't have to go to London. You can move back home, find a night job, and go to university during the day.'

'I don't want to do that.'

He waved his hand without looking at her. 'I've already made an appointment for you with the dean at UNSW. Next week. He's willing to meet with you to discuss enrolment.'

'Then unmake the appointment. My ticket is booked.'

'Cancel it.'

'No,' she said, her voice rising. Beside her, Grace winced.

Edward glanced up sharply, his eyes narrowing. 'Excuse me?'

'I won't cancel my ticket. And I won't be at that appointment at UNSW. I'm going to London because for the first time in a long time, I want to do something for myself instead of doing what everyone else thinks I should do.'

He turned his eyes to Grace. 'Did you know about this?'

'No, I didn't. But Edward—'

'You're not going,' he said, his jowls quivering as he pushed the words through clenched teeth.

Belle lifted her chin. She really was becoming tired of people telling her what to do. 'Yes, I am. I'm thirty-five years old. I can decide for myself what I want to do with my life.'

Edward's fist connected with the table, making the plates and cups rattle. 'Four generations of Hamiltons have attended university. Are you going to be the one to ruin tradition? For God's sake, Grace, talk sense into her.'

Grace sighed. 'Edward, it's a small trip in the big scheme of things. Let her have a year off. After what Ben did to her, she deserves to go. She's not a child.'

Edward turned puce, close to exploding with anger. He let his fork and knife clatter onto the plate, wiped his mouth with his napkin and left the table, storming out of the dining room. Somewhere, down the opposite end of the house, Belle heard his office door slam shut.

She turned in her chair and cast her mother a sheepish look. 'Sorry. I knew he wasn't going to take it well, but I didn't think he'd react like that.'

Grace gave her a small smile. 'He'll get used to the idea.'

'I don't want you to get into trouble for it later, though.'

'Don't worry. I can handle him.' She placed her napkin on the table, her long fingers smoothing over the linen. She had always seemed young for her age, a woman who dressed well and cared for her figure, someone who exuded a quiet strength, but not for the first time, Belle wondered how she put up with Edward.

'You have the patience of a saint, Mum.'

Grace chuckled. 'If you mean your father, I've had decades to get used to it.'

'I'm surprised you've lasted that long,' Belle murmured.

'He wasn't always like this.'

'He's impossible to please. Believe me, I've tried and failed my whole life.' She played with her napkin too, her appetite souring.

'That's not true,' Grace said firmly. 'You haven't failed at anything. Sure, some things haven't gone to plan, but Belle, maybe that's because you put everyone else first. You're kind and generous, occasionally to your detriment. You need to put yourself first now.'

'So you think I should go?'

'Of course!' Grace said without hesitation. 'I would be disappointed if you didn't.'

'The only Hamilton in decades not to attend university,' Belle mumbled in her father's voice. 'He's never going to speak to me again.'

Grace patted her hand. 'He'll get over it.'

Later, after hugging her mother goodbye, Belle drove away from her parents' house, heavy-hearted. Even if she stayed and did all the right things, went to university, moved back home, or even moved back in with Ben, it would never make her father happy.

Disappointment had settled between them long ago and gone were the conversations where it didn't edge into his voice in some way. He reserved his steeliest eyes for her, his sharpest tones for their conversations. Thinking back to when she was a child, it had always been there, simmering beneath the surface, and she could never comprehend what she'd done to warrant such harshness.

It was almost a relief to leave it all behind, start fresh somewhere new, even if just for a few months. Her only regret was saying goodbye to her mother, who she'd long suspected led the loneliest kind of life, despite her pristine armour.

SEVEN

The next two weeks passed in a blur, but if Belle could take comfort in anything, it was the sudden orderliness that had returned to her life. She had lots to do but, more importantly, she had a purpose, which kept her distracted and moving.

She quit her job, sold her car, dusted off her passport and, when Ben and Olivia were at work the day before her flight, she borrowed her mother's car and drove to the terrace in Pyrmont to pack up the rest of her belongings— clothes, cookbooks and her kitchen utensils and appliances —to store at her parents' house.

She breathed a sigh of relief when her key still worked in the door, grateful that Ben hadn't yet changed the locks, and walked down the hall, hit once again by Olivia's heavy and lingering perfume.

Although Ben had offered her half the furniture, she had declined, leaving it behind as a gesture of goodwill. She had no use for it anyway and there had been little time to sell it and recover the money. But as she moved through the house, she was shocked to see that most of it was gone anyway.

Belle's cream linen sofa had been replaced with a new bulky leather recliner, and her vintage elm dining table was gone, a large black table with a heavy glass top and black suede chairs in its place. Belle's delicate pastel prints had been replaced too, with huge pieces of black and gold abstract art in thick bronze frames that hung on the walls. Olivia's style was vastly different from Belle's, traces of her gawdy handprint all over the beloved terrace.

The closet held a similar story. Belle's clothes had been carelessly tossed to the side or on the floor, and Olivia's coats, suits and evening dresses hung in the centre. There were designer shoes and bottles of perfume cluttering every surface and a leopard print quilt had replaced the pretty floral coverlet that had once been on the bed. It seemed Ben and Olivia were determined to eradicate the ghost of the woman who'd lived there.

Once Belle had loaded her bags and boxes into the car, she walked back inside, stepping through each of the rooms. She glanced around, remembering the good times they'd had—when they'd first moved in and had made love in every room, when they'd attempted to paint the walls and had accidentally chosen the most horrendous colour, when Ben had professed his love day after day, night after night, with the promise of children and a future so blissful it had made Belle wonder how she could ever have been so lucky. But it had all fallen apart. She hadn't seen it coming, hadn't felt the first dangerous ripples of his unhappiness. It had washed over her before she'd had time to draw a breath.

She sighed now and returned to the kitchen. Digging the house key out of her pocket, she set it down on the bench for

Ben to find later. She'd considered pairing it with a hand-written note, to thank him for their years together, to be the bigger person and wish him all the best, but it would be a lie. She was still too hurt for that, unwilling to absolve him of his indiscretions. Instead, she committed all she could to memory, of a life once happy there, then she pulled the front door closed behind her, heard the deadbolt latch, and drove away.

BOARDING the flight felt incredibly surreal, like Belle had fallen through the woven threads of a dream and at any moment might wake to find herself back in Riley's spare room, staring up at the ceiling counting the hours until morning. As she and Riley took their seats and other passengers filled theirs around them, Belle kept glancing down at her boarding pass and passport, then out at the plane's wing beside her. She had to remind herself that it wasn't a dream, that she was going away and didn't know when she would be back. Spontaneous, open-ended, and so un-Belle like.

'Are you okay?' Riley asked, casting her a worried look.

Belle nodded. 'I think so. Actually no, I'm not sure.'

Riley patted her arm. 'Don't overthink it. We need this.'

Belle let out a steadying breath. *Yes, we need this*.

The plane taxied down the runway, then lifted with a jolt, circling high above the city. Belle craned her neck, trying to seek out her beloved Pyrmont terrace from the maze of cluttered rooftops below, but everything looked the same, and she couldn't discern the street or the roof or even the grand old trees that towered over it.

Maybe it was for the best, for it wasn't *her* beloved terrace anymore. It belonged to the woman who had taken her place. *Olivia*. Nothing in that city was Belle's to call home and she wiped away a solemn tear from her cheek, as the aircraft pulled her north, away from everything she'd ever loved, and into the unknown.

———————

AFTER A LAYOVER IN SINGAPORE, they were back in the air for the last leg of the flight to London. They were allocated new seats and this time were positioned in the window row with a young woman. Her eyes were closed, her head lolling against the headrest, as the girls dropped into their seats beside her. When the plane launched into the air, her eyes popped opened and she pressed her face to the glass, looking out over the lights of Singapore below. She made a few soft sighing noises and gave the outside a wave as they circled the city once, then flew into the night.

'Well, that's that,' she said, throwing Belle a grin, who was seated next to her.

Belle returned the smile, then trained her focus on the screen in front of her as she searched for a movie to watch.

'Did you enjoy Singapore?' the girl asked, ready for conversation, turning completely in her chair to face Belle. Her hair was long and blonde, woven into two messy plaits, and there was a splatter of freckles on her nose. She was young, early twenties, perhaps, and her accent was Canadian. Her big blue eyes searched Belle's with an almost youthful exuberance, and Belle, not wanting to appear rude, dragged her attention away from the screen.

'We didn't stay in Singapore, actually. It was just a layover from Sydney.'

'You're Australian?' Her eyes widened as she clapped her hands together. 'I've never been to Australia before. I've always wanted to go but my parents said it was too far. I was lucky to get to Singapore.' She sat up in her seat, hardly pausing for breath. 'I was in Thailand for a week, then I finished in Singapore where I met friends from back home. They left yesterday to return to Vancouver.'

Belle's brow creased with confusion. 'But this flight's bound for London. You're not going home to Canada?'

'Oh, I don't live in Canada. Not now, anyway. I'm staying with my uncle and cousin in Rome. That's where I'm heading to.'

Feeling intrigued about the girl beside her, Belle abandoned the idea of a movie. 'You live in Rome?'

'My uncle owns a trattoria in the city, and my cousin and I work there. If I'm honest, they're slave drivers, but I have my own apartment near Piazza Navona, so I can't complain.'

'It sounds incredible.'

'My parents thought a gap year might be good for me,' she continued. 'I left school and was finding it difficult deciding what to do next. I come from a long line of doctors on my dad's side, so it was medical school or a whole lot of arguments.'

'I guess you chose a whole lot of arguments?' Belle said with a knowing smile. Although this girl was surely younger than her by fifteen years, Belle knew all about fathers and their impossibly high standards. She was thirty-five and still her father couldn't part with the idea that she didn't want to study law.

The girl giggled and nodded. 'Exactly. My parents are living in hope that a few years in Rome will warm me to the idea of med school.'

'Is that what you really want to do?'

She shrugged and twirled one of her plaits around her finger. 'I don't know. I'm a bit of a wanderer. I love travelling and culture and people. I'd love to star on one of those travel shows. I would even eat witchetty grubs and wrestle a crocodile in Outback Australia. That's how rogue I can get. I'm not kidding.'

Belle laughed so loudly she drew stares from the other passengers. Riley became aware of their conversation and tugged her headphones off, glancing curiously across at them.

'Are you travelling alone?' the girl enquired.

Belle leant back and pointed at Riley, who waved. 'We're travelling together. This is my best friend.'

'Hi,' Riley said.

The girl waved too. 'What brings you both all this way?'

Belle gave her a rueful smile. 'A story not so different from your own, I'm afraid. I felt the need to go rogue too.'

'With or without the grubs?'

Belle chuckled. 'Without! Are you boarding a connecting flight to Rome once we land?'

'No, I'm going to stay in London for a few days. I'm meeting friends there.'

The flight attendants moved through the aircraft with the evening meal, and all through dinner, Belle and the girl talked. Even long after Riley's movie finished, and she pushed her seat back to sleep, they continued to converse in whispers.

At one point, the girl put her hand up to her mouth. 'How silly are we? We haven't introduced ourselves yet.'

Belle grinned at their oversight. But even without knowing the girl's name, she felt like she'd known her a lifetime. 'You're right. I'm Belle Hamilton. And my friend is Riley Alexander.'

The girl shot out her hand and shook Belle's warmly. 'I'm Avery Sinclair. It's *so* nice to meet you!'

EIGHT

It was six-thirty in the morning when their flight touched down on a Heathrow runway. The sky was thick with clouds, a light drizzle washing out everything below.

Outside at the taxi rank, amidst a flurry of hugs, Avery said goodbye to Belle and Riley. 'I'll be staying in London for a week, then heading back to Italy after that. Call me while I'm here and we can meet up for a drink.'

They hurriedly exchanged numbers before she climbed into a black taxi, waving eagerly from the back seat as it pulled away from the curb. Belle and Riley hailed the next taxi and fell into it. While Riley had slept soundly on the flight from Singapore, Belle had stayed up most of the night talking with Avery. Jetlag nudged at the corners of her brain, but she was still too excited to contemplate sleeping, as the taxi swung into morning traffic, and they began their journey into central London.

They followed the motorway through the outer suburbs, modern airport hotels and blue-glassed industrial buildings relenting to pebbledash houses, then, finally, the classic facades of Victorian terraces, so like the one Belle had left behind in Pyrmont.

The driver navigated them through London's stubborn peak hour, braking sharply and gesticulating at other drivers when they cut in front of him, before double parking out the front of their hotel in Mayfair, where he unloaded their luggage and bid them good day. Belle's excitement slowly began to wane and a deep longing for sleep took over. It was nine o'clock in the morning in London, seven o'clock in the evening in Sydney. She'd been travelling for over twenty-four hours and her body was now a muddled array of time zones.

They checked into their room and Belle kicked off her shoes, collapsing into a heap on one of the beds.

'The quickest way to combat jetlag is to avoid napping,' Riley announced matter-of-factly when Belle fluffed out a pillow to get comfortable. 'You'll adjust quicker if you stay awake until bedtime.'

'Says the person who slept for six hours on the plane.'

'You shouldn't have stayed up talking,' Riley said, hands on her hips.

'Yes, but Avery was lovely. And it's bedtime now, some-where.' Belle yawned. Her eyes grew heavy, and she allowed them to close for a second until a cushion clipped the side of her head and she jerked.

'Come on, lazy bones.' Riley was having none of it. 'Up you get. We'll find coffee and something to eat.'

They washed their faces and changed clothes, then Riley dragged her outside to walk. Belle pushed through her exhaustion, surprised to find a second well of energy.

As they wandered from the hotel, her eye was drawn to many things. She knew the buses would be red, of course, that every corner might host the familiar tube station signs, that buildings as old as time would grace cobbled lanes but seeing it in person was not the same as imagining.

Sleep was forgotten as they trailed charming back alleys and ducked beneath bow-necked lamp posts. At one point, she reached absentmindedly for Ben's hand to point out Buckingham Palace, only to find Riley's instead.

They bought tall takeaway coffees on Grosvenor Street, then wandered into Hyde Park, as a gentle spring sun emerged from the clouds to warm the grass. They found a spot beneath a silver maple and sat.

'I always thought I'd make this trip on my own, but I have to say, kid, I'm pretty glad you came,' Riley said, taking a long sip of her coffee and crossing her legs.

'I'm glad too,' Belle said, turning her face up to the sunlight before another cloud sailed past.

'How long do you want to stay here for?'

They hadn't made definite plans beyond the first weeks in London. Belle was happy to drift, a rarity for her since she wasn't much of a drifter. But making that pivotal break from her old life had changed her. What else was there to do when you had little left to hold on to?

Her only concern was that the money Ben had given her might not last and she would be forced to find a job to support herself. 'Maybe a week or two, then we could go to Scotland,' she suggested.

'I was thinking Paris or Amsterdam.'

'As long as I'm distracted,' Belle said. 'I don't want to think about Ben anymore.' Or his infidelity, or that this trip could have easily been their honeymoon. Every thought of him weighed her down and frankly, she was tired of it. She didn't want him there with her, his memory rattling her like aftershocks.

'Distraction I can do,' Riley said, nodding as though she

were making it her mission to keep Belle busy.

Belle's stomach rumbled loudly, and she clutched it. 'Whoops.'

'We should eat,' Riley said, 'or this coffee is going to go straight to our heads.'

Probably not a bad thing, Belle thought, as jetlag began to drag her muscles down again.

They climbed to their feet, tossed their empty coffee cups into a bin, and found a path that led back to the street. On the way to the hotel, they stumbled across a late-Edwardian pub. It had been hours since Belle had eaten, and the time difference, the flight and now the walk had made her ravenous. It was a pleasing change, this onset of appetite, when for the past two months food had only been an afterthought.

They sat inside a warm dining room of dark oak panelling and lager-soaked carpet, ordering roast beef and Yorkshire pudding. The sun relented and a light shower tapped on the glass panes, rain falling on a city that wasn't like Sydney at all. And Belle decided, after everything she'd been through, that was certainly a good thing.

———

BELLE KICKED off her shoes and collapsed onto her bed, Riley mirroring her effort across the room. Their day out in Bath had been long, starting early that morning, as most of their day trips did, in what had been a cumulative cycle of sightseeing.

Their first two weeks in London had passed quickly, but with the distraction Belle had desperately sought. She'd never yearned for the road less travelled with Ben, thoroughly content, as he'd been, for the most part, to exist only to each other. She wasn't at the point of declaring their split a blessing in disguise—no, definitely not—but she couldn't deny that spreading her wings had been like a soothing balm for her soul when all else had threatened to sink her.

She stretched her arms above her head and yawned. Endless day trips had left her exhausted, although happily so. Her only niggling concern now was the state of her bank account, and she rolled over, plucking her phone from her backpack on the floor and sinking back into the pillow. She logged into her account and winced at the balance. 'We need to plan our next move.'

From the opposite bed, Riley opened a sleepy eye. 'I was thinking Cornwall for the weekend.'

'No, I mean about money. I'm burning through it. I won't be able to stay in this hotel for much longer.'

Riley finally opened both eyes and dragged herself up into a sitting position. 'It was always our intention to find work, but so soon?'

'Not just yet, but we should start looking. It could take weeks before we find something. And we need a cheaper place to live. This hotel is bleeding me dry.' She could ask her father for a loan, but she was certain he'd refuse, and besides, she cradled her pride close. She wouldn't give him the satisfaction of knowing she was on the other side of the world, broke.

Riley flopped back down onto her pillow and closed her eyes again. 'You're right, it could take a while. London is full of foreign workers. We should travel up north where we might have a better chance.'

'Maybe we should have done some research on this before we came.' The first hints of panic gnawed at her. She'd been in such a daze before leaving that she'd left a lot of the trip to chance. What if they couldn't find work?

What if she ran out of money and couldn't afford the flight home?

Riley gave an airy wave. 'You worry too much. We'll be fine.'

'But what if we're not?'

'What's the worst that can happen?'

Belle could think of several things, but her reply was interrupted when her phone, still in her hand, began to ring. The number flashing across the screen was Avery's, the Canadian they'd met on the plane, and she smiled. The first few weeks in London had passed by so quickly, she hadn't had a chance to call her.

'Avery, hi,' she said.

'Hey, Belle.'

'I meant to call you, but it's been crazy,' she apologised. 'You must be back in Rome by now.'

'I'm still here, in London!' Avery yelled down the line, exuberant. 'But I'm going back tomorrow. Want to catch up tonight?'

'We'd love to.' Belle glanced at Riley, who had no trouble hearing Avery's voice from across the room and gave the thumbs up.

'I have someone with me though. My cousin. He's a total bore. Is it okay if he comes along?'

Belle smiled. 'Of course. Where shall we meet you?'

———

AVERY HAD SUGGESTED a pub in Marylebone that Belle and Riley located easily. They were the first to arrive, settling into wingback brocade armchairs beside a fire to wait. The pub was warm, smelling of ale and roast dinners lathered in gravy. It was still early, the dining room filled mostly with the chatter of diners, while the area of armchairs and tables around the unlit fireplace remained quiet.

They'd only been seated a few minutes when the door to the pub pushed open and a blast of cool night air rushed in. Avery and a man, who Belle presumed was her cousin, stepped inside, their eyes scanning the pub. She stood and waved from the armchairs and Avery skipped over, engulfing her in a fierce hug. The young girl wore the widest grin and there was an energy she exuded that seemed to electrify the air around her. Her hair was woven into plaits like she'd worn on the plane and her cheeks were flushed pink from the cold outside.

'Isn't this exciting?' she exclaimed. 'I didn't think we'd see each other again.' She shrugged out of her cardigan and tossed it over the back of a chair, then jabbed her finger towards the man standing next to her. 'This is my cousin, Andre.'

Andre was tall and dressed in dark jeans and a buttoned shirt. He wore his hair slightly longer than Ben's, wavy and brown, and had dimples in each of his cheeks that hollowed as he smiled at them. His eyes were the deepest brown, like pools of chocolate, framed by long lashes.

Belle stuck her hand out to him. 'Hello, I'm Belle and this is Riley.'

'*Ciao*.' He took it up, shaking it warmly. 'It's nice to meet you both. I am Andre.'

The accent caught her at first, heavily Italian, but then she noticed the way he pronounced every consonant, the way the vows rolled from his lips, and she thought it was the loveliest sound she'd ever heard.

They took a seat in the circle of armchairs, while Andre walked to the bar to order drinks. Avery was beside Belle, and she was already leaning forward talking. 'I'm so glad I managed to catch you before you moved on. I meant to call earlier but was busy.'

'We've been busy too,' Belle said. 'But I'm surprised you're still here. We thought you'd be back in Rome by now.'

Avery groaned dramatically. 'I was meant to be, but I got side-tracked. Then my uncle sent the henchman to come and get me.' She rolled her eyes as Andre returned with a tray of gin and tonics.

'I heard that,' he said, setting them down on the table between them and handing them out. The seat beside Belle was free and he lowered himself into it with his drink.

'You were meant to.' Avery threw him a look, then turned to Riley, launching into a fresh conversation about Edinburgh and Dublin, and all the places she'd visited while she should have been back in Rome.

Belle picked up her gin and tonic and sipped from it, before casting Andre, who sat almost rigid with his hands folded in his lap, a smile. He was clearly shy, overwhelmed by the gaggle of girls around him and perhaps the language barrier. 'Avery tells me your father has a restaurant in Rome,' she said, attempting to break the ice.

He nodded, his hands relaxing. 'Yes, it's not quite a restaurant though. It's a *trattoria*.' His tongue rolled over the word like a song.

Avery overheard and turned around again. 'We serve pizza and pasta. Uncle Benito isn't very adventurous with his cooking. It's a fun place but it would do a whole lot better if he offered more on the menu.'

'He is the only one in the kitchen,' Andre explained. 'He can barely keep up with the menu we have.'

'Why doesn't he hire a sous chef or a kitchen hand?' Belle asked.

Andre laughed, exposing a row of straight white teeth. 'This is my father we are talking about. It's his kitchen. His cooking. His way. He would probably drive the poor person mad.'

'He's a slavedriver,' Avery interjected again.

Andre shook his head at her. 'You should be quiet. You are in enough trouble as it is.'

'Do you work there too?' Belle asked him.

'I run the bar,' he said.

'He gets the easy job,' Avery retorted.

Andre frowned. 'Maybe if you stopped looking at your phone during service and actually did some work, you'd see how busy the bar gets.'

Belle watched their exchange with a smile. She liked their dynamic. It was far from heavy-handed or aggressive, but instead like sibling playfulness, something she'd never encountered before, being an only child. There was a clear age difference between them—Avery was in her early twenties with Andre closer to Belle and Riley's age—and it was hard not to feel sympathy for him. He'd obviously been sent to locate his wayward cousin and drag her back to Italy, something he could be forgiven for resenting.

The time edged on, and Belle was enjoying herself, as the pub grew noisier, and she talked for hours. She hadn't had stimulating conversation with people in years, her world largely consisting of Ben for too long. But it was over all too soon when Andre stood just after midnight and announced that he had to get Avery to bed. 'We have a plane to catch in the morning,' he explained. 'I need her to be sober.'

Belle giggled, then hiccupped. The gin and tonics had

gone to her head too. 'It was wonderful to meet you. It's a shame you aren't staying in London longer. We could have gone out again.' Once the words were out, they sounded forward and flirtatious, rather than the innocent platitude she'd intended, and her cheeks grew pink. His did too, as he smiled, then jammed his hands into his pockets.

Outside the pub, Avery threw her arms around Belle and Riley and held them close. 'Promise me you'll come to *Roma* soon. Promise me!'

Belle hugged her back. 'We'll try, but money's a bit tight at the moment.'

'You can stay with me! I have a spare bedroom and all you have to do is pay for your flight.'

'That's very kind. We'll think about it.'

Andre dragged Avery into a taxi and once she was inside, he turned back to Belle and Riley, smiling apologetically. 'It was nice to meet you both. Enjoy the rest of your trip.' He climbed in after his cousin and the taxi pulled away.

Riley wove her arm through Belle's as they strolled away from the pub and back to their hotel. 'Avery is a bundle of energy,' she said, 'but I like her.'

'I like her too,' Belle agreed, looking up at the sky. There were no stars to be found, London's lights washing them away, but the moon was out, a glowing orb balancing over the city. 'Do you think a trip to Rome would be possible?'

Riley glanced at her with surprise. 'You want to go to Rome?'

Belle shrugged. 'It's an idea.'

'It's a great idea, but earlier today you were concerned about money.'

'I still am, but we could go for the weekend, then come back and look for a job. Avery offered her spare room.'

'I must say,' Riley said, nodding her approval, 'I like this new Belle. The one that makes plans on a whim. We should keep her around.'

'Very funny.'

'I'm going to put it out there,' she stated matter-of-factly. 'Ben finding Olivia might have been the best thing that ever happened to you.'

Belle pulled a face. 'I wouldn't go that far.'

NINE

They wasted little time booking a flight and, two days later, their plane soared into Rome amidst a clutter of terracotta rooftops and towering church spires. Avery was waiting in the arrival's concourse for them, in the exact spot where she said she'd be and, to Belle's surprise, Andre was with her, a wide grin on his face.

Avery broke from her cousin and dashed towards them, throwing her arms around them both as though they were long lost relatives she hadn't seen in years, rather than new friends she'd just left in London.

'I can't believe you're here!' she said, loud enough to attract glances from others in the concourse. 'How was your flight?'

'It was fine,' Riley said.

Andre reached them and this time, instead of shaking Belle and Riley's hands, he leant in and kissed each of their cheeks. '*Ciao. Benvenute a Roma.*'

'Thank you,' Belle replied, although she wasn't quite sure what he'd said.

'It means welcome to Rome,' Avery explained.

'Can I take your bags?' Andre asked. He collected the handles of each of their suitcases and rolled them behind him, the muscles in his tanned arms taut and lean.

They followed him outside to the carpark, the wheels of their luggage clacking over the concrete. The rush of hot air that greeted them was not like London at all, with its cool shadows and gentle warmth. It was only eleven in the morning in Rome, but the sun was already high and glowering, and the bare skin on Belle's shoulders began to tingle with burn.

They reached a white Alfa Romeo and Andre retrieved a set of keys from his shorts' pocket, clicking it to unlock the doors. He lifted their luggage easily into the boot as Belle climbed into the back seat with Riley, and Avery climbed into the front.

Before long they were on the autostrada for the thirty-minute drive to Rome. As they sped along, Belle gazed out the window, entranced by meadows of sunflowers rolling by. She had to squint to find their end on the horizon, for they seemed to roll on forever, an abundant sea of yellow.

'Pretty, aren't they?' Avery said, turning in her seat to face Belle. 'Italy has loads of sunflower fields.'

'They're beautiful. I've never seen anything like them,' she replied.

'You're still staying with me, aren't you? You didn't do anything silly like book a hotel room.'

'We're staying,' Riley said, 'if you'll have us.'

'Of course she'll have you,' Andre said. 'Avery befriends people all the time. But you might regret your decision after the first day. She has no mute button.' He threw his cousin a playful smile and she punched his arm.

'Are you trying to scare them off?' she said. 'I knew I shouldn't have brought you.'

'Ah, but you needed my car.'

'That was the only reason, I assure you. It wasn't for your company.' Avery folded her arms petulantly.

Belle exchanged a glance with Riley, then they broke into laughter as Avery and Andre continued to antagonise each other in the front seats. She wondered how Andre found the patience to deal with his younger charge. Avery was fun and wildly spirited. Having to constantly remain one step ahead of her seemed like an impossibly endless task. Still, he seemed to take it all in his stride. He had one hand on the wheel, the other resting on the gear stick, relaxed and focused on the road. His window was partially down, tossing his hair around, his eyes hidden behind dark aviator shades. Yes, they were certainly an intriguing duo.

Belle smiled and returned her focus to the window, watching the sunflower fields roll by, as every mile carried them closer to Rome.

AVERY LIVED at the top of a three-story, terracotta-coloured building on the charming Corsia Agonale. Piazza Navona was at the end of the corsia, so close Belle could hear water trickling in fountains.

Andre's car was restricted from entering the historical parts of the city, so he parked it two blocks down and they walked the remainder of the way to Avery's apartment. Belle didn't mind at all, even when her suitcase was a challenge to manoeuvre over the uneven cobblestones. Rome, in all her ancient glory, was like walking through an open-air museum, and she wasn't sure where to cast her eye as they passed monuments and crumbling buildings, and nonnas high up on balconies hanging washing beside pots of basil and tumbling oregano.

When they climbed the steps of Avery's apartment block to drop their bags in her doorway and she suggested they head straight back out to explore, she didn't need to say it twice.

Belle inhaled as they strolled down to Piazza Navona, the scent of tomatoes and citrus, garlic and coffee permeating the air. The square itself was a pedestrian precinct, filled with restaurants and bars and three magnificent fountains erected in the middle. The square was lined with *baroque palazzi*, lovely big Italian mansions in colours of rust and amber, and the Sant'Agnese in Agone church, with its fanciful Baroque façade made of brick and limestone, provided an impressive backdrop.

They walked around the square, stopping to observe the cast of street artists and hawkers plying their trade, Andre giving a proud crash course in Roman history, while Avery shook her head at him. 'He thinks he's a tour guide.'

When their stomachs began to growl, they chose a pizzeria near the Fountain of Neptune and sat under a large white umbrella to eat. The sun was warm, a delicious smell lingering in the air and Belle felt like she'd been deposited right into the motherland of pizza. They ate cheesy calzone, drank pitchers of negroni and afterwards Andre talked Belle into drinking a *caffe doppio*—two shots of espresso in a small glass that left her eyes wide and her heart racing.

After lunch, Andre farewelled them in the square and returned to his father's trattoria, and Avery led the girls back to her apartment. It was a small flat situated up three narrow flights of stairs on the top floor, with two bedrooms, a bare kitchen, a bathroom featuring a cracked porcelain sink and shower, and a living area housing a threadbare sofa and a small coffee table. The walls were a faded olive green, and the terracotta floor tiles were a cool reprieve on tired, hot feet.

Belle and Riley collected their suitcases from where they'd parked them in the front entrance earlier and followed Avery to the spare bedroom.

'I'm hardly ever here,' Avery explained as she flung open the door. 'I'm usually working at the trattoria or out with friends.'

Belle peered inside the room. It was just large enough for the double bed and small mahogany closet. The walls were olive green too, and a small window framed with plain white curtains offered a view of the apartment block and laneway behind them. Belle grinned. It was perfect.

'This room is meant to be for my parents when they come to stay. Which is never,' Avery said, rolling her eyes. 'I hope it's okay. It's a bit small, actually.'

'It's great,' Belle insisted.

'Yes,' Riley agreed. 'We appreciate you letting us stay.'

Avery beamed. 'Help yourself to anything you like. There's not much in the way of food. I can't cook to save my life but anything that's there is yours.'

Avery showed them the balcony next. It was the apartment's hidden gem—a quaint wrought-iron balcony that overlooked the corsia below, afternoon sunlight streaming in through timber French doors to cast patterns on the tiles. While standing out there, if Belle craned her neck far enough, she could see a sliver of the Fontana dei Quattro Fiumi—the Fountain of the Four Rivers—in Piazza Navona, and the towering Agonalis Obelisk glinting in the sunlight.

'Wow,' she said, but it came out in an awed kind of whisper.

Riley leant over the balcony railing to peer below. 'How can you afford this place?'

'Well, it's hardly a palace. And I don't spend a lot on food or utilities because I'm hardly here.'

'I can't imagine you'd ever want to leave,' Belle said, gazing out at the busy lane, filled with people walking or crowding around tables draped in red and white checked cloths, drinking shots of espresso. She was breathless with exhilaration, her focus unable to settle on one thing. While London had been a frantic attempt to distract herself with activity, Rome felt embracing—a place to lose herself in colours and smells.

'As much as I complain about my uncle and Andre, I do love it here. I have a lot of freedom and I'm independent,' Avery said.

They spent a few minutes more on the balcony, then she indicated that they go back inside. The air was considerably stuffier in the living room without the convenience of an air conditioner, and she tugged on a cord to turn the ceiling fan on.

'I don't have to work tonight,' she said, dragging a hand across the sweat on her brow. 'I'll take you to Trastevere. It has lots of bars and restaurants. But I'm rostered for lunch and dinner tomorrow. You could visit me at the trattoria.'

'Sure,' Belle said.

'And since you're only here for two days, you should do some sightseeing while I'm at work.'

'Okay.' Belle didn't want to talk about leaving already. As she and Riley unpacked clothes from their suitcases and hung them in the narrow bedroom closet, she had a sudden urge to cram in as much as possible. In the pursuit of distraction, London had been an effective pastime, but she could already sense that Rome had the power to be all-encompassing, to chase away the chill in her heart with its intoxicating energy. To love her in a way that Ben couldn't.

TEN

The cobblestones were already baking under the morning sun when Belle, Riley and Avery set out from the apartment the next day. The trattoria was only a short walk away, across Piazza Navona, and although it was early, the square was alive with tourists and hawkers.

'What's the trattoria called?' Belle asked. They passed the Fontana del Moro—the Moor Fountain—cool water gurgling from the mouths of the Tritons.

'Valentina's,' Avery replied. 'It was Andre's mother's name.'

'*Was*?' Belle glanced at her abruptly.

'Aunty Valentina passed away when he was five,' she explained. 'I'd never met her because she died before I was born, but from what I understand, she was sick with cancer.'

'Oh.' Belle's heart grew heavy for Andre at the thought. 'That's awful.'

'After she died, Uncle Benito bought the trattoria here in Rome and called it Valentina's.'

'It's been around for a while, then?' Riley asked.

'About thirty years,' Avery said, as they left the square,

stepping onto Via di Pasquino. 'And believe me, it's showing its age.'

'The place must mean the world to Andre and Uncle Benito,' Belle said.

'It does, but it's in desperate need of a makeover. Uncle Benito has been cooking the same old food since the day it opened. I know he's protective of his little trattoria, but the business is going downhill.' She groaned theatrically. 'Restaurants in Rome need to adapt to the times. The culinary movement has taken off here. Whoever doesn't keep up will get left behind or worse, they'll go bankrupt.'

They arrived at a laneway off Via di Pasquino, bordered by ancient stone buildings and rows of potted lemon trees and pink petunias. Avery led them down the cobbled path, past unassuming bars where locals sipped coffee, to a white striped awning. By the front door, affixed to the trattoria's exterior, was a rectangular bronze sign, the word *Valentina's* inscribed on it. Cluttered around the awning was a collection of small circular tables draped with red and white checked cloths.

Avery pushed through the door, and Belle and Riley followed, stepping across the threshold. Although it wasn't lunch yet, the trattoria pulsed with activity. There was an air of organised chaos as tables were set with glasses and cutlery, and an espresso machine whirred near the bar. The room was noisy, the sound of rapid English and Italian filling the air, people laughing and joking, the *swoosh* of tablecloths, a song on the radio.

'They're preparing for lunch,' Avery explained.

Belle took in the frenzy with a wide grin. It was nothing like the sedate café she'd left behind in Sydney, with its lethargic atmosphere. This trattoria was energetic. And although Italian waiters were rushing around, she thought she heard the acoustics of other accents too, Russian, and American. 'Does your uncle employ foreigners?' she asked.

'Yes. Everyone in Italy does,' Avery replied. 'It's cheaper than employing someone from the EU. That's how Uncle Benito can afford us all. It's illegal, of course, but cash is king here. Money always exchanges hands.'

Belle turned to gauge Riley's reaction to this but found that she was no longer by her side. She'd drifted towards one of the tables and was in conversation with an Italian waiter who was laying out dishes of parmesan. His dark eyes and playful smile were fixed on her, and when he said something, Riley must have found it amusing, for she threw her head back and laughed seductively.

'I'd introduce you to Uncle Benito, but he's probably busy in the kitchen,' Avery said with apology. 'Lunch starts in an hour.'

Belle returned her focus to her. 'Oh, that's okay. I don't want to disturb him.'

'I'll see you later then, after midnight. That's when I finish. Do you have your key for the flat?'

Belle patted her backpack slung over her shoulder. 'I have the key.'

'Great.' Avery threw her arms around Belle and hugged her tightly. 'I'm so glad you came to Rome!' She skipped away, disappearing into the chaos.

While Belle waited for Riley, she cast her gaze across the trattoria. Aside from the tired whitewashed walls and dated furniture, it had classic Italian charm. Leafy dwarf olive trees in terracotta pots dotted the four corners of the room, an abundance of coloured olives on twiggy stems, and walls were lined with canvases depicting Naples, Venice, and the Amalfi Coast. A woodfire pizza oven roared, a deliciously smoky smell emanating from its cavern.

Her eyes swept across to the bar where she saw Andre with his head down polishing glasses, expression serious, a strand of hair dangling over his eyes. When he glanced up and their gazes locked, his face broke into a wide smile.

'*Ciao*,' he mouthed to her, for there was no way to hear his voice above the noise.

'*Ciao*,' she mouthed back, then dropped her eyes when her cheeks unexpectedly flushed.

Riley returned to her side. 'Ready to go?'

'I am, but are *you*?' Belle asked with a knowing look.

Riley grinned like a Cheshire cat. 'Yes, let's go.'

They stepped back out into the laneway, the morning sun fierce over the city. First on their list to explore was the Pantheon, a five-minute walk from Valentina's and, along the way, they stopped at a small bar for espresso and *zeppole* —a deep-fried sugary dough ball topped with custard and Nutella. No matter where locals headed in Rome, they always drank their coffee at the espresso bars dotting the sidewalks. Ordering takeaway coffee was considered sacrilege, as was sitting down at a table like a tourist where the cost was inflated, and so everyone stood at the bars and drank.

'Did you see it?' Belle asked, deciding to raise what had been on her mind since leaving the trattoria.

'See what?' Riley paid for their espressos and *zeppole*, then took a cautious sip of her coffee.

'The waiters at Valentina's. They weren't just Italian. They were American and Russian. Andre's father employs foreigners outside the EU.'

'I hadn't noticed.'

'And I don't think they have working visas.' She dropped her voice to a whisper, although it was unlikely that she would be overheard. Everyone in the bar was talking in rapid Italian and the fan above them whirred noisily. 'Avery said lots of businesses in Italy hire foreigners without visas.'

Riley lifted an eyebrow. 'Isn't that illegal?'

'Illegal, yes. Enforced? I don't think so.'

Riley reached for a dough ball and tore it in half, stuffing it into her mouth. 'Where are you going with this exactly?'

Belle popped a chunk of dough into her mouth too and dusted her hands of the sugar. 'What if I got a job here instead? In a restaurant. It might be easier than going back to London to find one. We could stay with Avery—I know she wouldn't mind. We could help her with rent and utilities.'

'You want to stay in Rome?'

'I think so.'

'What would I do for work?'

'There are hundreds of art galleries here. With your experience, they'd fall over themselves to hire you.'

Riley shook her head as though the conversation was still taking her by surprise. 'Wait, just so we're clear, you want to *stay* in Rome. Long-term?'

Belle took a fortifying breath. She wasn't accustomed to making grand decisions in such a way. She'd always left that sort of thing to Ben, but there was no Ben anymore, and Belle had to carve her own future. Rome felt right; it had from the minute she'd stepped off the plane. She watched Riley's reaction carefully as she said, 'Yes. I want to stay.'

Riley took another sip of her espresso, which felt interminably long, her expression contemplative. Finally, she said, 'I suppose there's no harm in staying for a few months, if that's what you want to do.'

Belle gasped. 'Really? You would stay with me?'

'Well, I'm not about to leave you here.' Riley looked offended at the suggestion.

Belle threw her arms around her friend. 'Thank you. This means a lot to me.'

Riley hugged her back. 'I know it does, kid.'

They finished their espressos and *zeppole* and left the small bar, hitting the scorched pavement again.

'Where are you going to apply for work?' Riley asked as they walked.

Belle consulted Maps on her phone, directing them onto Via del Teatro Valle. The street was narrow, old stone buildings rising to block out the sun and drench them in welcome shade. 'I'm going to ask Uncle Benito.'

'Andre's father? You want to work at Valentina's?'

'Yes,' Belle said, dabbing the sweat that had gathered on the back of her neck. 'It seems a good place to start. And I already know Avery and Andre. Maybe they could vouch for me.'

'And I know Leo.'

Belle raised her eyebrow. 'Was that the waiter's name?'

Riley's smile was coy. 'Maybe.'

———

THEY ARRIVED BACK at the apartment later that afternoon. While Riley sat on the balcony with a Peroni and her phone to search art galleries, Belle raced across Piazza Navona to Valentina's. The lunch shift had ended, and staff were redressing the tables for dinner. The trattoria smelled of woodfired pizza, coffee beans and the unmistakable scent of sambuca.

'Hey, you're back.' Avery bounded towards her, her plaits askew. 'I'm due for a break. Let's have a quick espresso.' As swiftly as she'd appeared, she disappeared again, back into the frenzy of the trattoria.

Belle glanced around for Andre, hoping to say hello, but found herself disappointed when he was nowhere in the dining room. Avery returned a few minutes later carrying two short blacks. She led Belle outside to the empty tables in the laneway, and they sat.

'Tell me all about your day,' Avery said, sipping the crema from her espresso.

Belle sipped too, feeling the bitterness of the coffee flood her tastebuds. She was still getting used to coffee as strong and black as the Romans drank it. 'Amazing. We visited the Pantheon, then had lunch in Piazza della Rotonda. I think I had the best espresso I've ever tasted in a little bar right on the square's edge.' She'd had so much coffee that day, she thought her nervous system would implode.

'The Rotonda has the best coffee in the world,' Avery said, enunciating every word for dramatic effect.

'I may not sleep tonight. I've had a fair bit of it today.'

'But that's okay.' Avery spread her arms wide, slipping into an Italian accent. 'No one sleeps in *Roma*. We drink coffee all day and make love all night.'

Belle giggled, taking another sip. 'I did want to speak to you about something, though,' she said, setting her glass back down. 'You mentioned earlier that your uncle employs foreigners to work in his trattoria.'

'That's right. Half the wait staff are international workers.'

'I was wondering if he was hiring. If he'd consider hiring me.'

'You want a job here?' Avery's eyebrows shot up.

'Yes,' Belle said. 'I have experience working in a café

and I wouldn't expect to be paid much. Just enough to get by on.'

'You're considering staying in Rome then?' Avery's eyebrows had relaxed but her smile broadened.

'Yes. We'd like to.'

Her squeal of delight was ear-splitting. 'The trattoria has a high turnover of staff because foreigners come and go. I'm sure he'd have something for you. Why don't you come back with me tomorrow morning? We'll speak to him together before the lunch shift.'

'Really?' Excitement bubbled in Belle's stomach. She tried to quell it, not wanting to get her hopes up. 'That would be great. I can serve food and drinks, wash dishes, scrub floors. I can even cook if he needs me in the kitchen.'

'No.' Avery shook her head firmly. 'Uncle Benito doesn't let anyone in his kitchen. He's very protective of it. You'll be confined to the dining room, waiting tables.' Dinner guests began meandering down the laneway towards them and Avery stood, collecting their empty glasses. 'I'd better go. Service is about to start. I just hope you know what you're signing up for. I don't want to deter you, but the shifts here are long. Most days you'll be working fourteen hours.'

But the thought didn't deter Belle. She hugged Avery and left the laneway, stepping onto Via di Pasquino and slipping into the southern entrance of Piazza Navona. As she walked back to the apartment under the glowering sun, she couldn't wipe the smile from her face. Chance may have delivered her to Rome, along with a broken heart, but a job in that beautiful, messy city would provide the purpose she sought.

And a place to take a breath, just for a while.

ELEVEN

Belle hardly slept that night, too excited for what the morning would bring. When it was time to leave for Valentina's with Avery, she farewelled Riley, who was sitting on the balcony, long legs up on the railing, eating jam toast and scrolling through her phone. 'Good luck,' she called out to them, her voice still thick with sleep.

Piazza Navona was already teeming when they reached it. At the Fontana dei Quattro Fiumi, a gaggle of tourists had gathered, tossing their coins into the water and casting wishes to the four rivers.

Minutes later, they reached the laneway off Via di Pasquino, then walked through the front door of Valentina's. Like the day before, waiters inside were preparing for the lunch shift.

'Wait here. I'll get Uncle Benito.' Avery skipped in the direction of a set of swinging doors that led to the kitchen while Belle waited by the entrance, trying to keep out of the way of the staff.

It wasn't long before she emerged again, followed by Andre and an older man with a shock of grey hair and a round belly that protruded behind his apron. Yet it was when he stood next to Andre that Belle noticed their similarities—the strong jaw, perceptive dark eyes, and thick, wavy hair.

As Uncle Benito approached her, her stomach flipped with nerves. It had been a long time between job applications, and she wished she'd rehearsed a few polished lines for what could possibly become an impromptu interview. She was glad, at least, that she'd worn her prettiest floral dress and had set her hair in two neat French braids.

Andre smiled warmly as they reached her, his eyes sweeping over her outfit.

'So you must be Belle,' Uncle Benito said, standing before her and placing floury hands on his hips. 'My son told me all about you last night.'

Andre blushed profusely.

'Yes, I'm Belle. It's a pleasure to meet you,' she said, holding her hand out to shake Uncle Benito's.

He accepted it warmly in his. 'My niece, Avery, says you're looking for a job.'

'Please. If you have anything available.'

'You work hard?' he asked, narrowing his eyes.

Belle nodded eagerly. 'Yes. *Si.*'

'You work in a restaurant before?'

'Not exactly. More like a café. *Un bar.*'

Andre leant towards his father and relayed something in Italian.

Uncle Benito nodded with understanding. 'Okay, okay, I see. You work in bar. Well, we serve more than just espresso and *pasticcini* here. We are a trattoria. You will serve hot food, wait tables, and clear and redress them before each shift. And the hours are long. I don't pay much.'

'That's fine,' she said quickly.

'Do you have a working visa?'

Belle's shoulders slumped with disappointment. 'No, I don't.'

He made a small sound which Belle couldn't decipher, and she felt the opportunity slipping away. Finally, after agonising silence, he nodded. *'Va bene*. You don't tell anyone you work here without a visa, eh?'

She brightened. 'Of course.'

'Then come back this afternoon. We will see how you go during dinner. If you can do half as good a job as Avery, you're hired.'

BELLE WASN'T EXPECTED back at Valentina's until five. She raced across Piazza Navona, along Corsia Agonale and climbed the stairs two at a time up to Avery's apartment. She wanted to tell Riley about her trial at Valentina's later that night, but when she let herself into the humid flat, she found Riley out on the balcony with a tall man. As she neared the balcony doors, she realised it was Leo, the waiter from Valentina's.

'You're back!' Riley said as Belle stepped outside. 'How did it go?'

'I have a trial tonight,' Belle said, squinting up at Leo. Backlit by the sunlight, she noticed dark eyes and hair, and a charismatic smile. It wasn't lost on her that he was much younger than Riley, but by the way his eyes rarely left hers, he was clearly smitten.

'Belle's going to work at Valentina's,' Riley explained to Leo. 'You'll be colleagues.'

'You will like it there,' he said with a thick Italian accent. 'It's fun, like a party.'

'So does that mean we're staying?' Riley asked. Her question betrayed a hint of hope as she glanced at Leo.

'If we both get a job, I think we should,' Belle said.

Riley beamed. It was obvious she wanted to, and that perhaps this young waiter was part of the reason. 'Leo has the day off today. We're heading to Naples. Want to come?'

Belle would have loved to explore colourful Naples, but it was already mid-morning, and she didn't want to risk being late for her first shift. 'I better not. We might not make it back in time.'

'We'll do something together soon, okay?' Riley engulfed her in a hug and kissed her cheek. 'Good luck at Valentina's. I want to hear all about it later.'

They collected their backpacks and Riley called out, '*Ciao, bella!*' as they left the apartment.

From her spot on the balcony, Belle listened to their footsteps echo down the stairwell, then watched as they emerged through the front door and out into the foot traffic below.

She smiled. It had been a long time since Riley had appeared interested in a man. Her interactions with the opposite sex were usually restricted to one-night stands, a self-imposed rule that saw her slinking away before dawn, never answering their calls again. But that was the beauty of Rome. She was charming and seductive, and you could be forgiven for forgetting who you once were, as she folded you in her arms and changed you.

The heat of the day was already penetrating the apartment and with hours to kill before her shift started, Belle decided to leave the stuffy flat and explore Rome. She wiped the dampness from her face and reset her braids, then changed into shorts and swapped her sandals for sneakers.

The air was heavy when she stepped back outside, but she still paused for an espresso at the bar next door to the apartment. She stood at an outdoor table to drink, watching people stroll past, mostly tourists in these parts, with the corsia's proximity to Navona, then she headed off on foot.

She meandered the streets, gazed at the shopfronts, became happily lost in the maze of cobbled laneways, then stumbled upon the Trevi Fountain, tossing coins into the water, and wishing she could stay forever. She allowed the sights, smells and sounds of Rome to guide her and for once, it felt liberating to walk without plan or purpose. Once upon a time, she would have balked at the idea of exploring on her own. She would have waited for Ben to join her. But singledom had thrust Belle into a new world of independence, and as daunting as it had once seemed, it now felt empowering, like she was the master of her own fate.

As the afternoon drew to a close, she stopped for one last espresso near Piazza di Montecitorio, then headed back to the apartment to get ready for work.

THE STAFF WERE REDRESSING the tables for the dinner shift when she arrived back at five. New cutlery was being laid out, along with fresh napkins, salt and pepper, and dishes of parmesan. Avery bounced to the door to greet her and placed a black collared shirt in her hands with the word *Valentina's* embroidered in white font on the front.

Belle beamed, clutched the shirt to her chest and disappeared into the female washroom to change. When she returned to the dining room minutes later wearing her new uniform, Avery directed her to the head waiter, Angelo, for training.

The doors opened promptly at six, and service trickled to life as diners meandered their way to tables. They placed drink orders, followed by entrees and mains, and the food began to flow from the kitchen pass.

Belle was slow to begin with, uncoordinated in the art of carrying larger plates than she was used to, and deciphering the menu, which was worded solely in Italian but may as well have been written in Egyptian hieroglyphs for all she could understand. But she was competent with the coffee machine whenever Andre needed help and, to her immense relief, she didn't drop a single plate or glass during the shift.

By the middle of the evening, she found her rhythm enough to speed up a little and could begin to pronounce certain dishes on the menu. She rarely saw Uncle Benito except at the kitchen pass where he barked orders, a permanent sheen of sweat on his brow as he worked furiously to keep up, despite the trattoria only filling half its capacity. It wasn't busy, but it was enough to test a solitary chef.

When the last customer had left and the doors closed, Belle collapsed into a chair. She was tired, her feet aching, and her mouth parched.

'*Signorina*,' Andre said, appearing next to her, flicking a dish towel over his shoulder. 'You did well tonight.'

'Thank you,' she said, looking up into warm eyes.

'In *Italiano*, we say *grazie*,' he said.

'*Grazie*.' She smiled at him, then blushed when a deep yawn escaped her. 'Oh, pardon me.'

He chuckled, amused. 'Is it your first time doing a long shift like this?'

'Sort of. I've never worked until midnight before. I used to work day shifts. And I was stationed at the coffee machine mostly.' She realised he was watching her face intently and she blushed. She must have looked a mess—shabby braids, tired eyes, a pink nose from the sun that day. 'Avery's meeting up with friends after work, but I think I'll head straight home.' She climbed to her feet and pushed the chair in.

'Head home? Now? But you haven't had dinner yet.'

'Dinner?' She scrunched up her nose. 'It's midnight.'

'This is dinner time for us,' he said with a grin.

She turned and noticed the staff were stripping away dirty tablecloths. Old cutlery and dishes were being whisked away too. The male waiters pushed together several of the tables to form one long line, then they were wiped clean and redressed. The head waiter, Angelo, collected bottles of red wine and sambuca from behind the bar, placing them with glasses up and down the tables.

'See, you can't go home yet, *signorina*,' Andre said, beckoning her to join him, 'because now it's our turn to eat.'

Valentina's staff gathered along the line of tables. Avery was across from her, deep in conversation with a Russian waitress called Natalya, and someone had turned on the radio, filling the air with loud music. Belle had been so busy during service she hadn't realised how hungry she was, and she took the seat proffered by Andre, aware of her empty stomach.

A few people passed by to congratulate her on her first successful service. Someone poured her a wine and shoved it into her hand. Two staff members retreated to the kitchen pass and returned moments later with trays of pizza, pasta and bread, which they spread out along the tables, the aroma of garlic, basil, and cheese wafting through the air.

Uncle Benito emerged from the kitchen, hanging his sauce-splattered apron on a hook by the swinging doors, and the room stood and clapped for him. Andre handed his father a glass of sambuca, and Uncle Benito held it high in the air, shouting, '*Saluti!*' before knocking it back in one swift motion.

'*Saluti!*' the table responded with a loud fervent cheer, signalling the beginning of the meal. Everyone dove in, platters of food, glasses and wine bottles being passed this way and that in what could only be described as joyful chaos.

'Is this a special occasion or do you do this every night after service?' Belle asked Andre.

'We do this every night, seven days a week. We're a family. And families eat together.'

As she looked around the table at everyone, she understood what he meant, for they looked and felt exactly like a family, with all the love and togetherness that made families whole. They drank wine, broke bread, ate food, and laughed at each other's jokes.

It made Belle question if she'd ever truly been part of a family. She'd always been aware of it, her father's conditional love and Ben's unwillingness to commit. She'd never fit their mould and so they'd punished her by restricting love and acceptance, never quite letting her in.

She marvelled at how easily these people had allowed her into their lives. She was a stranger, yet they had opened their hearts, their homes, and their trattoria to her, all without strings attached. She was waiting for the penny to drop, for someone to say, *wait a minute, you need to be an achiever to win our love.*

She popped a chunk of bread into her mouth and looked up to find Uncle Benito peering down at her.

'*Bella,*' he said, nodding his approval. '*Ben fatto.*'

She looked to Andre for translation, and he smiled at her. 'He said, "well done".'

Belle swallowed the bread and smiled too. 'Thank you.'

'Would you like to come back tomorrow?' Uncle Benito asked.

'That depends. Are you offering me a job?'

He blinked and grinned, his eyes crinkling.

'You can take that as a yes,' Andre said with a laugh.

Belle squealed as Uncle Benito patted her shoulder and shuffled back to his seat at the head of the table. She couldn't believe it. She'd found herself a job, and while the hours would be long and the pay meagre, she wouldn't have turned it down for all the world. She'd discovered a place to plant her feet, somewhere to call home and rest her weary soul, to forget about Ben and her broken heart. The feeling of belonging to this beautiful and vibrant family ... well, that was just the icing on the cake.

TWELVE

Days soon became weeks and between Riley's new job at the National Gallery of Modern and Contemporary Art— where she worked three days a week as an exhibit designer —and Belle's long shifts at Valentina's, they rarely saw each other. Whatever free time Riley had, she usually spent with Leo and, as Belle worked most days and nights, the weeks began to pass with little more than a hurried hello and goodbye as they departed in different directions.

But Riley was happy, and that made Belle happy, so she didn't feel guilty about throwing herself into her new life in Rome. And Avery was delightful company. They often walked through the piazza together to work, then laughed through shifts, balancing plates of food and drinks until midnight. Between shifts, Avery showed Belle the locals' Rome, licking *gelati* as they abandoned the beaten path to find small, fairy-tale-like neighbourhoods that were free of tourists, like the utterly enchanting Quartiere Coppedè, with its whimsical architecture and chandeliered archways.

'Avery's like the little sister I never had,' Belle told Riley one morning as they set out early to visit the fresh produce markets in Piazza Campo de' Fiori. It was less than a ten-minute walk from the apartment and they passed through Navona on their way, the early heat cloying.

Belle had a rare Saturday off and she had told Riley in no uncertain terms that she wanted to spend it with her.

'Did you hear her get in at four this morning?' Riley asked as she linked her arm through Belle's.

Belle adjusted her burlap tote to avoid it knocking against Riley. 'Was that what time it was? I knew it was late. Or early.'

'I don't know how she does it—parties all night after Valentina's, sleeps a few hours, then works until midnight again.'

'It's called youth.' Belle chuckled.

'Yes, but you shouldn't be walking home late at night on your own.'

'I don't walk home alone. Andre walks me whenever Avery goes out.'

Riley's eyebrow lifted. 'I see.'

Belle nudged her with her elbow. 'It's not like that. He sees me safely to the door, we talk for a bit, then he leaves.'

'Okay.' Riley was smiling now.

'Believe me, there's nothing exciting about my love life to tell. On the other hand.' She threw Riley an expectant look, hoping she would take the bait, but she glanced the other way, finding convenient interest in a gypsy selling a necklace to an elderly tourist.

'I've hardly seen you,' Belle persisted when Riley wasn't forthcoming. She didn't want to badger her, since she'd been equally as busy. She just missed Riley, especially when they lived together under the same roof but rarely saw each other.

'I know and I'm sorry,' Riley said, giving up on watching

the gypsy and turning her attention back to Belle. 'I've been occupied.'

'You don't have to apologise,' Belle said. 'I have been too. Double shifts every day for the past three weeks.' She sighed with mock irritation. Truthfully, she was enjoying her work at Valentina's even if it was exhausting. 'Things seem to be going well with Leo.'

A hint of a smile tugged at Riley's lips. 'They are. It's been a whirlwind, actually. I wasn't prepared for it. But he's fun and sweet. He makes me laugh.'

'How old is he?' Belle wasn't oblivious to the age difference.

'Old enough,' Riley said with a wink.

Belle laughed. They left the southern end of Piazza Navona and crossed over the busy Corsia Vittorio Emanuele II, the sun beating down on their bare shoulders.

'You know me,' Riley said. 'I'm not the relationship kind. I'm not the girl that men take home to meet their mothers. And that's fine. But it's different with Leo.' She dropped her head briefly, not before Belle caught the look of vulnerability on her face. 'He talks constantly about marriage and children and buying a vineyard just outside Rome. He's intense and emotional; he wears his heart on his sleeve. He makes me talk about things I would never normally talk about.'

'Have you met his family?'

'Not yet. But I sense that he wants me to. He's close to them, especially his mother. It scares me a bit, but in a good way.' Riley had little contact with her parents, her mother living in Seattle with her new husband and children, and her father retreating to Western Australia decades ago to live out his life in the mines. It hadn't occurred to Belle that she might crave the comfort of a big family, for Riley had always seemed content on her own.

'Have you slept with him?' she asked.

Riley cast her an earnest look. 'No. We've just kissed. We both want the first time to be special.'

Belle tried not to look gobsmacked as a niggle of envy worked its way into her conscience. She'd spent twenty years trying to make Ben wear his heart on his sleeve, to commit to children and a life together. Riley had never wanted any of those things and there they were, dropping uninvited into her lap. Then, in the next breath, Belle berated herself for being petty. Riley deserved happiness just as much as anyone, the chance at love, at finding a soul mate. Leo had made her smile again, had grounded her in a way that few people had ever been able to do. Belle couldn't resent that.

They reached the bustling marketplace in Piazza Campo de' Fiori, and a ripple of excitement shot through her. Restaurants and espresso bars lined the square, and the monument of Giordano Bruno stood boldly in the centre. Stalls were clustered around him, large umbrellas erect, and crates overflowed with nuts, fruits, and vegetables. There were bowls laden with crusty bread, jars of pickles and sauces, tubs of dried pasta, and buckets brimming with flowers.

She grabbed Riley's arm and tugged her forward, stopping at a stand filled with every type of cheese known to Italy. She grabbed a wedge of pecorino and raised it to her nose, breathing in its nutty aroma. Pleased with her first selection of the day, she moved on to a tub of ricotta.

'You really love it here, don't you?' Riley said, watching her relish in the cheeses like a child in a candy store.

Belle smiled with the same fondness she'd grown to

associate with Rome. 'I loved it from the moment I stepped off the plane. I can't explain why; it just feels like the right place for me.'

'Because of the food?'

'Not just because of the food. I belong here, like I have purpose. That probably sounds silly.'

Riley was quick. 'No, it doesn't. I feel it too.'

Belle studied the ricotta in the tub, inspecting its dimply surface, before ordering a kilo of it, along with the pecorino wedge. She handed the attendant some coins, glad that she'd taken the time to convert larger euro bills into *spicci*—small change—before coming, for it was the preferred transaction at outdoor marketplaces. Andre had forewarned her that large bills would be frowned upon.

'You know Andre likes you,' Riley said unexpectedly.

Belle blinked in surprise. 'How could you possibly know that?'

'Leo told me.'

'And how would he know? I can't see Andre pouring his heart out to Leo.'

Riley snorted. 'He doesn't need to pour his heart out. Apparently, it's written all over his face every time you walk into that trattoria.'

Belle ignored her, but her heart hummed a strangely pleasant beat as they moved to the next stall, where rows of wicker baskets were filled with nuts and seeds. 'We should go on a day trip soon. The five of us. Maybe the Vatican or Cinque Terre if we can all get the same day off.' She tipped a scoopful of *marrone del Mugello*—a sweet vanilla-flavoured chestnut—into a brown paper bag and paid the lady.

'Sure. Just let me know when.' Riley raised an eyebrow as Belle paused at the next stall and lifted a giant eggplant to inspect. 'What in the world are you buying? And what are you going to do with all this food?'

'This is eggplant, *melanzane* in Italian. And I'm going to cook it,' Belle said.

'In that tiny kitchen at Avery's?'

'All I need is a good pan, some bench space and an oven or stove. And yes, we need food in that apartment. I've never seen such empty cupboards before.'

'Good luck!'

'Maybe one night you could stay home and cook with me. If you can tear yourself away from your boyfriend,' Belle teased.

Riley threw her head back and chortled. 'I don't cook. And I think it's a bit premature to be calling Leo my boyfriend.'

But as they moved to the next stall, Belle noticed Riley wore the widest grin.

THE NEXT MORNING, Belle wove her hair into her usual braids, threw on her black Valentina's uniform, and bounced down the stairs of the apartment block with Avery. They pushed through the door at the bottom to find Andre waiting on the pavement.

'Andre!' Belle said in surprise.

'*Ciao*,' he said, with an awkward half-wave.

'What are you doing here?' Avery blurted, as though the sight of him on her doorstep was completely puzzling.

'It's a beautiful day,' he said. 'I thought maybe we could walk to work together.'

Avery scoffed. 'You already walk her home at night. Do you need to walk her in the mornings too?'

Andre's cheeks flushed red.

'Besides, I've been here a whole year and you've never once picked me up for work.' She huffed her offence and flounced ahead, quickly becoming lost in the sea of people on the corsia.

Andre let out a slow breath, sliding embarrassed eyes towards Belle. 'Sorry,' he said. 'I hope you don't mind that I came here.'

She smiled reassuringly. 'Of course not. I just hope it's not too far out of your way. She's right, you already walk me home in the evenings. I don't want to take up all your time.' Andre and Uncle Benito lived on the other side of the city. Walking her home occasionally at night was one thing but looping back around to collect her in the morning was surely an inconvenience.

'It's fine for me. I like to walk, as long as you don't mind the company either.'

They rounded the corner of the corsia and stepped into Piazza Navona. The square was already heaving with life. The morning sun burned brightly, making the water in the fountains glisten, and tourists wandered aimlessly, melting *gelati* in one hand and cameras in the other.

'I like this thing you do with your hair,' he said, pointing to her.

'My braids?' Her hands reached up to touch the ends of her French braids, two neat gleaming ropes cascading over her shoulders. She'd worn her hair that way for years and was an efficient braider.

'Yes. They suit you,' he said. 'In Italian we say *carina*. Cute!'

Her cheeks flamed at the compliment. It seemed whenever she was around Andre, she was permanently blushing. 'Thank you.'

They sidestepped a tour group gathered around an artist drawing a caricature. Some of the square was still drenched in shade, but the sun was quickly chasing it away, baking the ground.

'About walking me home at night,' Belle said, 'I hate putting you out. At two am, it's a bit much.'

Andre chuckled. 'Please, don't feel bad. A woman should not walk across the square on her own at night. Rome is safe, of course, but I'm not willing to take that chance.'

'Have you ever walked Avery home? I think she was a little offended earlier.'

'I've walked her home many times. She's my cousin and I want to keep her safe too. But mostly she goes out with friends after work. Honestly, I find it difficult keeping up with her.' He scratched his head, a perplexed look on his face.

She understood what he meant. Avery had more energy than Belle ever remembered having at her age. Although, to be fair, at the same age, Belle had already been in a five-year relationship with Ben. Sometimes she felt like an old maid, having missed out on the social experiences of her youth, trading parties with friends for quiet dinners at home. Avery was living her best life, having fun at an age when it was crucial to spread her wings and gain her independence. Belle's one regret was that she'd never spread her wings and she'd never been independent.

'I see she hasn't convinced you yet to go out after work?' Andre said.

'Sadly, my party days are over,' Belle quipped. 'Not that I ever did much of it in the first place. I missed out on all that.'

He tilted his head questioningly.

'I'd been in a serious relationship since I was sixteen,' she explained. 'It ended recently and ... well, twenty years down the drain and here I am.' She hadn't meant to sound cynical, but it had crept in unconsciously. One could easily argue that she'd learnt a lot in those twenty years, but somehow, she'd yet to find the lesson in any of it.

Andre nodded slowly, chewing his lip. 'Is that what brought you all the way here, *signorina*? A broken heart?'

Belle was surprised to find her throat clogged with emotion. It had been weeks since she'd thought of Ben. Occasionally, something would remind her of him, and he'd drift into her thoughts uninvited, although he was becoming less of a presence these days and more an apparition. Still, when he did flit through her mind, it was with the dispiriting realisation that his betrayal was still raw.

Andre was watching her, and she forced a smile. 'Yes, a broken heart brought me here. A broken dream. A broken life. Everything felt apart.' Her voice wobbled and she cast her eyes forward, afraid that if she met Andre's gaze, she'd crumple into a heap.

They reached the end of the piazza, Via di Pasquino stretching ahead of them and the laneway to Valentina's around the corner. She was surprised when Andre's fingers found hers, a slight brush, then a light squeeze.

'Whatever brought you here, Belle, whether it was a broken heart or wanderlust, or to chase all those missed opportunities, you're going to be fine. I know you will be.'

His voice held such certainty and kindness that her eyes welled, and she had to look away for fear of letting him see her tears. They reached the laneway, then eventually Valentina's, and before they stepped through the trattoria's door, she caught his smile, one so hopeful and honest, that every part of her believed him.

THIRTEEN

Belle reached for a tray of hot margherita pizza from the pass and delivered it to a waiting table where an elderly man and his wife sat. They were loyal customers, part of a handful of regulars who frequented often, but aside from them and a few other occupied tables, Valentina's was quiet.

It had been a slow shift, a slow month, Rome plunged into a cool autumn as tourists retreated to their usual lives. Even so, Valentina's had never experienced the kind of roaring trade that the other trattorias did, the ones that offered interesting menus and had more chefs in the kitchen. Even at the height of summer, Valentina's was often overlooked for the more favourable restaurants that lined the piazzas.

Belle returned to the pass to check on a plate of garlic bread she was waiting for, Avery loitering beside the potted olive tree nearby, checking her phone. 'Slow night,' she mumbled.

Belle made a sound of agreement. 'Is it always like this in the off-season?'

'Compared with other restaurants, yes. Even in winter they're busy, while we struggle.' Avery pushed her phone into the back pocket of her pants. 'Uncle Benito's barely paying the bills.'

Belle glanced around the trattoria. Only half the wait staff were working that night. Josh, Natalya and Chase, all foreigners like her, were staving off boredom, talking by the register, while Avery loafed about unenthusiastically. Valentina's was a shadow of herself. She could have been thriving, with crammed tables and conversation that was musical, with wait staff frantically delivering plates of food. Instead, peak and off-seasons had blended to create a humdrum atmosphere, and Belle wondered how the trattoria managed to stay afloat at all.

'It's the menu,' Avery complained, watching her. 'It's the most boring menu in Rome. But try telling him that.' She rolled her eyes in the direction of the kitchen and Uncle Benito. 'He's as stubborn as a mule.'

The plate of garlic bread arrived on the pass, Uncle Benito pushing it towards her before scurrying away again. Belle threw Avery a commiserating smile, then reached for the plate and delivered it to the waiting table. Satisfied that her section of the dining room was under control, she walked to the bar, where Andre was preparing a tray of espressos.

His eyes lit up as she approached, the machine shooting jets of coffee into small cups. '*Signorina.*'

'Hello,' she said.

'Slow night.'

'It is.' She glanced at the tray. 'Can I take that for you?'

'Please. Table ten, since Avery is doing nothing again.' He frowned at his cousin who was still by the olive tree, engrossed once more in her phone. 'Is she going out tonight?'

'I believe so.'

'Then I'll walk you home,' he said.

Belle suppressed the urge to grin so obviously. She looked forward to her nightly walks with Andre, across the empty piazza to the door of Avery's apartment. And despite the late hour—for it was always two in the morning by then— they'd linger outside on the steps in the dark to finish a conversation, remaining there until one of them stifled a yawn. Sometimes, if they were still out there when dawn arrived, Avery emerged from the piazza, rolling tired eyes their way as she dragged herself past them and up the stairs to the apartment.

'I have a day off next week,' he said, placing four cups of espresso and two shot glasses of limoncello on a tray. 'I'll change your shift on the roster too. We can go somewhere.'

He'd been gracious about taking her places, ensuring that she saw all of Italy's beauty. He'd wandered the Vatican and Pompeii with her, and had driven her to tiny boutique vineyards, the kind that only the locals knew about. Their day trips often commenced at sunup, long before Avery or Riley were willing to stir, and ended when the moon was high. For this reason, it was often the two of them journeying out of Rome, which Belle didn't mind at all. Andre was lovely company, and they could fill a whole day with conversation that was neither stilted nor awkward.

'How about Venice?' she suggested, a city she'd been dying to visit. 'Can we do it in one day?'

He nodded with a thoughtful expression. 'It's a ten-hour roundtrip journey. We'd have to leave early, and we'd get back late. We probably wouldn't see everything.'

'It's quiet here. We could ask your dad for two days off.'

He glanced at her with a bemused expression. 'You mean we should stay overnight?'

Her face burned with her insinuation. 'Well, yeah, I mean, we could ask Riley and Leo to come too. And Avery.' Her intention had been to get the most out of Venice, but she'd made it sound like a romantic getaway instead. She dipped her head, letting her braids fall around her face to hide her flushed cheeks.

'I see,' Andre said. He looked mildly disappointed.

'Us girls could share a room, and you could share with Leo. We could have two days there instead of one, and we wouldn't have to rush. It's just an idea.' She was rambling, still cringing at how she'd embarrassed them both.

'No, it's a good idea,' he said quickly. 'I'll sort out the roster so we can all take the time off.' They shared a smile as she collected the tray of espressos and limoncello to take to the table. But when Andre's gaze broke away from her to fall on the front door beyond her shoulder, she turned and followed it. Three men had entered the trattoria, dressed smartly in dark blue uniforms.

'Belle, leave the tray.' His voice was suddenly firm. 'Take Natalya, Josh, and Chase with you. Go through the kitchen and out the back door. Nice and slow. Wait for me there.'

'Why, what's wrong?' Belle set the tray back on the bar. She could see the concern on his face, and something fluttered unpleasantly in her stomach.

'It's nothing to worry about. But can you send my father out?'

Belle nodded, her eyes straying to the uniformed men by the door again who were scanning the trattoria.

Natalya was beside her in an instant. 'Come with me,'

she commanded, folding her hand around Belle's, and leading her to the kitchen.

Josh and Chase were close behind them as they pushed through the swinging doors.

It was hot in there, pans and pots covering every inch of the stove and benchtops, the ovens blazing with bread and pizza. Belle had never been inside the kitchen before, only glimpsing it from the pass. Despite the urgency that had arrived with those men, she glanced around curiously, taking in the industrial appliances and the refrigerators, the trays of fresh pizza dough, and containers of prepped vegetables.

'What is this?' Uncle Benito barked at them in surprise. 'What are you doing in my kitchen?'

'There are some men in the dining room. Andre wants you out there,' Belle said, moving quickly past him, her hand still firmly in Natalya's, with Josh and Chase following behind.

Uncle Benito wiped the sweat from his brow with a paper towel. He muttered what she was sure was a series of expletives before he removed pots and pans from the gas burners on the stove, washed his hands at the sink and dried them, then barged through the doors into the dining room.

'Come,' Natalya insisted in a Russian accent. 'We will wait in the back alley. This should not take long, I hope.'

They left the kitchen behind them, exiting through a single back door into the alleyway behind Valentina's. It was unlike the laneway at the front, which was rustic and charming, decorated with chairs and potted plants and small bars. This alleyway serviced the backdoors of the bars and trattorias. Crates and boxes were piled high on either side and the smell of rubbish from the dumpsters was over-powering.

Once they were all through, Natalya pulled the back-door shut. Chase kicked an empty box off a crate, sat down and pulled a packet of cigarettes from his pocket. He lit one, took a deep drag, then offered the packet around.

'Those things will kill you,' Natalya said, wrinkling her nose at them.

'Everything will kill you,' Chase said, his voice thick with a Mississippi drawl.

'What happened back there?' Belle asked. Her hands trembled, although it was nothing to do with the cool night air.

'Italian immigration,' Josh said, another American waiter, from California. 'They're looking for illegal workers.'

Belle straightened in alarm. She'd always known it was a risk to work in Italy without an approved visa, but she'd allowed the thought to wither since nobody else had seemed overly concerned. She cursed herself now for not sorting the paperwork out sooner. The last thing she wanted was to be deported back to Australia or worse, sent to an immigration camp.

'It's fine,' Natalya said, sensing her panic and waving her hand. 'More a nuisance than anything.'

'What do you mean?' Belle asked, her heart pounding rapidly. She thought it might burst from her chest.

'Money will exchange hands, the officers will go away, and we'll all be fine for a few more months.'

Belle glanced worriedly at each of them, but her concern wasn't mirrored in their faces.

Chase dragged lazily on his cigarette. 'Don't worry about it. Uncle Benito will buy their silence. It's not a big deal.'

'As long as you're not parading out there in front of

them, they can easily turn a blind eye,' Josh added. 'That's why we come out here until they leave.'

'But...' Belle was still trying to make sense of it. 'Why would Uncle Benito be willing to risk that for us?'

'Because seasonal workers are cheap to pay,' Josh said. 'We don't demand the wages of locals or visa-holders. Even with the bribe on top, it's still cheaper than paying full wages. And have you noticed we work harder? We pick up every shift we can. We work double shifts and long weeks without a break. Yeah, we're *cheap* all right.'

'This place is hardly profitable,' Natalya said soberly. 'Uncle Benito needs to save all the money he can.'

Andre appeared at the door and beckoned them inside. 'They're gone. You can come back now.'

Belle gave him a weak smile as Chase crushed out his cigarette and they trudged back through the kitchen to the dining room. Uncle Benito was at the cash register, counting notes and scratching his head, a defeated look on his face.

'Is everything all right?' Belle asked Andre, following him back to the bar. The tray of espressos and limoncello was gone, already delivered to the table by Avery, so she slipped behind the bar to stand beside him.

Andre positioned himself by the coffee machine again. 'Just a small problem. It's fixed now.'

'Were they immigration officials?'

'Yes.'

'Am I in trouble?' she asked. Despite the lack of worry from the others outside, it was hard to shake the concern. She'd never been a rule-breaker, always one to toe the line.

But Andre smiled in a way that told her everything would be all right. 'No *signorina*, you're not in trouble.'

She let out a semi-relieved breath, still searching his face. 'Are you sure?'

'Yes. My father has an arrangement with them. It's fine. They are happy again.'

'It would be easier if I just applied for a working visa,' she said. 'I never expected to work in Rome, but now that I'm here, I should make it official.' In fact, she would suggest that Riley do the same, and Natalya, Josh, and Chase. It would avoid the stress of having immigration officials arrive every few months.

Andre shook his head sadly. 'You can't apply for a working visa here,' he explained. 'You have to apply at the Italian embassy in your home country, like Avery did before she came. Only when it's approved can you come to Italy. I'm afraid it's too late. You will have to stay with this arrangement.' He patted her arm gently. 'Don't look so worried. I won't let anything happen to you.'

The determined look in his eyes told her that he meant it.

FOURTEEN

Thanks to the sluggish off-season, Andre managed to secure all of them two days off. Riley requested leave from the art gallery too and, the following week, they piled into Andre's Alfa Romeo for the five-hour drive to Venice.

The sun was just creeping over the horizon as they left Rome behind, reaching the autostrada and following it as it climbed north. Avery was still waking up, nursing large dark sunglasses and a rare macchiato to-go from the espresso bar next door to her apartment. In the backseat beside her, Riley leant into Leo, his arm around her, but the air around them seemed strained and deflated, as though they were recovering from a quarrel.

The front seats were livelier, Belle and Andre full of conversation. They'd stayed up late the night before, talking on the steps until three in the morning, before Andre had conceded he'd need a few hours' sleep before returning to pick them up for Venice.

They stopped for coffee and breakfast in Orvieto, a small cliff-side village in Umbria, an hour and a half outside of Rome, before resuming the journey. Avery came to life after a second macchiato, and Riley and Leo's tension thawed enough for them to join the conversation.

Several hours later, they reached the Venetian Lagoon, crossing the Ponte della Libertà—the Bridge of Liberty— which connected Venice's islands to the mainland. Cars were forbidden from entering the historical parts of the city, so Andre parked the Romeo in a car station, and they collected their overnight bags, walking the rest of the way to their hotel near Piazza San Marco and the Ponte dei Dai.

They checked into their rooms, Andre, and Leo's suite down the corridor from the girls', agreeing to meet downstairs again for lunch in an hour.

'God, I'm hungover,' Avery groaned as she tossed her bag onto the floor and collapsed on the bed.

Riley was quiet as she pulled a blouse and cable knit from her bag and hung them in the closet.

'Is everything okay?' Belle asked her as she did the same, collecting a cardigan and jacket and slipping them onto coat hangers.

Riley shrugged. 'Fine,' but her tone sounded hollow.

'Did something happen with Leo?' Belle persisted. 'You guys were quiet in the car.'

Riley shook her head, her lips pressed into a forced smile. 'It was nothing. I got a little angry with him last night.'

'What for?'

Riley sighed. She left the closet and walked to one of the beds, lowering herself down onto it. Her green eyes looked immensely sad. 'It was his mum's fiftieth birthday yesterday. The family had a dinner to celebrate. A big dinner. Everyone was there.' She glanced down at her lap. 'Everyone but me.'

'You didn't go?'

'I wasn't invited.'

'Oof,' Avery murmured, her head buried in a pillow. 'That's rough.'

Belle finished hanging her clothes, then left the closet too, sitting down beside Riley. 'Oh, Ri.'

'It's not a big deal,' Riley said quickly. 'I overreacted.'

'I don't think you did. It was dinner with his mother, his whole family, and he didn't invite you.'

Riley chewed her lip. It was hard to ignore the emotion in her eyes, how much Leo's rejection had hurt. 'It's just that we've been seeing each other for months now. I haven't met his mother yet, or anyone from his family. It would have been a nice opportunity. But it didn't even occur to him to ask me.' She let out an exasperated breath. 'Is there something wrong with me? Maybe I embarrass him.'

Belle scrunched up her nose. 'Don't be ridiculous. There's nothing wrong with you. You're perfect.'

'Then what's the problem?'

'Meeting the parents in Italy isn't like meeting the parents where we're from,' Avery said, lifting her head from the pillow. 'It's a big deal here. A few months of dating doesn't qualify for something as serious as that.'

'What qualifies, then?'

'It would be easier if you were Italian,' she said, grimacing apologetically. 'Culturally, you're going to have an uphill battle.'

Riley slumped, looking even more deflated.

'Why don't you talk to him about it?' Belle suggested.

'I have, but he's full of excuses.'

'You need to be firmer with him.'

Riley blinked. 'I'm not sure how to do that.'

'Be diplomatic but assertive.'

'Ugh. Relationships are horrible,' she moaned, flinging herself backwards onto the bed.

Belle patted her friend's knee sympathetically. Poor Riley. She was hopelessly inexperienced when it came to relationships, the concessions and complexities that had to be navigated as part of the journey. Throw in a little tradition and Riley was out of her depth. Belle wanted to pull Leo aside and shake sense into him. No one should have to feel the demoralising effects of inadequacy, least of all from the ones who professed to love you the most.

Belle knew better than anyone how damaging that could be.

———

THEY SPENT the day exploring Venice, riding gondolas down canals and traipsing through squares. The historical parts of the city reminded Belle of Rome, except that in Venice it was almost guaranteed one would get lost amidst the wandering waterways and narrow lanes, every turn of the corner looking like the last.

Later at dinner, Riley was quiet, and afterwards, as they gathered in the laneway outside the restaurant, Leo leant down and whispered in her ear. She nodded, then cast Belle an apologetic look. 'We're going to go for a walk by ourselves. Do you mind?'

'Of course not,' she said. 'I'll see you up in the room later?'

'Okay.'

She watched them leave hand in hand, hoping that Venice would bring them common ground and that Leo would see how wonderful his world could be if he'd let Riley in.

'I need sleep,' Avery said, nursing her head. 'I'm going to bed. See you in the morning.'

Belle hugged her. 'Can you find your way back to the hotel?'

Avery waved her hand, unperturbed. 'I've been to Venice dozens of times. I know it like the back of my hand.' She farewelled them, then disappeared into the crowds.

'Then there were two,' Andre said, scratching his head. 'I wasn't expecting everyone to separate on our only night in Venice.'

The evening was pleasant and cool, and although it was close to midnight, Belle wasn't tired, the upshot of working regular late shifts. 'Would you like to walk with me?' she asked.

His face lit up. 'I'd like nothing better.' They left the restaurant and began strolling, bridges carrying them over chalky green canals and cobbled passageways, steering them through the centre of buildings. Wrong turns led to the water's edge or down narrow lanes that proved tricky mazes to encounter. They giggled as they became hopelessly lost, Venice outsmarting them.

'It's been a long time since I've walked around this city,' he said, as they found themselves unexpectedly in a quiet courtyard, presided over by shabby amber apartment blocks with wrought-iron balconies and potted herbs. 'Were Riley and Leo okay tonight? They both seemed preoccupied. Even in our room, Leo wasn't himself.'

Belle wondered how much she should divulge. It wasn't her story to tell and yet, she decided if anyone would have good advice, it would be Andre. 'It was his mother's birthday yesterday. Leo didn't invite Riley to dinner. In fact, after months of dating, he still hasn't introduced her to his family.'

'I see. And she's upset by this?'

'Of course she is. She thinks something's wrong with her.'

They retreated from the courtyard, retracing their steps back onto a main walkway that led them to the Bridge of Sighs.

'Leo is a nice boy,' Andre said. 'He comes from a good family.'

'I don't doubt that, but is he playing games?' Belle asked. 'Riley doesn't give her heart away easily. I'm worried that she's given it to Leo and he's going to break it.'

Andre nodded; brows drawn pensively above his dark eyes. 'You know, in Italy, meeting the family is a big milestone. It's not considered an informal occasion like it is in Australia, after just one or two months of dating. It means the relationship is serious enough to be taken to the next level. It means you are considering marriage and a life together. Casual dates do not get introduced to nonna.'

'Avery said this also. Does it mean Riley has nothing to worry about?'

He shrugged. 'I can't be sure, for I don't know what goes on behind closed doors. But if meeting the family is the only problem they have, she needs to be patient. She's a foreigner and Leo's parents do not speak fluent English. If she is serious about this, she will need to learn the language. I don't just mean the pleasantries, but proper lessons. And she will need to learn how to cook. The women in his family will want to exchange baked goods and recipes with her. There are many cultural barriers that will need to be overcome.'

Belle wondered if deep down Riley had the patience for Italy's 'cultural barriers'. 'I only hope that Leo's intentions are good. I'd be disappointed if he was stringing her along.'

'Italian families can be complex,' Andre said. 'But he is the one she needs to talk to. You and I can only speculate.'

'That's part of the problem. She's not sure how to talk to him. Riley isn't good with relationships. She's certainly not good with *those* kinds of discussions.'

Andre smiled. 'I understand. But he is the only one who knows what's going on.'

They reached the Rialto Bridge, its ornate renaissance design spanning the Grand Canal. By day, the canal was a teeming waterway snaking through the island, splitting it in two. By night, gondolas bobbed idly on the edges and the damp, musty water rippled bottle green under the moon.

They crossed the bridge, heading back towards their hotel, passing through Piazza San Marco. Fewer people crowded the square at that hour, but Caffè Florian's orchestra was still playing a spirited rendition of Vivaldi's *Four Seasons*. Belle and Andre paused outside to listen to it. Belle, still steeped in the three glasses of wine she'd indulged in at dinner, boldly slipped her arm through Andre's. For a moment, he seemed startled, then he relaxed beside her.

'Thank you for bringing me here,' she said. 'Venice is magic.'

'You're welcome, *signorina*. Summer brings to Venice everything that is intolerable. Humid days, smelly canals, swarms of tourists, but fall...' He sighed. 'Fall is the most beautiful time of the year here.'

She sighed, too, with contentment. It had been the most wonderful day already, the most wonderful evening.

'Are you finding all those missed opportunities?' he asked softly as the strains of music circled the square.

'I am. And more.' Belle turned her head and gazed at him. His eyes were alight, and she couldn't be sure if it was the music or the kind of closeness they shared that had him looking as happy as she felt.

He caught her gaze and smiled down at her. For a moment, she wondered what it would be like to kiss him, to slip his shirt from his body, to trail her fingers along his tanned skin. Maybe the alcohol had gone to her head, but she wondered, hoped, that he would drop his lips onto hers.

When he seemed about to say something, to do something, to lean down and kiss her, she held her breath, but to her immense regret, a flicker of hesitation crossed his face, and the moment vanished.

Andre cleared his throat, then put his arm around her. 'You must be cold. Should we head back?'

Belle blinked away her confusion. 'Oh... right. Sure.'

They left the orchestra and the piazza behind, the sound of cellos and clarinets trailing them. Belle tried not to feel the sting of disappointment, but she'd wanted that kiss more than she'd realised. Maybe Andre had wanted it too, but nerves had got the better of him. Or maybe he hadn't wanted it at all and had tried to let her down gently. Uncertainty swarmed all the way back to the hotel.

Outside her room, he smiled down at her. 'I had a wonderful night, Belle.'

She tried to smile as well. 'Me too.'

'I will always remember Venice for the time we shared here.' His lips were soft as he leant in to graze them along her cheek. When he pulled away, the trail he left on her skin blazed softly. '*Buona notte*. I'll see you in the morning.'

'Goodnight, Andre.'

Had she imagined the moment they'd shared in the square? The look between them, the promise of a kiss? She must have, for Andre gave her one last fleeting wave before turning and walking down the corridor to his room.

FIFTEEN

They returned from Venice the following evening. The next day, Belle was back at Valentina's for a double shift. It was another sluggish dinner service as she waited by the bar, Andre preparing a tray of *aperitivi* for one of her tables, a pre-dinner drink that often opened a meal. She watched as he mixed Aperol, Prosecco and a spritz of sparkling mineral water in tall glasses of ice, dropping slices of orange in afterwards. Belle had yet to taste an *aperitivo* as nice as Andre's.

'Did you enjoy Venice?' he asked.

'It was superb,' she said. They hadn't discussed the 'almost kiss', if that's what it could be called, allowing it to drift into oblivion as if it had never happened. Belle decided it was for the best. Her friendship with Andre was special to her and she shouldn't have allowed herself to be swept up in the moment, thinking there could be more.

'How are Leo and Riley?' He set the drinks on a tray.

'Much better.' Their talk that same night had obviously smoothed over the tension, for they'd been smiling again the next morning at breakfast. Avery had also recovered from her hangover, and they'd spent the day exploring Saint Mark's Basilica and the Doges Palace, followed by several hole-in-the-wall *bacari* that Belle had dragged everyone to. They'd stood outside at counters, sipping frosted glasses of bellini, and snacking on *cicchetti*—tapas plates of olives, velvety meatballs, grilled baby squid, and crostini heaped with porcini and ricotta. It had been with full stomachs and regret that they'd all piled back into the car that afternoon to make the journey home to Rome.

'Your drinks are ready, *signorina*,' Andre said, pushing the tray towards her.

His voice broke through her reverie, and she smiled at him, collecting the tray with both hands, and delivering it to the waiting table. The diners, a regular group of four that frequented after work, chatted with her in Italian as she set the drinks down. After three months, she was able to converse in small talk with patrons, but she was still learning, and they were always forgiving when she got the words wrong.

After leaving the table, she drifted past another, where an older gentleman was dining alone. He'd finished his *aperitivo* and entrée but his main course, the linguine *con gamberetti*, sat abandoned. He stared at it, looking immensely displeased.

She walked over to him. 'How is your meal this evening, *signore*?'

'The *con gamberetti* is undercooked. Look at the prawns here.' He lifted a sliced prawn with the tip of his knife, and Belle instantly noticed the translucent flesh. 'It's still raw. I cannot eat this.'

Belle swiftly lifted the plate from his table. 'I am terribly sorry,' she said, placing the plate on the *aperitivi* tray she still carried. 'Let me fix this for you right away. And I'll have a glass of red wine sent to you on the house.'

'There is no need. I am leaving.' He tossed down his napkin.

'No, *per favore*,' she said. 'I will have it fixed for you in a couple of minutes. And I'll have the glass of wine sent over.'

He sniffed, then indicated with a slight nod that he was willing to wait.

Belle hurried to the pass and set the dish down, poking her head through the open window, looking for Uncle Benito. He was wedged behind one of the ovens, cursing the appliance's death mid-service. She grimaced. She didn't want to bother him with the complaint, but the dish needed to be fixed—the customer at the table was staring at her.

She glanced around for Andre's help, but he had Avery and Chase at the bar waiting for drinks and she knew he wouldn't be able to leave his post. She was perfectly capable of fixing the dish herself, but did she dare? It was a risky move entering Uncle Benito's kitchen to cook, for the rules were clear—no one should. On the other hand, diners were few and far between at Valentina's and she hated to lose one over something as careless as uncooked shellfish.

Before she had time to regret her decision, she picked up the plate and pushed through the swinging doors into the kitchen. She'd only been in there once before, hurrying through to the back door when the immigration officials had arrived. Now, with Uncle Benito still wedged behind the oven, she figured she could be in and out again before he realised she'd been there.

She placed the meal down on the stainless-steel countertop and studied it. It was an easy dish to construct, an old Italian classic—linguine and prawns in a tomato-base sauce.

She could see the undercooked prawns, the slightly translucent flesh, and she cringed. Serving undercooked shellfish was dangerous in any restaurant. Besides that, the dish was varying degrees of red and brown, and if there was one thing Belle knew about cooking, it was that people ate with their eyes first. The meal lacked vibrancy and love and showed Uncle Benito's stress on the plate.

Keeping one eye on him still yelling expletives from behind the oven, she fired up a stove plate and tossed the *con gamberetti* back into a frypan, listening for the sizzle of the prawns. Something inside her, a fierce passion for cooking that had always been difficult to contain, ignited as she gripped the handle of the frypan and gave it a shake.

She found a container of sliced chilli at the prep station and threw a touch in, then sliced a lemon and squeezed the juice into the pan, catching the seeds. She tasted the sauce, adding more dry white wine and cherry tomatoes, then she corrected the seasoning. Before finishing, she checked the prawns' firmness to ensure they were cooked, satisfied that they were perfect, and that the linguine was not overdone. She gave the frypan another good shake, reached for a clean fork, twirled it in the pan, then carefully transferred it to a new plate.

When the linguine held its position she grinned, adding bright green rocket leaves, a grating of lemon zest and a good grind of pepper. She finished it with a drizzle of olive oil and fresh parsley and was out of the kitchen and back to the customer's table before Uncle Benito had any idea she'd been there.

When she set the plate down, the man's eyes infinitesimally widened, and a small smile tugged at his lips. He nodded and thanked her. She promptly delivered his complimentary glass of wine and returned to the bar, finally releasing a trapped breath.

Andre glanced up at her as he worked the coffee machine. 'Are you okay? You look worried.'

She shook her head as she nervously watched the man eat his meal. 'I'm fine.'

New customers walked in and were shown to tables in her section, and she became distracted again, taking orders. She didn't notice the man rise from his table and speak to Uncle Benito at the pass until it was too late. The man was smiling, smacking his lips against his thumb and forefinger with a resounding *belissimo*! Then he turned and pointed her out.

Uncle Benito looked past him to glare at her, as her stomach lurched sickeningly into her throat. The man eventually left the pass, paid the bill with a wide grin, and thanked her on his way out.

Although the rest of the evening passed uneventfully, Belle felt like she was moving through fog, so distracted with thoughts of getting into trouble, that she could hardly concentrate. She'd disobeyed Uncle Benito and had let herself into his kitchen, a place that everyone knew was off limits. Maybe she'd even insulted him, transforming one of his dishes into something the customer had loved. Compliments to the chef were rare at Valentina's, Uncle Benito holding fast to his collection of safe, plain dishes that he could solely manage in the kitchen.

She hardly ate at the staff dinner, feeling his eyes boring into her the entire evening. Any hope of scurrying out the door unnoticed was dashed when, after the meal, he threw his napkin down and called her into the kitchen. She rose slowly from the table and followed him in through the swinging doors, aware that everyone was watching her. Oh,

God! She was about to be fired. She'd blatantly disobeyed him and now she was to suffer the consequences. Her heart thumped as she stepped into the kitchen, her mouth as rough and dry as sandpaper.

When he stood before her in front of the stove, his hands on his hips, asking her exactly what she thought she'd been doing in there, her voice shook in reply.

'It's just that... I mean the prawns were...' She cast her eyes down. 'Oh, I don't know. I'm sorry. You were busy and I didn't want to disturb you.'

He stared at her while she stood waiting for his lecture, the repercussions, the loss of her job, but then he smiled. It was a small smile that started in his eyes, lifting his cheeks, and finally pulling at the corners of his mouth. 'Where did you learn to cook like that?'

She was still waiting to hear that she'd been fired, and she sputtered for a moment, wrong-footed. 'Uh... it's just something I've always enjoyed.'

'You're not a trained chef?'

'No.'

'How did you know what that dish needed?'

'I've cooked it once before. It's a summer dish, so it should look like summer on the plate. Colour, flavour, and it should be light to eat.' She shook her head. 'Wait, am I fired?'

He grunted, then grabbed her elbow and tugged her towards the pantry, a long narrow room at the back of the kitchen. He flicked on the light and led her inside. 'Tell me, what do you see in here?'

She glanced around at the shelves of tinned food, bottles of oils and vinegars, bags of coffee beans, and jars of herbs and spices. As one would expect of a commercial pantry, there was a plethora of produce in there, but it was haphazardly arranged, without a clear system. Oils were scattered higgledy-piggledy, baskets of garlic, potatoes and onions mixed together, and containers of flour and sugar were void of appropriate expiry labelling. She didn't want to offend Uncle Benito, but she was shocked at the disarray.

'It's a pantry with lots of stuff in it,' she said politely.

'Ha! It's a mess!' He threw his hands up in the air. 'Everything is everywhere. There is never time to fix it.'

She took a step inside, inspecting the shelves closely, running her fingertips along packets of ladyfingers and amaretti stacked precariously on top of packets of dried bay leaves, that were stacked again on top of blocks of dark chocolate and a tub of what she was fairly certain was arborio rice. How he found anything in that clutter was a miracle. If his pantry system was failing him, the rest of the kitchen would feel the stress. Was it any wonder he was serving undercooked prawns?

'What are some small things I can do to make it better?' he asked, watching her intently.

She scratched her head. 'Uncle Benito, I'm not an expert in commercial kitchen management.'

'Just some thoughts.'

'Well,' her eyes swept the shelves, 'if it were my pantry, I wouldn't attempt shortcuts here. I would pull everything out, clean the shelves, go through all the produce, throw away expired goods, and put it all back. I would properly label these containers, put similar foods together, place bulky items at the bottom. You have lots of large tins, but let's face it, they don't stack well. You need tin racks. They will change your pantry!'

He narrowed his eyes but allowed her to continue.

Her confidence grew for if there was one thing she could pride herself on, it was her organisational skills. Her

pantry back at the Pyrmont terrace had always been immac-
ulate. Albeit it was of a smaller scale than this one, but a
system was a system, and she revelled in order. She moved
to the random jars of herbs and spices scattered chaotically.
'You use lots of dry herbs and spices. You need to store these
properly, in ingredient bins. You can put flour and rice in
them too. You don't need to try and pour from these heavy
bags.' A large bag of flour rested on the floor, and she kicked
it gently with the toe of her shoe.

Uncle Benito was still staring at her, and she blushed
suddenly at the uncertain look in his eyes. Had she gone
too far?

'Anyway, that's what I would do,' she said quietly,
chewing her bottom lip.

He cleared his throat. 'And you know how to do this
kind of thing?'

'I kept an organised pantry back home and at the small
café I used to work at. This is on a grander scale, but yes, I
could do it.'

'You could come in, say, every morning for one week
and do this for me?'

A small smile played on her lips. 'Yes. I could reorganise
your pantry in a week if you'd like me to.'

He nodded slowly. 'And how much would you expect
me to pay you for this?'

She glanced around the pantry. There was a lot to be
done. She'd have to design a new stacking system, pull
everything out, transfer most of the ingredients to appropriate storage, label it all, sort through the root vegetables,
discard what had perished, then put everything back again.
There were hours of work there, plus her double shifts in
the dining room straight after. She faced him again. 'Aside
from the cost of the ingredient bins and the tin racks and

any additional shelving you might need, I don't want money for my work.'

He looked confused. 'You don't want me to pay you for this?'

'No.' She smiled. 'I want something far better. I want to cook in your kitchen.'

'And he said yes?' Andre looked gobsmacked as he walked Belle through Piazza Navona to Avery's apartment, and she relayed all that had happened that evening.

'He did!' Belle was just as astonished. 'He's going to let me help him prep every morning for one week.'

It had taken a long time to convince Uncle Benito to allow her to cook in his kitchen in exchange for organising his pantry. After some hours, and after all the staff had left and Andre waited patiently at the bar to walk her home, he'd finally relented.

To anyone else, it would appear she was giving her time away, rearranging his pantry, then helping at the prep station for not a single extra euro. Most people would consider her mad, but Belle felt as though she'd struck gold. Somehow, she'd worked her way into Uncle Benito's fortress, even if through the entire negotiation he'd worn the look of someone in extreme discomfort.

'This won't be easy for him.' Andre confirmed her thoughts, as they strolled through the deserted piazza, a light breeze whipping up. It was already three am, but Belle wasn't tired. On the contrary, adrenalin coursed through her so that she felt neither the late hour nor the cool night air. 'He's protective of his kitchen. He hasn't had a person in there to cook with him since Valentina's opened. Not even me. I just get the fun jobs, like cleaning the ovens.'

'It's only for a week. I'll go in early, work on the pantry, then help him with some prep before my shift starts. I'm hoping he'll see the value in my work and offer to let me do it permanently.'

Andre whistled softly. 'I hate to disappoint you, but it's unlikely. That pantry is a mess, and he's been desperate to fix it. Letting you reorganise it is one thing, but he will never let you keep cooking with him beyond the week. He's too set in his ways for that.' He glanced at her with a mix of apology and admiration. 'Still, you must have impressed him tonight with that *con gamberetti* you fixed. You even impressed me. I didn't know you could cook like that.'

Andre touched her hand gently to let her know he was halting. He fished in his pocket for a coin and tossed it into the Fontana del Moro, the coin breaking the fountain's surface before sinking to the bottom, the promise of a fulfilled wish too much for even a local to resist.

'I thought he was going to fire me,' she said, shaking her head as they continued walking. She recalled the moment she'd been led back into the kitchen, expecting to be yelled at. 'I never thought he'd ask for my advice about the pantry.'

'Papà is struggling,' Andre said. 'He cannot run the trattoria, do all the cooking by himself and make the business a success. It's too much for one person. I know he'd love to cook different dishes, better dishes, dishes that he can take pride in, but he is too stubborn to let anyone help!' His voice rose with frustration.

'He's a good cook,' Belle said. 'A great cook, in fact, but

you can get traditional pizza and pasta everywhere in Rome. He needs to shake things up, modernise the menu, or Valentina's won't last.'

'Modernise the menu?' Andre repeated with a chuckle. 'This is Benito we're talking about, right?'

Belle smiled. 'I know Valentina's means a lot to him. But it could be so much more if he let people help him.'

Andre's expression grew serious. 'I agree. We're in terrible debt, the bills are paid late, and there's never any money for renovations or new furniture. We struggle to get customers in. We are simply existing. Sometimes, I don't know how we stay open.'

Belle knew things were difficult at Valentina's, but she hadn't realised the full extent of it. *Late bills, simply existing?* Uncle Benito's pride, 'ways' or whatever it was that he held fast to were sinking his beloved trattoria. Protecting his late wife's legacy by keeping a tight rein on every aspect was doing more harm than good.

'Now, tell me about your cooking,' Andre said. 'Did you work in a restaurant back in Sydney?'

'No, just the café. I served coffee and pre-made sandwiches.'

'Have you never felt the desire to work in a commercial kitchen?'

'Oh, I have,' she said. 'But I put a lot of things on hold for someone I loved, thinking we might start a family. It was stupid, of course, for after twenty years he left me.'

They exited Piazza Navona, rounding the corner into Corsia Agonale, a mantel of mist settling over the lane. Moments later, they arrived at Avery's apartment block and sat down on the front steps. Andre slid out of his jacket and placed it around her shoulders to ward off the chill. Belle nestled into it, smelling the fresh soapy scent that clung to the fibres. She'd grown accustomed to his smell, having worn his jacket on previous cool evenings, and she liked it, one that she associated now with comfort and familiarity.

'Did he not want the same things you did?' Andre asked.

'I thought he did, but then he ended it and I realised how unhappy he'd been. Ben was my first love, my only love. And I was his, until I wasn't.' She glanced down at her hands, the sting of humiliation still raw, even after all these months. 'He cheated on me with another woman. Before I'd even had a chance to get my head around it, she'd moved into our house, and I'd become homeless. Then the café I worked at was going to put people off, so I was about to become unemployed too. Everything unravelled quickly.'

'And now here you are.'

'Now here I am,' Belle said, smiling. 'And it was the best thing I ever did. Scary, but worth it.'

Andre's gaze was still fixed on her. 'That Ben is a fool.'

Belle shrugged. 'I used to think that too, not so long ago. But as hard as it was at the time, I've come to realise that he did us both a favour. I loved our life together, but he was never going to ask me to marry him. I was just someone he was passing the time with.' It surprised her to utter those words, until she realised how true they were.

'Do you feel like you wasted all those years?'

She took time answering the question, for it was something that couldn't be defined so easily. 'Yes and no. I don't regret my time with him. He was my best friend, my soul mate, the person I went home to every day. I loved him with my whole heart. But did he waste my time? Did he ruin my chances of meeting someone, marrying and having a family while he spent all those years working out if I was the one? Yes, he did. I have to start all over again.' And for someone who was thirty-five and had wanted children for as long as she could remember, it was a bitter pill to swallow.

'I'm sorry this happened to you, Belle,' Andre said.

She shook her head. 'Don't be. It was my fault. I was living in a dream, taking his monogamy for granted. I didn't put enough effort into maintaining what we had.'

'This is not your fault. There were two people in your relationship.'

'Or in our case, three.'

He smiled sadly at her quip. 'Don't be disheartened, *signorina*. He wasn't the one for you. Your one is still out there somewhere.'

'Maybe. Or maybe not. It scares me a little to find out.' She may have made peace with the collapse of her relationship, but she'd be lying if the thought of giving her heart to someone new didn't make her anxious. Handing it over so completely, with the explicit trust that they'd handle it with care, filled her with unease.

A few dry leaves scattered across the cobblestones, the mist swirling on the corsia. It was almost dawn.

'I was engaged once,' Andre said.

Belle turned to look at him. 'You were?'

'Yes.'

'Oh.' Her interest piqued. 'How long ago?'

'Earlier this year. I broke it off with her the day I left for London to bring Avery home.' He drew his knees up to his chest and wrapped his arms around them.

Belle tried to hide her surprise. She'd never considered that Andre might have had another life before she came to Rome. A relationship. A fiancée. And so recently. 'What happened?'

He shrugged. 'We grew apart. Some things aren't meant to be.'

'What was her name?'

He seemed amused by her question. 'Mary. Her name *is* Mary.'

The way he referenced Mary in the present when Belle had referred to her in the past made her back stiffen. As if Mary were still in his life. 'Do you still see her?'

'Yes. We're good friends and our parents are close. It didn't end on bad terms.'

Belle concentrated on the zipper of his jacket, an uncomfortable clarity prickling beneath her skin. She was jealous of Mary.

'So it seems we've both suffered the loss of a relationship,' Andre said.

'Will you and Mary ever work things out?'

He glanced at her, his eyes deep pools of brown that she couldn't tear her gaze away from. 'No,' he said softly. 'Not now.'

His words sent her heart soaring and clenching at the same time. *Not now?* Not now because he'd met Belle? Or because he still loved Mary in his own way and was trying to figure it out? She remembered their 'almost kiss' in Venice and felt more confused than ever. They shared a special friendship, but Andre was hard to read sometimes, and she wasn't sure her heart was ready for such a perplexing dance.

Andre tore his gaze away and looked up at the sky. 'The sun will be up soon.'

'Yes,' Belle said regrettably. But she didn't want the sun to rise. She wanted their moment on the steps to stretch forever.

'Are you tired?'

She shook her head.

'You should try to get some sleep anyway. You have a double shift today.'

He rose to his feet, and she did the same, slipping out of his jacket, which she handed back to him. He accepted it and leaned forward to kiss both her cheeks. She met him halfway, savouring his touch on her skin. When he pulled away, his eyes locked on hers, his gaze so complete that her breath caught.

'*Buona notte*, Belle,' he said.

'Goodnight, Andre.'

He closed his eyes, then opened them again, sighing, it seemed, with indecision. A moment passed, then two, until he nodded. 'Yes, I should go.'

Belle wilted with disappointment, as she watched him turn and walk towards the piazza, a thousand unsaid words still on her lips.

SEVENTEEN

On Belle's first morning working in Uncle Benito's kitchen, she arrived promptly at seven. She'd only managed a few hours of sleep the night before, and still had a double shift afterwards to get through, but this didn't prevent her from skipping across Piazza Navona with a grin on her face.

Uncle Benito was already in the kitchen when she entered. He grunted at her, a sign that his heart had still not caught up yet with the agreement they'd made, no matter how desperately his pantry needed reorganising.

'The ingredient bins and tin racks you ordered arrived yesterday,' he said, pointing to a stack of boxes next to the pantry door. 'I put everything over there.'

'Great!' she said, slipping out of her jacket and scarf.

She wasted little time getting to work, clearing shelves, and shifting produce to ingredient bins, throwing it away if it had expired, or repositioning it in a more suitable spot. She concentrated on one shelf at a time, keeping the area tidy while she moved items around, aware that Uncle Benito still needed access to the pantry, and that creating a mess during the reorganisation would only irritate him.

The previous week, she'd designed a system for the pantry, transferring her ideas to a sketch. She'd taken suggestions from Andre too, before getting Uncle Benito's tick of approval. She worked methodically now and at a swift pace until Uncle Benito walked into the pantry two hours later.

He put his hands on his hips and assessed the shelves she'd been working on. 'Yes, this side looks good. *Mi piace molto*!'

Belle grinned with relief. He liked it very much.

'Now, come have coffee and calzone,' he said, 'then we start cooking.'

They ate together at the stainless-steel bench, but the meal was quick. Uncle Benito wasn't accustomed to pausing for breaks, and Belle's mind was already on the prep task ahead. When they finished eating, he showed her around the rest of the kitchen, cautiously at first, explaining where the knives and pots and pans were kept, how to use the oven and stove, and most importantly, how *not* to get in his way while they worked. Then he seemed to warm to the idea of her presence, moving about with ardour, showing her what foods they prepared early, how the pass was run, and lastly, how he managed the refrigerators and product orders, which Belle noted were also a mess.

At nine-thirty, he slipped his apron on and collected another from a drawer, handing it to her. 'Let's prep!'

They worked side by side for the next few hours. While she sliced vegetables and herbs—menial tasks—he prepared batches of fresh pizza dough, tossing it through the air with agile hands. He was a joy to watch, his preparation like pure theatre. Belle set her knife down, paying rapt attention, as he explained the importance of twirling the dough, for it was the best way to form a thicker crust, as opposed to rolling it out which produced a thinner one. Next, he moved onto a batch of fresh pasta dough he'd prepared earlier, separating it into several smaller portions, then dusting the bench with flour and rolling each portion out with the longest rolling pin Belle had ever seen.

'Wouldn't a pasta machine be easier?' she asked.

He grunted his offence. 'Pasta machine? Ha! The worst invention ever. Find me a nonna in Italy who has one and I'll give you my trattoria.'

She giggled to herself, watching him roll the dough into thin circles. Once he was finished, he began to slice the pasta into strands and drape them over damp tea towels. She suspected, from the thickness and shape, that he was cutting strands of tagliatelle and linguine.

'I could put a pot of potatoes on, and we could whip up some fresh gnocchi,' she suggested, feeling emboldened. She had finished slicing the vegetables and herbs and they were set neatly in containers on the prep station ready for service.

He shook his head emphatically as he sliced the pasta, sweat gathering on his brow. 'Gnocchi is not on my menu. And besides, it takes too long. There's no time.'

'But I know how to make it,' she insisted. 'I could have it ready for the dinner service. We could put it up as a special. Gnocchi with tomato and mascarpone or gnocchi with lemon, garlic, and parmesan.'

'No!' he said with vehemence. 'We stick to the menu.'

Although he'd cited lack of time, Belle had finished her prep well before the lunch service and could easily have made the gnocchi. She was left looking for things to do, watching enviously as he draped long strands of pasta over the tea towels. What she wouldn't give to be allowed to help. She offered to make the pizza sauce for him, or to prepare the dough for the garlic bread, or to throw together a batch of biscotti. All her attempts to be useful were met with resistance until Uncle Benito finally shooed her out of the kitchen and told her to help Andre instead.

The rest of the week passed by in the same way. She finished her work in the pantry, then helped Uncle Benito prep in the kitchen. She easily completed the humble tasks he gave her, like chopping or slicing the vegetables, and always finished well ahead of schedule. Every day she offered to help him with the pasta or pizza dough and was even brave enough to suggest creating other meals that weren't on the menu—mussels in white wine and garlic broth as well as individual tiramisu pots and a ricotta and jam crostata. There were no desserts offered at Valentina's, other than biscuits and dessert liqueurs. Belle had to bite her tongue every time an idea whirred in her brain, or she risked being kicked out of the kitchen at the mention of something new.

When she raised the idea of stuffed calamari or pan-roasted artichokes as an entree, Uncle Benito grumbled that her time was up, and she should help Andre. Belle sighed defeatedly, hung her apron on the hook and pushed through the kitchen doors into the dining room. It was too early for the wait staff to arrive; only Andre was behind the bar, setting up.

He smiled sympathetically at her downcast face and placed an espresso in her hand. 'Here, I had this ready for you.'

She took it from him, appreciating his thoughtfulness. 'You knew I was going to get kicked out of the kitchen again?'

He shrugged. 'Benito is Benito. He will never change.

But I like that you're trying.' He picked up his espresso and a copy of the culinary magazine *Romeing* and nodded towards a table. 'Shall we sit and drink?'

'Sure.'

They pulled out a chair each and sat. While Andre perused the magazine, Belle played absentmindedly with her braids, her thoughts returning to the kitchen. Her work in the pantry was almost finished and she had one day left of prepping with Uncle Benito before their agreement expired. While she'd enjoyed the experience, it had also been frustrating—his unwillingness to consider new ideas, to improve the menu or to accept help. Belle hadn't suggested anything outrageous, just a dish here and there to pull Valentina's out of its slump, but his stubbornness seemed almost irrational.

Then she berated herself. Who was she to march in and demand changes? She'd only been there four months and was hardly positioned to cast judgement on the way he ran his trattoria, nor was she an expert in Italian cuisine. She enjoyed cooking it and was proficient with the basics, but Uncle Benito had lived and breathed it his entire life.

She argued back and forth like this until the whole situation gave her a headache.

'*Mama mia!*'

Belle jolted from her reverie and glanced up sharply as Andre's mouth fell open. 'What? What is it?'

'This can't be.' His eyes swept frantically across the page he was reading.

Belle craned her neck for a better look. 'What? Tell me.'

He glanced up, a smile spreading across his face. 'The *con gamberetti.*'

'Huh?'

'The *con gamberetti*. The one you corrected for that man.'

'What about it?'

'He was a *Romeing* reviewer. He reviewed the dish and gave it four-point-seven stars out of five. He's put Valentina's in the magazine.'

'Let me see that.' Belle pulled the copy of *Romeing* towards her. Although the article was written in Italian, she translated the headline easily. 'Style Meets Tradition at Valentina's.' Beneath it was a photograph of the man she'd served the *con gamberetti* to and, next to that, was a shot of the outside of Valentina's, as well as a close-up of the dish Belle had served him. The rocket looked glossy, the prawns fat and pink, the cherry tomatoes bright and the parmesan flaky.

Belle gaped in disbelief as Andre laughed. 'You have to read it to me,' she cried. 'I can't possibly translate it all.'

Andre pulled the magazine back towards him and began reading. 'Valentina's may just be the next hidden gem,' he began, 'tucked away off Via di Pasquino, in the historical part of the city, with somewhat unassuming décor. The menu is basic and dated, but with all the classics one might crave mid-week.

'The linguine *con gamberetti* was the highlight of my visit. It came to life on the plate, a tantalizing fusion of style and tradition—old meets new—served by dedicated and passionate wait staff. I would go as far as to say it was the best *con gamberetti* I've ever tasted. Please don't tell Nonna.'

'Oh my God.' Belle was on the edge of her seat, listening to Andre's translation.

'Silky linguine, zesty sauce, crisp, bitter rocket, and perfectly-cooked prawns all delivered with sublime plating.

Although I had to send the meal back initially for corrections, it was returned to me completely revitalised with the perfect balance of sweetness, saltiness, citrus, and spice. An utterly resplendent and colourful dish. Rome, you are on notice. With more dishes like this, Valentina's could be the next big hit.'

Belle sat back in her chair, her mouth gaping open with disbelief. 'Is that really what it says?'

'Yes!' Andre was beaming, his lips caught between a smile and a laugh. 'I can honestly say Valentina's has *never* made it into *Romeing* before. This is incredible.'

The kitchen doors swung open, and Uncle Benito emerged, his forehead shiny with sweat and his apron splattered with sauce. 'Andre,' he called, wiping his hands on a dishtowel before flicking it over his shoulder. 'Make your papà an espresso.'

Andre jumped to his feet and held out the magazine. 'Papà, you have to come see this!'

Uncle Benito pursed his lips. 'What is it?'

'Come.'

He walked to them as Andre held up the review in *Romeing*. 'Read this.'

Uncle Benito reached for the magazine and held it far out in front of him, squinting as his eyes swept over the words. He was silent for a moment, his face impassive. Belle couldn't tell if the review pleased or agitated him. Finally, he glanced up at them. 'Did you know this was going to happen?' he asked.

Belle and Andre shook their heads in unison.

'So, you didn't put this in the magazine?'

'The man Belle served was a *Romeing* reviewer,' Andre explained. 'And he loved the dish. He wrote the article.'

Uncle Benito glanced at the magazine again, eyes narrowed.

'It's nice, no?' Andre said.

Uncle Benito grumbled indecipherably, then dropped the magazine onto the table, scowled at them both, and marched away, back through the swinging doors into the kitchen.

EIGHTEEN

The review wasn't mentioned again and the next morning, Belle completed her final session in the pantry and at the prep station. Before she left the kitchen, Uncle Benito cast his eye over the clean, organised shelves, as she walked him through the system again and how to maintain it. He looked pleased, rewarding her with an uncharacteristic smile and a pat on the back.

'*Un lavoro ben fatto,*' he said, congratulating her on a job well done. While it pleased her to make him happy, she was disappointed that it didn't seem to extend to her work at the prep station. Some mountains were just too difficult to climb.

It was already eleven, so she hung her apron, said goodbye to Uncle Benito and Andre, and left Valentina's. She had the lunch shift off and needed to catch up on groceries and laundry before she was due back for the dinner service.

Later, as she was returning to the apartment with a basket of clean clothes, preparing to put them away, her phone rang. She rummaged through her bag for it and saw Andre's name on the screen.

He sounded frantic when she answered. 'Belle, it's me. What are you doing right now?'

'Putting laundry away,' she said. 'Why?'

'I think the review has done something.'

'Done what?'

'The trattoria—it's busy. Everyone is asking for the *con gamberetti*.'

She gulped. 'Really?'

'Can you come in? I know you're not working this shift, but Papà needs you to show him how to make it the way you did last time.'

She couldn't help the huge grin that had spread across her face. Maybe some mountains weren't so impossible. 'I'll come now.'

She left the basket of clothes on her bed, changed into her uniform, refixed her braids, and raced back across Piazza Navona. The sky was laden with clouds, threatening rain, and the air whipping up around the piazza was cold, but she hardly noticed it as she side-stepped the lunch crowd, turning quickly down Via di Pasquino and into the lane.

There was a group of customers gathered in the entranceway of Valentina's, Leo trying frantically to seat them all. Belle excused herself politely, traversing around them to get through the door. Avery, Natalya, and Chase were running between tables taking orders, and Josh was behind the bar helping Andre prepare trays of *aperitivi*. Belle's eyes widened at the sight. She could only guess as to how Uncle Benito was coping in the kitchen, for she had never seen so many people in Valentina's before.

Andre glanced up as she approached the bar. 'It's gone crazy in here!' he said. 'He's waiting for you in the kitchen.'

Belle nodded and strode quickly to the kitchen doors, pushing through them. Uncle Benito was furiously slicing lemons and chilli while pans of prawns sizzled and linguine boiled in pots of bubbling water.

'Your *con gamberetti*,' he called out, wiping sweat from his brow with the sleeve of his chef's jacket. 'It's all they're asking for!'

She dropped her bag in the corner near Andre's backpack, collected her apron still hanging on the hook, and slipped it over her head. 'I'll take care of the sauce and prawns; you keep the linguine coming.'

Uncle Benito looked relieved as he left to roll more pasta, and Belle washed her hands at the sink before taking over at the stove. For the remainder of the lunch shift, they worked relentlessly to keep up with the orders, as noise from a packed dining room filtered in through the pass window and dishes of vibrant prawns and pasta left the kitchen. Time seemed both stagnant and turbo-charged, as an endless carousel of *con gamberetti* went out until finally, the last order left the kitchen, and Belle let out an exhausted breath.

As soon as lunch service was over and the last customer had left, Belle loaded the industrial dishwasher and scrubbed down the stove and countertops. Uncle Benito had disappeared into the dining room, returning twenty minutes later as she hung her apron on the hook.

'The dishwasher is stacked, and all the surfaces have been wiped,' she said. 'And I've set out clean knives and chopping boards for you so you can prep again.' All the prep containers had been bled dry after the surprise rush.

'*Grazie*,' he said, a thoughtful expression on his face. 'Except, dinner will probably be busier than lunch, no?'

'Yes, it could be.'

'Then you come back. You prep with me, then we cook tonight.'

Belle tried not to beam so obviously. 'You want me to cook with you again?'

'*Si*,' he said. 'But just for today.' He wagged his finger at her with a smile. 'No getting any ideas, eh!'

DINNER SERVICE WAS, unsurprisingly, busier than lunch. Word had got out about Valentina's famous linguine and prawns, and it became the most desired meal on the menu. At the pass, all other dishes paled in comparison with its vibrancy, and Uncle Benito looked embarrassed at the grey carbonaras and uninspiring pizzas that left the kitchen.

The following morning, before she'd even wrestled her eyes open, her phone rang. She groaned, rolling over to collect it from her handbag then sitting up, seeing Andre's number on the screen.

'He wants to know if you can come in at eight,' he said when she answered.

She rubbed her eyes, then sank back into her pillow, drawing the quilt over herself and burrowing down deep. 'I thought I was only allowed to help yesterday.' And she was still sleep-deprived from leaving Valentina's at two, then talking to Andre on the apartment steps until sunrise.

'He doesn't want to talk about that,' Andre said. There was a smile in his voice. 'Will you come?'

'Will you have an espresso waiting for me?'

'A double, *signorina*.'

They ended the call, and she gave a small sigh as she kicked off the covers and ran a hot shower, trying not to think of the sleep she was missing. As Avery snored softly in the next room and life barely stirred on the corsia below, she dressed and left the apartment. It was October, and the morning air was brisk, the leaves crisp and golden. She walked quickly across the piazza, retreating into her warm jacket as her sneakers hit the black cobblestones.

When she reached Valentina's, she found Uncle Benito sitting at a table in the dining room with the menu and a pen. She glanced at the bar where Andre was making coffee. He noticed her and smiled brightly.

She returned the smile and waved, then walked to Uncle Benito's table. He rose, kissing each of her cheeks. '*Boungiorno*, Belle. *Come stai?*'

'*Bene grazie*, Uncle Benito.' She unwrapped her scarf and slipped off her jacket, draping both over the back of the chair. She dropped into it as Andre brought their espressos to the table with a plate of warmed *cornetti*.

'I have to go to the market and run a few errands,' he said.

'Okay. Thanks for the espresso,' she replied, taking a grateful sip.

He winked at her, then grabbed his jacket and left.

'Right,' Uncle Benito said. 'Let's get down to business. We need to change the menu.'

Belle choked on her espresso. 'Excuse me?'

'This just won't do anymore,' he said, waving his pen at it. 'People do not want boring food. They want excitement. They want colour. You cook with both. So, what do you suggest?'

She set her cup down and glanced at the menu. It was a

moment she'd only ever imagined—Uncle Benito asking her opinion. But while she was bursting on the inside to share her ideas, she was achingly aware that the task had to be approached carefully. He watched her with such apprehension, his thick fingers locked together anxiously, that she couldn't let every idea tumble from her mouth unbridled.

'Well,' she said cautiously, 'I think the menu is lacking some variety. You have four of the classic pasta dishes on here, as well as several pizzas. And you do them all well,' she added quickly. 'But what's missing are meat dishes, entrees, a soup. Dishes with flair and appeal. People eat with their eyes first.'

'Flair and appeal,' he repeated, nodding slowly.

'Let me show you.' She slid the menu towards her and wrote minestrone, veal scallopini piccata and a Caprese salad. They were simple dishes, for she was hardly an expert in Italian cooking, and Uncle Benito would need to manage the extra work on his own, but it was variety she had in mind. She knew people would flock to Valentina's for them, and he was more than capable of cooking them. 'I think these could liven things up.'

Then she suggested a few changes to the existing dishes, some colour to the pale carbonara and extra flavour to the bolognese, so that they wouldn't be overlooked in favour of the new dishes.

Uncle Benito's eyes flickered over her writing, the dishes she'd crossed and circled, the notes she'd made on the side, and she realised with a sinking feeling that perhaps she'd gone too far. The changes were bold, and the last thing she wanted to do was overwhelm or insult him.

But to her surprise, he gave a nod. He took the pen from her and leant across the table, crossing out two of the pasta dishes and one pizza.

'Get rid of them! No one orders them anyway,' he said with conviction.

Belle smiled her approval.

He cast his eyes to the ceiling, the pen poised in his hand, then he began to scribble on the menu.

'We can add a rabbit and couscous here. An artichoke risotto here. Oh! And I know a good pan-fried squid dish with lemon and *pangrattato*. We can add that here.' He made more notes as the pen became an extension of his ideas and he began to write furiously, possessed, it would seem, with the relief of finally giving into much-needed change.

When he finished, Belle glanced over the menu. It was barely recognisable. There were five dishes from the original menu still there—three pizzas and two kinds of pasta, the linguine *con gamberetti* being one of them. The rest of them had been scribbled out.

New to the menu were the rabbit, squid, risotto, two different fish dishes, veal scaloppini, three salads and a winter minestrone soup. He'd also jotted down ideas for desserts which, they both agreed, they would need another session for.

Uncle Benito shook his head slowly at the menu. 'But it's impossible. I can't do all this on my own.'

'We can add one dish at a time,' Belle suggested. 'We'll take things slow.'

'No,' he said. 'We need all this now. Valentina's is barely surviving. I can't lose the love of my life twice.'

Belle swallowed back the sadness she felt for Uncle Benito and glanced solemnly at the menu. The changes *were* extensive. How could he possibly manage them on his own?

'You could help me,' he said, as if to answer her question.

She looked up in surprise. 'Help you? You mean, do a little prep before service?'

'No. I mean help me. You could be my sous chef during service.' He smiled at her astonishment.

'Your sous chef?'

'I can't do all this on my own,' he reiterated, looking down at the menu. 'It's too much. And, well, I trust you in my kitchen.' He looked sheepish at the revelation, as she blinked, stunned. 'I know, it's a surprise to me too, but I do.'

It was a marvel at how far he'd come that morning, from nervously watching as she made a few minor corrections to completely overhauling the menu himself. Now he was inviting her to become his sous chef.

'I can give you a small pay increase, but I can't offer you much,' he said.

She shook her head, still making sense of his offer. 'That's fine. I'm just... well, I'm...' She didn't know what she was. Thrilled. Overcome. Terrified. It was everything she'd ever dreamed of, but what if she failed miserably by his side, if she'd talked a big game, then couldn't deliver? 'It's just that... I've never been a sous chef before.'

'You will be okay.'

'I don't want to disappoint you.'

He placed his hand over hers with grandfatherly gentleness. 'You could never disappoint me, Belle.'

She smiled as tears began to well in her eyes. It was the words she'd waited a lifetime for her father to say.

NINETEEN

Belle and Uncle Benito agreed to launch the new dishes the following week once she and Andre had purchased the ingredients and the recipes could be tested in the kitchen. Then they would trial them on a specials board to determine what was popular with the customers before redesigning the menus.

'We need a specials board inside and one at the top of the lane,' Belle suggested, as Uncle Benito stood poised over a notepad, making a list. 'Otherwise, how will people know you have all these amazing new dishes? We love your regular customers, but we want the tourists too!'

Uncle Benito liked the idea and he added two boards and a box of liquid chalk to Andre's growing list of items to buy.

After the staff dinner that night, Belle and Andre walked home across the piazza. She babbled the whole way about the week she would spend in the kitchen with Uncle Benito, trialling the new courses, her excited voice echoing across the empty square.

'I'm not even sure how you convinced him to make

those changes,' Andre said, shaking his head. 'He can be a stubborn old man.'

'I think he convinced himself in the end. He just needed a little encouragement, and maybe the *con gamberetti* showed him what was possible.'

'You have been a breath of fresh air, Belle. You have shown me what is possible, too, if I'm brave.' Andre cast her such a fond look that she flushed. She wasn't sure if he was talking about Valentina's anymore or if he was talking about *them*, and she was surprised at how much she hoped it was the latter. She wasn't good at reading his signals—an accidental brush of his arm, a hand on her back, the gentle looks he sometimes gave her. What did they all mean? If that 'almost kiss' in Venice was anything to go by, apparently nothing more than the actions of a devoted friend. It had been a long time since she'd had to interpret a man's body language and she feared she'd misread Andre's at every turn.

They reached Avery's apartment block and although she was still running on adrenalin and wouldn't have minded sitting on the steps with Andre, he gave her an apologetic smile.

'I have to get home. I still have a couple of hours of bookkeeping to do.'

'Oh.' She tried not to let her disappointment show.

'Believe me, I wish I could stay.' His look of longing was equally regretful.

She forced her face to brighten. 'No, that's fine. I'll see you tomorrow then?'

'Always.' He leant down to kiss both her cheeks, before touching her arm gently and turning to head back towards the piazza.

She sighed. It was two in the morning, and she should

probably have a shower and go straight to sleep, but she was still humming from her day at Valentina's and going to bed was the last thing she felt like doing.

She climbed the stairs to Avery's apartment and let herself in. Avery was out with friends and the stark silence caused a pang of homesickness to wash over her. It had been a few weeks since she'd spoken to her mother and it was the quiet times, when everything stopped spinning, that she felt her absence the most.

Belle kicked off her shoes and dropped down onto her bed, retrieving her phone from her back pocket. She tapped her mother's number, Grace answering on the second ring.

'Darling!' She sounded happy to hear from her, and Belle settled into her voice like arms wrapping around her.

'Mum, how are you?'

'Everything's fine here. How are you?'

'Good. Great in fact. Uncle Benito offered me a job in his kitchen.' The news came pouring out.

'He what?' Grace let out a whoop. 'That's wonderful. Will you help him with more than pantry organisation this time?'

Belle chuckled. Grace had enjoyed the pantry story on their last call. 'Yes. I'll be his sous chef. He even wants to try some of my ideas for the menu.'

'I'm proud of you, sweetheart. You're doing it; you're living your dream.'

'I haven't felt this happy in a long time.' And it was the truth. Never had the prospect of going to work before been an exciting one. Her only regret was that she seemed to see so little of Riley. Glancing around their shared bedroom, it was hard to ignore how Riley took up less and less space these days, most of her belongings transferred to Leo's apartment.

'You'll have to pass on my appreciation to Uncle Benito, Andre and Avery,' Grace said, bringing Belle back to the conversation. 'They're taking such good care of you.'

Belle nodded into the phone as she peeled off her socks. They smelt of coffee and red wine. Her entire wardrobe was steeped in the aromas of Valentina's.

'You've been gone such a long time.' Grace's voice sounded wistful. 'I can't believe it's almost Christmas.'

'Six weeks to go,' Belle confirmed, tossing her socks into the clothes hamper. 'The weather has cooled here.'

'And it's warmer here. We're going to have a stifling summer. Are you coming home for the holidays? We'd love to spend them with you.'

Belle wondered just how much of the 'we' was her mother talking. She couldn't imagine her father lamenting over a Christmas without her. The delicate threads of their relationship had finally snapped when she'd left for London. 'I would, it's just that I've accepted this job now. It wouldn't be right to leave Uncle Benito with the menu when we're about to launch it.'

'Maybe you could come home for the week of Christmas, then go back to Rome before the new year. Doesn't Italy shut down over a holy holiday?'

Belle hesitated. The job was only part of it. How did she explain to her mother that she didn't want to go back, to face her father and his constant discontent towards her, to drive down streets saturated in memories of Ben that she had no interest in revisiting? Not to mention the minor hiccup of being an illegal immigrant in Italy.

'Darling?'

'I'm here, Mum,' she said.

'Well?'

'I don't know.'

'If it's your father or Ben—'

'It's not just them. The problem is if I leave now, I won't be allowed back into the country. I'm kind of working... illegally.'

There was silence on the other end, then, 'What do you mean you're "kind of working illegally"? You don't have a working visa?'

'No.'

Grace sounded confused. 'Why not?'

Belle cringed. She'd always followed the rules, and the idea of breaking the law in Rome had never sat well with her, even when she'd forced it to the back of her mind. 'Well, it all just happened quickly. I was offered the job and Uncle Benito said it was fine to work off the books.'

'Nevertheless, you should apply for a visa straight away.'

'I can't,' Belle said. 'It's too late. I'm already here. I can only apply for one in my country of residence.'

She could feel her mother's frown from across the oceans. 'Belle, working illegally in a foreign country was not what I had in mind when I encouraged you to go. If you're caught—'

'I won't be. Uncle Benito has an arrangement with the authorities.'

Grace inhaled sharply. 'Oh, for heaven's sake!'

Despite her reservations, Belle couldn't resist a smile. 'It sounds worse than it is. We have it under control. Money exchanges hands here all the time. It just means I won't be able to come and go from Italy freely. If I leave now, I might not be able to come back for a while.'

'Because the missing visa will be noticed on your passport?'

'Yes.'

'So you're stuck there?' Grace's voice rose. 'For how long?'

'For as long as I don't want to be stuck here anymore.' She sighed, softening her tone. 'Mum, you're the only reason I would ever come back anyway. I don't have anything else waiting for me there. Not Dad or Ben or a job. Even Riley has a life here. She wouldn't come back with me now.'

'But this is your home.'

'Is it?' Belle said. The exhaustion of the day began to sink into her bones, and she closed her eyes. It was late and maybe she was lacking sensitivity. The last thing she wanted to do was upset her mother. 'Why don't you come and visit me instead? For a couple of weeks. You could stay here at Avery's. She wouldn't mind.'

Grace murmured a half-hearted agreement. 'Yes, I suppose I could.'

But although she said the words, Belle knew she never would. She would never leave Belle's father behind, and Edward would never come. 'How's Dad?'

'He's good. Working a lot.'

'Does he approve of my trattoria job?'

Belle could almost see Grace's smile. 'You know him, always holding out hope that you'll carry on with tradition.'

'I'm thirty-five, Mum. If I haven't gone to law school by now, it's not going to happen.'

'I'm not sure he's made his peace with that yet.'

'Well, he needs to start to. Does he even ask how I am?'

'I tell your father about everything you're doing. He doesn't say much. He's hard to read sometimes.'

'He doesn't need to say anything. It's obvious in his lack of interest.' Talking about her father deflated her all over again. Ten thousand miles and four months away had done little to quell the hurt he could still cause. It seemed the longer she spent in Rome, around people who loved and supported her, the more she realised how lacking her father's love had always been.

Belle sighed and glanced at the time on her watch. It was almost three and she was starting to feel the combination of sleep deprivation and early starts at Valentina's bear down on her. 'It's getting late here, Mum. I'm going to sleep now.'

'Of course, sweetheart.' Grace paused, then, with a sombre tone, she said, 'Before you go, there's something I've been wanting to tell you. I've been putting it off, actually. I wasn't sure how to bring it up.'

'What is it?'

There was a heavy pause. 'Ben's engaged. To that girl, Olivia.'

Belle was certain her brain stopped working. Everything slowed down, including her reaction, so that the only reply she could muster was, 'Oh.'

'Yes,' Grace said. 'I thought it might come as a shock.'

'That he proposed to her after six months when he made me wait twenty years?' Shock didn't begin to describe it. She felt old wounds split open as new life was breathed into them. 'How did you find out?'

'Your father heard through the grapevine. He was disappointed by the news. I think he was hoping that if you returned and Ben got this Olivia girl out of his system, he may commit to you.'

'I'm not sure who Dad is mourning the loss of most, me or Ben,' Belle said with a satirical snort.

'Anyway, I didn't want you hearing it from somebody else. Now that it's out, you should keep moving forward.'

And she would. Ben hardly consumed a second of her

thoughts these days. Nevertheless, the news of his engagement to Olivia was hard to ignore, like a familiar dagger piercing her heart. Old ghosts had a way of slinking back into cold shadows and she wished more than ever that Avery was in the next room or that Andre had stayed on the steps with her. She didn't want to be alone with those ghosts.

As she said goodnight to her mother and they promised to speak again soon, there could be little doubt in her mind. Rome was exactly where she needed to be.

TWENTY

Belle arrived early for her first official day in the kitchen as sous chef. Uncle Benito was waiting for her, a wide grin on his face as he held out his arms and presented her with two sets of junior chef's whites.

She took them from him, running her fingers over the starched fabric, the occasion so momentous, she tried not to leak tears everywhere. It was an equally significant moment when she ducked into the female washroom to pull one set on, spending a full minute studying herself in the speckled mirror, before stepping out again, her feet hardly touching the floor.

She was a chef. Well, a junior chef, in a tiny trattoria tucked away in a little pocket of Rome, like a thousand other little pockets in Rome, but a chef, nonetheless. Every hope and dream that this might one day be her life was woven into the crisp threads of those new junior whites, which she wore so proudly, she couldn't wipe the grin from her face.

But Uncle Benito didn't allow her to float for long. He was all business again, instructing her to write up the specials board before joining him in the kitchen to start prep.

Andre had arrived early too and was unloading boxes and crates of food for the new dishes through the back door. They'd stayed out talking the night before as they often did, on the apartment steps, and she knew he'd then risen with the sun to buy fresh seafood.

'Did you actually sleep?' she asked him, helping him stack the produce by the refrigerator door.

'A little. Nothing coffee can't fix.' He gave her new whites a nod. 'I like the uniform.'

'You do?' She ran her hand down the fabric, still pinching herself that she was wearing it.

'It suits you.'

'Your father gave them to me this morning.'

'I know. I was the one who ordered them.' He threw her a warm smile as she took another box from him, loving the uniform all the more knowing Andre had arranged it for her.

Uncle Benito prepared them a plate of brioche buns with butter and jam alongside hot macchiatos. Work stopped for twenty minutes while they gathered to eat, conversation light as they discussed the day ahead before activity resumed once more.

At lunch, when the doors opened, a steady stream of diners flowed through. They eyed the new specials board by the entranceway with interest and, soon after, dockets for pan-fried squid, veal scaloppini and artichoke risotto began lining up on the pass.

Even from inside the kitchen, Belle could hear the mood lift in the dining room. The specials board at the top of the laneway was doing its intended job too, and diners began to fill the tables —winter tourists stopping through on their way to the Alps and locals who would normally find elsewhere to eat. Only an hour into service and a small line began to snake its way outside.

Uncle Benito worked tirelessly, but not with the exhausted and agitated look of someone who could barely keep up, nor with the resistance he'd exhibited weeks earlier when he'd begrudgingly let Belle help him with prep. This time he asked her to taste, sought her advice on plating and taught her how to manage her stations. Cooking at home was one thing, but juggling multiple orders, being the grill, pastry, fry, and sauté chefs all at once, and ensuring all components came together at the same time while not getting in each other's way was something else entirely. She sliced her fingers, burnt her hands, singed her eyebrows, but she shrugged it off, bandaged herself up and kept moving.

Dinner service was even busier, as locals and tourists emerged from their homes and hotels for a meal. Andre turned the music up loud and its beat filled the laneway, streaming out into Via di Pasquino, enticing people in. Belle thought half of Rome must have poured through Valentina's doors by the end of the night. She couldn't remember when she'd stopped for air or a bathroom break, and she hadn't eaten since the brioche bun she'd had for breakfast.

After service, she hung her apron next to Uncle Benito's on the hook and pushed through the kitchen doors to the dining room and rousing applause from the wait staff. As the dinner service had wound down and Uncle Benito had loaded the dishwasher, she'd fixed platters of couscous and veal scallopini to be served alongside the usual pizza and pasta for the staff meal.

She dropped into a chair beside Andre and was so ravenous, she quickly devoured two plates of food and several glasses of wine, the alcohol soaring to her head.

'Hungry?' he asked with amusement, watching her.

But her mouth was too full of couscous to reply, and all she could do was nod.

At one am, Avery rose and pulled her jacket on, throwing her arms around Belle and squeezing her tight. 'I'm going out. I'll see you in the morning. And by the way, you were friggin' awesome tonight!'

Belle hugged her back. 'Thank you. Be safe.' She watched her leave through the door, marvelling for the umpteenth time at Avery's inexhaustible energy. The only place Belle wanted to drop into was her bed.

'You must be tired,' Andre said, draping his arm across the back of her chair.

'Yes, it's been a long day.'

'Shall I walk you home?'

'I'd like that.'

They rose from their seats. Natalya and Josh volunteered to remain behind to clear the table, and everyone else pulled on their coats and scarves and clambered out the door. Andre helped Belle into her jacket, deft hands carefully relocating her braids so as not to catch them in the collar.

Uncle Benito appeared at their side, slapping Andre lightly on the back. '*Buona notte*, son,' he said, wearing a wide smile. 'I'll see you at home.' He turned to Belle. 'And *buona notte* to you, *bella*. I am so proud.'

The wine may have gone to her head, but even without it, she would have felt the same surge of emotion well in her eyes. *I am so proud.* No one had ever said those words to her before.

After saying goodbye to Uncle Benito, she and Andre left Valentina's under a clear, cold sky. They turned into

Piazza Navona, the crowds gone for the day, and the fountains gurgling to an audience of pigeons.

'You were remarkable today, Belle,' Andre said.

With her spare chef's uniform tucked under her arm, she smiled. The cold stung her cheeks, but it was intoxicating, as though she were standing on the edge of the world. And maybe she was. Working in that kitchen had sparked something long dead inside her, a sliver of hope that one day she might cook professionally. And it may have only been in a tiny trattoria tucked away in a small unassuming laneway, but she felt utterly blessed. Despite his earlier reservations, Uncle Benito had proven to be a generous and knowledgeable teacher and no cooking class could ever compare.

'What a day,' she said, revelling in the memory of it. 'What a ride this whole trip has been.'

'You enjoy cooking a lot, don't you?' Andre asked.

Belle smiled. 'It's in my blood. I can't explain it, but it's like I was born to do it, which is ridiculous when you consider that I come from a long line of lawyers. I should be in a courtroom somewhere fighting for justice.' She laughed. If only her father could see her now. 'But there's something about cooking, about colour and creation and making people happy through food, that I love.'

'Then that's exactly what you should keep doing. If you love it, you should live and breathe it.'

They reached the steps to Avery's apartment and Belle sighed with regret. Although she could have fallen into bed, she didn't want their time together to end, didn't want Andre to leave. She wanted to keep the night alive until the sun rose again. An idea popped into her head, and before she could consider how preposterous it was at this late hour, she blurted it out anyway. 'Bake with me.'

'Huh?' A smile eclipsed his bemused expression.

'Let's bake something upstairs, in Avery's kitchen.'

'You want to *bake* something?' He glanced down at his watch. 'Now? At one-thirty in the morning?'

'Yes!' She was breathless with the idea. 'Let's make biscotti and hot chocolate.'

He looked truly confused now. 'I thought you'd be sick of cooking for one day.'

'Never. Come on.' She tugged on his arm, feeling emboldened enough to lead him up to the empty apartment, when previously they'd only ever spoken on the steps outside.

She unlocked the door and let them both in. Flicking on the lights, she kicked off her shoes and shrugged out of her jacket. 'Just give me a second. I'm going to change. I'm wearing every dish on the menu at the moment.'

Andre's chuckle followed her as she headed for her bedroom. She closed the door and hung her clean uniform in the wardrobe, then she threw off her soiled one, covered in sauce splatters and oil, and tossed it on the floor to be soaked in the morning. Climbing into clean jeans and an oversized sweatshirt, she pulled open the door and walked to the kitchen, finding Andre with his shoes off too, pulling flour and sugar out of the pantry and lining them on the bench beside butter and eggs.

'Biscotti, right?' he said, glancing up as she entered.

'Yes.' She pushed her sleeves up and stood beside him. 'We can do an almond and citrus batch and a chocolate and vanilla batch.'

'Do you have chocolate pieces?'

'I do. And we can also melt them and dip the ends of the biscuits in later.'

He raised an eyebrow. 'I'm going home with a stomach ache, aren't I?'

'What Italian ever goes home with a stomach ache after eating biscotti?' she asked seriously.

Andre blinked, then they erupted in a fit of giggles, doubled over, their laughter coming out in snorts. Belle was certain the late hour, the sleep deprivation and the alcohol were making them loopy. Or perhaps it was just the inexplicable nature of their friendship that had always made them feel so comfortable around each other. Comfortable enough to snort while laughing.

When they'd regained enough composure to finally breathe again, they returned to the task, pulling ingredients, bowls, and utensils from the cupboards. Biscotti was easy to make, a combination of butter and sugar, combined with eggs then later, baking powder and flour. They made two separate batches, Andre presiding over the one with orange zest and almond extract, and Belle making the chocolate and vanilla batch.

They formed their doughs, talking and laughing, the ease with which they worked together in Avery's speck of a kitchen testament to their friendship. If Belle cast her mind back, she couldn't recall the exact moment Andre had become one of her dearest friends. He seemed to have always been there, like a constant fixture in her life, and not just for the four months she'd been in Italy.

When their dough was ready, they shaped them into flat logs and spread them out on paper-lined baking trays.

Andre stared at them; brow furrowed. 'They just need one other thing.'

'What?'

'Turbinado sugar.' He rifled through Avery's pantry and extracted a bag of raw sugar. 'It crystalises the top of them when they're baking in the oven.'

He opened the bag and Belle stuck her hand in at the

exact moment Andre did. Their fingers knocked together, then became stuck in the bag's opening. A frisson of energy shot up Belle's arm, the hair on the back of her neck rising at his touch. The air became charged around them, and his eyes locked on hers, a moment trapped in a heartbeat.

'Oh, sorry,' Belle said, snatching her hand back and blushing.

Andre blushed too. 'No, I'm sorry. You go first.'

'No, really, I'm taking over.'

'I don't mind if you do.'

'I have a terrible habit of it.'

Belle lowered her eyes, unable to hide her flaming cheeks. Andre swallowed, his Adam's apple bobbing. Suddenly, the kitchen became airless and small and a trifle hot, which was ridiculous, for it was not the first time their hands had bumped together, although it had never happened while they were alone in an apartment.

'We should get these in the oven,' Belle croaked.

Andre cleared his throat. 'Yes. Oven.'

They sprinkled turbinado sugar over the logs then squeezed one tray on the top rack and the other on the bottom of Avery's ancient little oven, Belle praying it would not give up the ghost halfway through. While the biscotti baked, they made small talk, leaning against the bench, skirting around the weird thing that had happened with their fingers.

Twenty-five minutes later, they took the trays out, set them aside to cool, then cut the logs into slices. They slid the biscotti back into the oven to bake for a further ten minutes, making hot chocolate while they waited.

Finally, with a plate of freshly baked biscotti and mugs of hot chocolate, Belle tugged open the balcony door and they lowered themselves onto chairs outside to eat.

'Are you cold?' Andre asked. 'I can get you a jacket.'

'There's a blanket on the sofa we can share.'

He disappeared inside, returning moments later with a thick woollen blanket that Belle sometimes threw over herself when the apartment was cold. He draped it over them both, and they huddled down under it, hot mugs and biscotti balancing on their laps. Exhaustion dragged at her muscles again, Andre's warm body beside her making her drowsy.

'It's beautiful at this time of night,' she said, glancing out over the quiet corsia, towards Piazza Navona.

'Rome has a tender side when you take away her grit and noise,' he said, staring out too.

'Would you ever leave Italy?' she asked.

He shrugged, cupping his hands around his mug. 'I don't know. My heart is here in Rome, in Tuscany, in Italy.' He glanced at her. 'I'm not sure I'm built for anywhere else. And my father is here. He hasn't had many days off in the last thirty years. Someday, I'd like to take over the trattoria so he can retire.'

'Then you'll be bound here.'

'There are worse places in the world to be bound.'

They shared a smile then fell silent, the soft crunch of biscotti and slurp of hot chocolate the only sound.

'Thank you for baking with me,' she said. 'Ben never used to do that.'

Andre raised an eyebrow. 'Not even once, in all the years you were together?'

Belle shook her head. 'He thought cooking was silly, certainly not as important as the things he did. He was happy to taste but would never roll up his sleeves and join me in the kitchen. It was a bit beneath him.'

'I'd be happy to cook with you every day of the week, Belle.'

His words wrapped her in warmth and, feeling sleepy, she rested her head against his shoulder, and he nestled his cheek against her hair. After Ben had broken her heart, the idea of being close to another man was something she'd only occasionally entertained. Twenty years of knowing someone, of them imbuing every part of your soul, could create a gaping void to fill. Months later, Andre had filled it, and the thought neither surprised nor troubled her. Rather, it made her heart swell, even if she wasn't sure she filled *his* heart.

When the sky began to pale and the first streaks of amber coloured it, Andre stood with a regretful look. 'I better go so we can get some sleep.'

Belle rose too, sad that their time was over, for she could have sat out there with him for a thousand sunrises. She collected the plate of biscotti and empty mugs and followed him inside, placing them down on the kitchen bench.

She ignored his pleas for her to stay in the apartment where it was warm and walked him down the stairwell. Out on the corsia, he looked at her with a tender smile. 'I had a wonderful night, Belle.'

'I did too.'

A second passed, then another, as their eyes held, and Belle's heart skipped a beat. To her surprise, when Andre leant in to kiss her cheeks, he skimmed her lips instead. She was too stunned to respond at first and she blinked, seeing surprise in his eyes too, as though he hadn't planned on doing that. Then, with an unexpected urgency, he wrapped his hands around her waist, pulled her to him, and kissed her.

Her breath fled as she folded into him, her intensity matching his with a dazzling fervour. She linked her arms around his neck, pulling him closer still, seeking his tongue, his lips, his whole mouth. It was everything she was afraid it would be. Exquisite, passionate—a desire that had confused and tormented her for months. No one had ever kissed her like that before, with such need that her stomach flipped and heat rose in places that left her breathless.

When they finally separated, Andre smiled. There was a satisfied, almost languid expression on his face. 'Sorry. I'm not sure you were ready for that, but I couldn't help myself.'

She pulled back to look at him, surprised by his apology. 'You don't have to say sorry.'

'It's just that, you're still recovering from a painful breakup. I know moving on can be difficult; I'm going through it too. I didn't want to scare you off.'

She shook her head, leaning in closer to him as his arms remained around her waist. 'You could never scare me off. I've wanted this too.'

'Really?' He looked thoroughly pleased. 'I've wanted you from the moment I met you, in that little bar in London.' He laughed sheepishly. 'It's hard just being your friend. I've tried to be patient.'

'You're the most patient person in the world,' she said, marvelling that all this time he'd felt it too, that sweet, taunting ache that came with adoring someone from a distance. 'In fact, I thought you didn't like me.'

'Don't ever think that. You haven't left my mind since that night. It's just that...' He grimaced, as though trying to find the right words in a language that wasn't his first, 'love might be complicated for us, Belle.'

'Complicated?'

'You have Ben, I have Mary.'

'I don't have Ben. And I hope you don't have Mary.'

He looked away. 'You know what I mean.'

She touched his cheek, turning his face back to hers. 'I'm not sure I do. But I want to come into this with an open heart, with the past behind me. Can you do the same?'

He stared at her, their gazes locked, his eyes so intense on her she thought he could see the most intimate parts of her soul. 'My heart is wide open.'

She nestled into his chest and closed her eyes with contentment, feeling the light thud of his heartbeat against her cheek. If only she could freeze time, halt its interminable tick, prolong the moment before he said goodbye. Now that she'd tasted him, she wanted more, a bubbling giddiness chasing the exhaustion of the day away and making her limbs tingle, her heart pound faster, her lips burn.

She sighed, soaked in the kind of happiness she had long forgotten. How swiftly life could change. How remarkable that a heart once shattered could heal and seek love again if you allowed it.

'You'd better get inside.' He rubbed her arms gently. 'It's freezing out here.'

'I don't want to leave you.'

He beamed. 'You don't know how happy that makes me.'

She smiled too, the luckiest girl in the world.

He kissed her cold nose, then her lips. 'Until tomorrow, *bella*.'

'Until tomorrow.'

He pulled away, his arms leaving hers regretfully, before he turned and walked back towards the piazza, disappearing into the dawn.

TWENTY-ONE

On the morning of Christmas Eve, Belle's eyes reluctantly opened. Stretching her fatigued muscles, she rolled over to check the time, groaning at the single digits that blinked back at her. Seven o'clock. She'd hoped for a sleep-in, to remain buried beneath the covers on a frosty morning after a busy night at Valentina's, but she could already hear Avery awake and banging around her room as she threw clothes into her suitcase. She was returning home to Vancouver for the holidays, and Belle and Andre were driving her to the airport.

Christmas had arrived in the blink of an eye. She would have barely registered its presence were it not for the coloured lights strung high above Piazza Navona and the towering Christmas tree she passed daily on her way to work. The air had turned bitterly cold too, the final weeks of December announcing themselves with a wintry gale.

Still, beneath Rome's frosty coat, she was glorious. Twinkling nativity scenes blinked in the piazzas and rows of Christmas trees, enormous and sparkling, lined the city streets. Belle's favourite by far was the tree that stood brightly outside the Colosseum by the triumphal Arch of Constantine, and every opportunity she got, she dragged Andre with her to see it.

Valentina's had closed for the holidays the night before. The final service had been manic, the glacial weather doing little to deter people from a meal out, especially as the new menu had thrust the trattoria onto Rome's culinary stage, enticing diners away from the busier piazzas and down into the little laneway. It had been so busy, and Belle so distracted with keeping up with dockets on the pass, that she'd hardly noticed the annoying arrival of the immigration officials for one last payday before the holidays until Natalya marched through the kitchen and tugged on her arm, dragging her into the back alleyway with Josh and Chase.

She sighed now, knowing she had to get up, but unable to find the will to push away the covers and let the cold air stream in.

'Belle, Andre's here!' Avery cried out.

She smiled. That was enough to tempt her up.

After a quick shower, she pulled on several layers of clothing, then greeted him in the living room.

'Sleep well?' he asked, grinning at her.

'I could have used a few more hours.' She was hoping he'd pull her into his arms for a proper hello, but he waited until Avery's back was turned before planting a hasty kiss on her lips.

Belle tried to hide her disappointment. It had been a few weeks since their first kiss on the corsia, and while she wasn't expecting to shout it from the rooftops, she'd hoped that by now they might have taken a few people into their confidence. Like Avery or Uncle Benito. But Andre seemed intent on keeping it between them. She saw it in the way he touched her arm discreetly, the way he avoided her eyes if his father was around, the way he'd dropped a kiss onto her lips just then, as soon as Avery's back was turned.

He's probably still working it out in his head, she told herself. She was doing the same, navigating the waters of a potential new relationship after a traumatic end to the last. If Ben's betrayal had taught her anything, it was that placing her faith in providence was infinitely harder to do these days. But she also couldn't completely dispel the niggle of misgiving that had worked its way into her mind.

Love for us might be complicated.

You have Ben, I have Mary.

Andre was watching her, and she forced a smile as Avery lugged her suitcase across the living room tiles and groaned. 'It's so heavy. I think I packed too much.'

He sighed, glancing at his watch. 'You're going to be late for your flight if we don't leave soon.'

'Okay, okay.' Avery's face scrunched up as though he were being entirely unreasonable. 'I'm ready.'

Down the stairwell they dragged her bag, stepping outside into the frigid morning air. Andre's car was parked two blocks away and they tugged the suitcase over uneven cobblestones, the wheels clacking with every bump. Icy blasts of winter whistled up the street, blowing through Belle's coat, as thick and ominous clouds churned in the sky. The news that morning had said that snow was coming.

The drive to the airport was a stop-start affair, holiday traffic grinding to a halt. When they eventually arrived, Andre parked the car, and they hurried into the departure terminal.

'I wish I was staying,' Avery said with a pout, as they stood out the front of the sliding doors that led to customs, her boarding pass and passport clutched in her hand. 'I don't want to go home.'

'At this rate, you're not going anywhere,' Andre said, running a hand through his hair with exasperation. 'Your flight is going to leave without you.'

She poked her tongue out at him and turned to Belle. 'Have fun in Tuscany,' she said, her pout remaining. 'I love that farmhouse. I'm completely jealous that you're going without me.'

She'd grumbled about it all week—the fact that Belle was spending Christmas and Epiphany with Uncle Benito and Andre at the Tuscan farmhouse they'd once shared with Valentina, their wife and mother, while Avery would be stuck at home in Vancouver with her parents.

'It won't be the same without you,' Belle assured her.

'It had better not be,' Avery said, wagging her finger at them both.

Belle laughed and hugged her, then pulled away to straighten her plaits affectionately. 'I promise we won't do anything fun until you get back.'

Avery looked only slightly mollified. 'Merry Christmas.'

'Merry Christmas, sweetheart.'

Andre ruffled the top of her head playfully. 'Be good to your parents,' he said. 'Don't get into mischief. *Buon Natale.*'

'*Buon Natale*, cousin.' She hugged him, then with a last wave goodbye, she disappeared through the frosted glass doors, lugging her suitcase behind her.

As Belle and Andre left the airport and drove back along the motorway towards Rome, the first flakes of snow began to drift down, tiny specks of white suspended on the breeze, like shimmering confetti. There was much to do, and Lady Luck was generous as they encountered little traffic heading back into the city.

Belle, Andre, and Uncle Benito would leave for the Tuscan farmhouse later that evening—Christmas Eve—and would return to Rome on January sixth, the day of Epiphany. The part Belle liked most about this plan was that Riley and Leo were coming for the entire two weeks. Although they texted regularly, it had been weeks since Belle had seen Riley, and months since Riley had stayed at Avery's.

They arrived back from the airport and Andre deposited Belle at the apartment. She had last-minute gifts to wrap, her bag to pack, then she had to box up all the food for Christmas Eve dinner. She had volunteered to manage the cooking at the farmhouse that night to allow Uncle Benito a chance at proper rest, although she doubted she'd be able to keep him out of the kitchen entirely.

For dinner, she planned to roast a macadamia and sage stuffed pork, served with golden roasted vegetables and spiced cherries with gravy. Fresh seafood that she'd sourced from the fish market chilled in the fridge and, for dessert, she would bake a chestnut cake with chocolate sauce, accompanied by deep-fried, sugary *ciambelle*. It was an ambitious menu, considering the late hour they'd arrive in Tuscany, and that she'd have to start cooking immediately upon arrival, but she was determined to prepare a Christmas Eve feast to remember. And she was certain nobody would go hungry, for Avery's kitchen was already groaning under the weight of all that food.

Andre kissed her goodbye on the front steps, and she

watched him hurry up the corsia under a light drifting of snow, towards Piazza Navona. He would spend the next few hours with Uncle Benito, scrubbing the ovens and cleaning out the refrigerators. At five pm they would collect her for an early Catholic mass then afterwards, they would return to Avery's apartment, pack the car, and begin the three-hour drive to Tuscany.

CHRISTMAS EVE MASS was held at Sant'Agnese in Agone in Piazza Navona. The church was filled with parishioners, the inside warm and bathed in soft light, the front doors closed firmly against the frigid air. The priest delivered his sermon in Italian to a rapt audience of the faithful, his words bouncing off the dark wood panels and stained glass. Uncle Benito was on one side of her and Andre on the other, his arm and leg resting against hers, the kind of touch that felt natural, if not slightly forbidden, with his father so close.

'You look beautiful tonight. I like your hair,' he whispered into her ear, sending her brain into overdrive. She could smell his cologne—fresh and masculine, as he sat beside her in a charcoal tailored suit and maroon tie.

She'd left her hair out, free of braids, and had brushed it until it shone. She'd worn her prettiest dress and heels, too, and had taken care with her makeup. It was refreshing to be out of her chef's whites and in feminine clothes, and the fact that he'd noticed her hair made her smile.

He was always considerate. Always kind. So unlike Ben in that respect. In fact, they couldn't have been more different from each other. Andre wasn't as self-assured, and he didn't measure life according to material wealth or success. He seemed happiest with the simple things—a slow walk to work, good food and company, an espresso at the start of the day, not to gulp it on the run, but to sit and enjoy it with someone he liked talking to.

She wondered what a life with him in Italy would be like. Would it be nurturing and protective? Would it be loving and gentle? Would it be fraught with challenges because *their love might be complicated*, whatever Andre had meant by that?

When the service was over, the heaving congregation spilled out onto the front steps and into the piazza. The cold did little to discourage people from wishing each other a merry Christmas, and Uncle Benito and Andre were quickly swept up in the mayhem. The native language was loud and rapid, too quick for Belle to follow properly, and she moved from circle to circle with them, until eventually, numb from the cold, she slipped away and began a slow stroll back towards the corsia.

When she turned around to check if Uncle Benito and Andre were almost finished, she noticed Uncle Benito in spirited conversation with a similar aged couple, while a young, slender woman with dark hair had led Andre away from the crowd and was talking to him by the Fountain of the Four Rivers. Her hand was on his arm, and when he said something to her, she threw her head back and laughed. After a few minutes, they embraced fondly and she returned to the older couple, but not before casting him a last lingering look.

Andre rubbed his jaw, then scanned the busy piazza. When his eyes settled on Belle, she waved, and he jogged over.

'Hey,' he said. 'I was worried I'd lost you.'

'Sorry,' she replied. 'I thought I'd keep out of the way.'

'It can get a little crazy after Christmas mass. We run into people we hardly see during the year. It's like a reunion.' He glanced across at his father, still by the steps talking to the older couple. 'He wants to stay.'

Belle glanced at Uncle Benito too. 'Stay?'

'He's changed his mind. He wants me and him to spend Christmas Eve with Mary's family and drive up to Tuscany tomorrow.'

'Oh.' Belle's heart plummeted. She studied the man and woman Uncle Benito was still deeply engaged in conversation with. 'So that's Mary's parents?'

'Yes.'

'And that girl you were talking to by the fountain. Was that Mary?'

He nodded slowly. 'Yes, that was her.'

'I see.' With a tightening in her chest, Belle's eyes dropped to her feet, stamping them against the cold. 'I knew you were still friends, but I didn't realise you were that close.'

He fell silent and when she looked up, he was studying her intently. 'I was supposed to marry her not so long ago.'

'It would appear she'd still want you to.' She hadn't intended to sound snippy, but her blood had begun to rush in her ears. 'Does she know about us?'

He dropped his head sheepishly. 'Not yet.'

'Does anyone know? Her parents? Your father?'

He released a long breath. 'You know they don't.'

She nodded, chewing her lip to quell a familiar rush of unpleasant emotions. Rejection. Uncertainty. Ben. That feeling, once again, of not being enough. 'Are you embarrassed by me?'

He recoiled. 'What kind of a question is that?'

'A valid one. We've been dating for weeks now, and no one knows. I'm starting to feel like your little secret.'

Hurt flashed across his eyes. 'That's unfair. I thought we were taking it slow. I didn't realise it was a race to tell everyone.'

'Not everyone. But a few would be nice.'

'I get that you want others to know, but I've just come out of a serious relationship, and I don't want to hurt people.'

'Like Mary and her parents?' she retorted.

He ignored the jibe. 'I'm not doing this because I want you to be my secret. I'm just trying to work out the best way to tell everyone without upsetting them, especially my dad.'

She glanced across the piazza, at the closed restaurants, at the fountain where he'd stood minutes before with Mary. Anywhere but his eyes. She hated being *that* person, the one who harped on about things, the one whose insecurities defined the relationship, but twenty years and a broken heart had taught her to tread cautiously.

'Belle?' he said, trying to catch her gaze. 'Are we okay?'

She forced her eyes back to his and nodded. 'We're okay.'

'Because I get the feeling you—'

'We're okay,' she assured him again. 'I promise.'

He gave her a rueful smile.

'But I won't keep you. It's freezing out here and they're probably waiting for you.' She hadn't expected to spend Christmas Eve alone and the idea of it, of Andre spending it with his ex-fiancée instead, left her feeling hollow inside. 'Will you stop past Avery's in the morning and pick me up for Tuscany?'

Andre looked confused, then shook his head. 'Wait,

Belle, I think you've misunderstood me. I'm not spending Christmas with Mary's family.'

It was Belle's turn to feel confused. 'You're not? But you just said—'

'I may be friends with them, but you're the one I want to spend Christmas with.' He placed his hands on her arms and rubbed them up and down to keep her warm. 'I've already told Papà I'm not going.'

'But you won't spend Christmas with him.' And she knew that Christmas Eve, or *La Vigilia*, was the most important day of the festive period. At midnight, church bells would ring out across the city and cannons would fire from Castel Sant'Angelo to celebrate the birth of Christ.

'It's just for one night. And I don't want you to be alone on Christmas.'

'Is that the only reason?' She bristled defensively. 'Because I'll be fine. I don't want you to feel sorry for me.'

He closed his eyes and sighed deeply. When he opened them again, it was with a look of strained patience. 'What I mean is I want to be with *you* at Christmas. I don't want to spend it with Mary and her family. I want you.'

His words warmed her from the inside and for now, she let them chase away the apprehension. 'Okay. As long as I'm not dragging you away from where you really want to be.'

'You're not. If I wanted to go with them, I would,' he said. 'But look, can we talk about this back at the apartment? My fingers have gone numb.'

She relented and smiled. 'Yes, of course. Let's go.'

They walked away from the church in the direction of Avery's, taking care not to slip on puddles of melted snow. 'What about Tuscany?' she asked.

'We'll still drive up tonight. Papà is going to meet us

there in the morning, and we can have lunch instead. That way we won't have to stay up all night cooking.'

'What about Riley and Leo? They're coming tonight.'

'Leo texted me. They're driving up tomorrow too. It looks like it'll just be you and me.' He glanced at his watch. 'We should hurry though. It's going to snow again, and we still have to carry the food two blocks to the car.'

TWENTY-TWO

A snowstorm blew in as they left the gridlock of Christmas Eve traffic in Rome behind and reached the motorway, driving north towards Tuscany. Thick flakes billowed down onto the windscreen and the wipers pushed them to one side with a monotonous squeak and thud.

It was a slow journey—families leaving the city, carefully manoeuvring through low visibility. With not much else to look at but dark and shadowy fields, Belle's head drifted towards the window, and she felt months of sleep deprivation claim her.

In what seemed like moments later, a hand gently shook her shoulder, and she wrestled her eyes open to find Andre smiling at her.

'We're here, Belle,' he said. 'You slept the whole way.'

She sat up in her seat and stretched. 'We're here already?'

'Yes. In Tuscany.'

Her groggy mind sought to catch up and she peered out the window, noticing a dark driveway and a house.

'I've already unpacked the car,' Andre said, planting a

kiss on top of her head. 'Come inside. I'll get the fire started.'

Belle slid her arms into her coat, pulled on her scarf, and opened the car door. Snow was still falling heavily, and it dusted her hair and turned her breath to fog as she jogged to the front door. With a fleeting glimpse of the farmhouse surroundings, she gleaned shadowy forms that looked like tall pencil pines lining the drive and dotted houselights on distant hillsides. But the night was heavy, the clouds too thick to glimpse much else, and she stepped with relief through the open doorway into a large room lit softly by lamplight.

It was the impressive high ceilings that she noticed first —rows of exposed dark oak timber beams. There were two comfortable-looking cream sofas and a large-patterned rug that covered the stone floor. The walls too were constructed of stone, and at the back of the room, a flight of stairs curved upwards to the second level. To the right, the floor sank beneath a large stone arch into a dining room and beyond that, the kitchen.

It wasn't what Belle had expected of a farmhouse. In her mind, she had imagined a little weatherboard shack sitting atop a hill, possibly surrounded by chickens and sheep. This was something else entirely. Built of stone and timber, it was enormous, sturdy and lovingly decorated, as though someone lived in it all year round, not just once or twice a year for the holidays.

Andre knelt beside the fireplace and tended to the fire as Belle walked around the room, admiring the paintings on the walls—Tuscan vineyards and fields of sunflowers.

'This is a gorgeous home,' she said.

Andre looked up. 'Thank you. I loved it here as a child. Someday, I hope to move back permanently.'

She came to rest beside him, at the fireplace mantel, to study a grainy photograph in a frame resting there, of a young boy and a woman. The image captured them in an open field of tall grass and wildflowers, the wind blowing through the woman's long dark hair. She was holding the little boy's hand and they'd been caught in a run, turning back to smile at the camera as they pranced through the grass.

'That's me with my mother before she got sick and died,' Andre said, rising to join Belle by the photo. He picked it up and gave the glass a gentle polish on the arm of his jacket. 'We always ran in the fields behind the house. After she died, my father bought the trattoria and we moved to Rome. I haven't run through those fields since.'

'Your mother was beautiful,' Belle said. 'And you were adorable.' They both shared Andre's dark eyes, the high, curved cheekbones, the wide, playful smile, and those deep dimples.

He gazed wistfully at the photo before returning it to the mantel and attending once more to the fire. 'Yes, she was beautiful.'

Belle touched his arm, and they shared a soft smile. While he concentrated on the fire, she slipped her coat off, laid it gently over the back of a sofa and looked around the room. 'Is there anymore unpacking I can do?'

Andre nodded, the wistfulness remaining. 'Si. In the kitchen. I've already turned on the refrigerator. You can unpack the food if you like.'

'Okay.'

Belle walked beneath the arch, through the dining room and into the kitchen. She found the boxes and bags of Christmas food and began pulling items out and putting them away. When she was finished, she stole a glance at the clock on the wall. It was almost midnight. She opened a bottle of Chianti she'd brought with her, found two wine glasses in the cupboard, and walked back into the living room.

The fireplace was crackling, and the warmth enveloped her instantly. Andre was by the window, peering out into the darkness. The snow was still falling, and he appeared lost in thought.

'It's almost Christmas,' she said, placing the wine and glasses on the table. 'I thought we could have a drink to ring in the birth of Christ.' She wasn't religious and Christmases back home were usually a quiet affair, alternating between lunch at Ben's parents' house or hers, with no church service. But the religious aspect was meaningful to Andre, and she wanted to honour that, especially as he'd chosen to spend Christmas Eve with her instead of his father, a sentiment that still touched her deeply.

She opened the bottle of Chianti and poured them each a glass as he slid out of his suit jacket and unknotted his tie, throwing both over the back of the sofa. It struck her how good he looked in a suit, the straight lines of his shoulders, the polished ruggedness it gave his jawline, even after hours of driving in the car.

He sat on the sofa beside her, and they clinked their glasses together, taking a sip. The wind outside rattled the windows, snow swirling in a fleece of white. But inside was warm and intoxicating, the fire crackling, the flames throwing shadows across the walls.

Over the rim of his glass, Andre met her gaze, dark, unfathomable eyes drinking her in. A heartbeat later, he placed his glass down and reached across the space between them, touching his lips gently to hers. She set her glass down too and responded, her mouth parting to let him in.

He tasted of wine, his hair carrying the faint smell of the fire. How good it was to kiss him again, to touch him and be touched, so openly after weeks of stealing scant moments together.

His fingers roamed her neck, down to her collarbone, like a whisper, sliding the dress sleeves off her shoulders so that the air hit her bare skin and she shivered, not from the cold, but from the way his breath grew shallow, from the soft moan that escaped his mouth, betraying his need for her.

Her fingers found his buttons, and she flicked them free one by one, running her hands over the tautness of his chest first, then helping him slide out of his shirt. She reached for his arms, drawing him down on top of her, pleasurably pinned beneath his weight. With deft hands, he slipped the rest of her dress away, followed by her underwear, and she pushed his pants off, so breathless her lungs ached.

His hands circled her hips and caressed her inner thighs, her head swimming as he murmured her name against her neck. She arched her body towards his, unbridled pleasure rolling over her like a wave, as he slid inside. Tilting her head back against the rush of sensation, she entwined her fingers with his, their lips a breath apart, their bodies moving as one.

THE FIRE WAS WARM, crackling against the logs. Belle lay beside Andre on the rug, her head resting on his chest, a blanket draped across their legs. She could hear the light thud of his heartbeat, drumming in time with her own.

'That was the best Christmas present I've ever had,' he

said, tracing his fingers along her shoulder blade and down her back.

She smiled lazily and turned her face towards his. 'You must have had some terrible gifts then.'

He laughed, a sound so beautiful that she nestled into him and held him closer. Andre had been every bit the generous lover she'd imagined he would be, and he'd seemed greatly satisfied with her too.

'Where's everyone going to sleep while they're here?' she asked.

'There are guest rooms upstairs, but we need to make up the beds. We should do that tonight, actually. Get it out the way.' He glanced at her. 'Are you tired?'

She shook her head. 'I slept in the car, remember?'

He chortled. 'Want to put the Christmas tree up with me afterwards?'

'Sure.'

It was almost two am and, as disappointed as she was to leave Andre's arms, and the warmth of the fire, where she could have stayed all night, there was still plenty to do.

They climbed to their feet and found their clothes, pulling them on, then Andre started up the stairs, headed for the attic where the Christmas tree and decorations were stored. Belle followed him up, locating the linen cupboard Andre had directed her to, to make a start on the beds. She found sheets, pillows and blankets and pulled them out. There were four bedrooms on the second level—a master room that belonged to Uncle Benito, a second room that looked out over the property, belonging to Andre, and two smaller guest rooms.

'Where am I sleeping?' she called out to him, as he disappeared down the stairs with a box of decorations.

'In the guest room next to mine. It has a double bed in it,' his voice echoed back from the stairwell.

'Am I sharing it with Riley?'

'Yes. She's not allowed to share it with Leo. Benito's orders.'

Belle chuckled to herself. Riley wasn't going to like being separated from Leo. On the other hand, Belle was looking forward to bunking with her, something they hadn't done in months.

She moved from room to room, making up the beds, then met Andre downstairs again in the living room. He indicated a pile of boxes that he'd stacked by the side of the hearth. 'Ready?'

She responded with a grin, and they sat on the floor, unpacking the decorations and tree parts from the boxes.

'Usually, we arrive in Tuscany before Christmas Eve, and we buy a live pine from the village,' he explained as he spread out the artificial parts of the trunk, ready for connecting. 'We always had a real Christmas tree when I was growing up. They smell beautiful, like the forest is in your house. My mother loved them. Even when they began to wither and die, she could never bring herself to throw them out. My father always complained about the pine needles on the floor. I was only young but for some reason, I still remember that.' A nostalgic smile pulled at his lips.

Belle reached across and touched his hand. 'You must miss her.'

'Everyday,' he said with a heavy sigh. 'The problem is, the older I get, the more I start to forget her face, her laugh, the way my hand felt in hers. I have photos of her, but they're not the same...' He trailed off. 'I do remember the Christmas trees and pine needles, though. That's part of the reason why I didn't want to spend Christmas in

Rome. Every Christmas is spent here because this is where she is. This is where my memories of her are strongest.'

Belle stared into the fire. The logs crackled and the flames licked the walls of the hearth. She was sad for him. For Uncle Benito. For Valentina who, in addition to being terminally ill, must have felt unbearable heartbreak at the thought of leaving her young child behind in the world. It made Belle think of her parents, how she'd called them to wish them a merry Christmas the day before and only her mother had come to the phone. Her father had been 'busy', tucked away in his office, with more important things than his daughter to tend to. The story of her life.

She watched as Andre slotted the trunk of the tree together until it was towering above them, then he spread the leaves apart. Opening a box, he hauled out a bundle of lights, carefully unravelling them. Belle climbed to her feet to help him.

'What you said to me earlier today,' Andre said, 'about you being my secret.' He circled the tree slowly, draping the lights across the branches. 'It hurts me to think you feel that way.'

Their eyes met and Belle winced apologetically. 'I'm sorry. I shouldn't have said that to you.'

'No, you should have. If that's the way I've made you feel, I'm the one who should be sorry.'

'It's a complicated situation. I know that.'

He paused, the lights still in his hands. 'It's just that, the whole Mary thing... and our families still being close... I should have warned you first.'

But you did, she thought.

Love for us might be complicated.

You have Ben, I have Mary.

'No, I get it,' she said. 'We both have baggage. Thankfully, mine's ten thousand miles away, but yours is here.'

'I just don't know if this will be easy for us,' he said.

There was a note of defeat in his words that made her heart sink. 'I still want to try,' she said. 'Do you want to?'

'Of course I do.' This time he had more conviction. 'I want you more than anything.'

A relieved smile burst onto her lips. 'Then that's all I need to hear.'

They hung the decorations next, handcrafted pinecones with tiny bells attached and little log houses with snow-covered roofs that had been in Andre's family for generations. They spent the next ten minutes hanging them, then Andre handed her the end of a piece of red tinsel and together they wrapped it around the tree. For the final touch, he held out a porcelain tree angel in a white dress with gold wings. Her halo sparkled and a small gold harp rested in her lap. 'This belonged to my mother when she was a child.'

Belle touched her fingers to the delicate angel. 'It's beautiful.'

He placed it carefully at the top of the tree, securing it firmly in place, and switched the tree lights on. They both stood back to admire their work—lights flickering and twinkling across the leaves, bells and pinecones dangling from the branches, Valentina's angel perched high at the top. Andre placed his arm around Belle and pulled her close to him. She let her arm drape around his waist and her head rest against his chest, as they stared at the tree, the fire quietly dying behind the grate.

When the clock on the wall chimed three in the morning, Andre sighed. 'It's getting late. We should probably get some sleep.'

'Yes, I suppose we should,' she said.

He locked the front door, extinguished the last of the dying embers in the fireplace, and turned off the lights. They walked upstairs together and by Belle's bedroom door, he bent to kiss her lips, deeply, unreservedly, with such intensity she felt her body thrum again.

'I'd love to sleep beside you tonight,' he said, grazing her cheek with the back of his hand.

'Me too. But can we risk it?' They couldn't be sure what time everyone would arrive in the morning and the last thing she wanted was for Uncle Benito to catch them in bed together. It would be disrespectful, not to mention mortifying.

'I'm almost willing to,' he said.

'It feels a bit hypocritical when Riley and Leo will have to follow the rules.'

There was a low groan in his throat as he threw his head back. When he looked at her again, his eyes were full of mischief.

'No,' she said, unable to hide her grin. 'Stop. You're a bad influence.'

He dipped his head towards hers and kissed her tenderly, then dropped kisses all along her neck.

'You're making this very difficult,' she said, laughing.

He laughed too, but not without a look of longing in his eyes. 'Okay, *signorina*, we will follow the rules.'

They kissed one last time, tender and slow, swaying to some unheard song, before he touched her cheek. '*Buon Natale*, Belle.'

'Merry Christmas, Andre.' The yearning to remain in his arms became almost unbearable, until she forced herself away, into the guest room.

TWENTY-THREE

Their sliver of solitude evaporated early the next morning when Uncle Benito arrived at nine in a flurry of snow and energy. Belle's eyes were just opening to the cold grey light when she heard the front door burst open downstairs and the windows rattle with the draught.

She pushed the covers away and swung her feet to the floor, scrubbing sleep from her eyes, then throwing on her robe and hurrying down the stairs.

Andre was already by the door, transferring bags and boxes in from the car, while Uncle Benito cursed the weather and the slow drive and the late hour he'd stayed up until the night before, drinking mulled wine with Mary's father.

After a shower, Belle joined him in the kitchen, where benchtops were already cluttered with ingredients for Christmas lunch. Although he'd had little sleep and lunch was supposed to be Belle's job, he still commanded the kitchen as he did at Valentina's, instructing her through prep. She didn't mind; they had a mountain to get through and it called for a comfortable rhythm they knew well.

While they cooked, Andre set the table and made espresso, then, at eleven, Riley and Leo arrived. The snow had moved on and the wind had settled as their car tyres crunched up the drive.

Belle quickly set down her bowl of cake batter, washed her hands and dashed into the living room to greet them. By the door, she threw her arms around Riley, sweeping her up in a hug. 'You made it!' she cried.

'We did. *Buon Natale.*' Riley wrapped her arms around her, holding Belle so close she almost squeezed the breath out of her. When they eventually parted, Belle caught a brief shadow of sadness that clouded her friend's eyes. As quickly as it appeared, Riley blinked, and it was gone.

'How was the drive?' she asked, taking Riley's jacket and scarf, and hanging them on the coat rack.

'Slow. The roads were icy. Wow, this place is beautiful,' she said, glancing back through the open door to the front of the property.

Belle glanced outside too, having missed the scenery the night before. The clouds were clearing and a cold, blue sky peeked through the white. Rows of pencil pines lined the driveway, their needles crystalised with snow, and beyond them, Tuscan hillsides rolled towards a whitewashed horizon.

She tugged Riley inside where it was warmer and closed the door. Uncle Benito and Andre greeted Leo and Belle hugged him before dragging Riley up the stairs.

'You're sharing with me,' she said, throwing open the door to their bedroom.

If Riley was disappointed that she wasn't occupying a room with Leo, she didn't let it show. She dropped her luggage on the floor and sat on the bed.

'Leo will be sleeping next door. Sorry, Uncle Benito's orders,' Belle said, by way of apology.

Riley tugged off her beanie with a downcast look. 'He's not staying. He's going back to Rome tonight to pack for a family trip to the Alps.'

Belle's eyebrows knitted together. 'But I thought you were both staying until Epiphany.'

'I am, he's not. I wasn't invited to go with him.'

Belle sank onto the bed beside her. 'He's going away with his family and he's not taking you?'

Riley waved her hand, her attempt at nonchalance failing. 'It's not a big deal. I'm getting used to it.'

'You shouldn't have to get used to something like that,' she said. 'Why didn't he ask you?'

'Because his family still doesn't know about me.'

'How can they not know about you? Didn't you spend Christmas Eve with them last night?'

Riley's eyes flashed with hurt before she blinked it away and straightened her spine. 'I had an early supper with him at his apartment, then he went to mass and dinner with his family.'

'Where did you go while he was with them?'

'I went to Avery's apartment and spent the night there. He picked me up this morning.'

'Oh Ri...' Belle's heart sank. Her friend had spent Christmas Eve alone in that empty apartment while families all over Rome celebrated together. If only Belle had known, she would have brought Riley with her to Tuscany. Even back in Sydney, Riley had rarely spent Christmas alone. Her father flew in occasionally from Western Australia to see her, or she would bounce around households visiting friends. Leo's world may have been complicated but abandoning her on Christmas Eve was unforgiveable.

'Have you asked him why he won't introduce you to them? It's been months now.'

Riley's smile was tight. 'I know the reason, Belle. I'm not one of *them*. I'm not fluent in their language or from a big family, I'm not Catholic, and I can't cook. And I realise this confuses him too because we love each other. We talk about family and children and me staying here long-term. But none of it matters if they won't accept me.'

'Then Leo should fight for you.'

Riley's expression grew sad. 'It's easy to say that, but more complicated than you think. He's being pulled in two different directions. He doesn't want to disappoint them, and he doesn't want to lose me, so what can he do? I'm constantly hovering at the fringe. He says one day soon he'll tell them about me. When the time is right. When they're ready to hear it.'

'And when will that be?'

'He doesn't know.' She shook her head and sighed deeply. 'Anyway, he's going to the Alps and I'm staying. For two whole weeks, if you can stand to have me that long.'

'Are you kidding? Two weeks won't be long enough.'

Riley reached across to squeeze Belle's hand. 'I've missed you, kid.'

'Don't get me started,' Belle said with a frown.

Riley managed a small laugh. 'I think the time apart will be good for me and Leo. He needs to miss me, to know what life might be like if he doesn't sort this out soon.'

'That's probably all he needs.'

Belle then confessed to Riley her intimacy with Andre the night before, but Riley didn't seem surprised. 'I'm wondering what took you both so long.'

Belle nudged her with her elbow. 'I really like him.'

'I know you do.' Riley smiled. 'Are you guys together? I mean, properly.'

'I think so. We first kissed a few weeks ago. But he hasn't told anyone yet, and I'm not sure he wants to.'

Riley nodded with a thoughtful expression. 'Give him time. Andre will do the right thing; I know it. And then, you're going to slot right into his family. Uncle Benito already loves you like a daughter, and you can cook and speak the language. It's nothing like me and Leo.'

'Yes, I suppose.' Uncle Benito might adore her, and she may have been considered part of the family, but deep down inside, Belle worried her situation was not all that different from Riley's.

UNCLE BENITO INVITED the local priest and some close family friends from the nearby village for Christmas lunch. By midday, the farmhouse was brimming with people, tree lights flickering and the crackle of the fire warming the rooms.

Belle and Uncle Benito's lunch adorned the dining table, replete with pork and crackling, spiced cherries and gravy, bowls of prawn and pasta salads, and a tray of golden roasted vegetables. There was hot, scented bread with herbed crust, pine nut couscous, and a crab and leek lasagne that Uncle Benito had been unable to resist 'whipping up'.

They had worked tirelessly in the kitchen, hardly noticing the festivities in other parts of the house. As everyone sat down to eat and dishes of food were passed around the table, glasses of wine steadily poured, Belle caught Uncle Benito's wink over the heads of the others and they shared a smile, one that was borne from trust and friendship in the kitchen.

Maybe Riley was right. Maybe she was overthinking the whole thing. All Andre needed from her was time and patience to tell people, especially his father, when the time was right. Pressuring him would do more harm than good.

After lunch, amidst the groans from those who had gorged themselves, the table was cleared and reset, ready for dessert. To allow their lunch to settle before the next course, everyone gathered around the Christmas tree, balancing glasses of wine precariously on laps as they sat.

Riley curled up beside Belle on the sofa and passed her a white rectangular box that she'd plucked from the pile of gifts beneath the tree. When Belle opened it, she discovered a crystal photo frame inside with a photograph of the two of them taken outside the gates of Buckingham Palace, during their trip to London in what felt like a lifetime ago.

'This was the last photo we had taken together,' Riley said, with an unusual amount of sentiment. 'And that's my fault, I know.'

Belle hugged it close to her chest. 'It's beautiful. Thank you. And for the record, we're both to blame for that.' She reached for her gift to Riley—a navy blue Balenciaga bag she'd bought in Milan with Andre, which Riley squealed at when she unwrapped it.

Belle gifted Uncle Benito a collection of Australian cookbooks and he gifted her a set of professional chef's knives. To Andre, she passed a small bag with cologne and a cashmere scarf inside. She'd deliberated at length about buying it. Her first instinct was to choose a gift of significance, a watch, or engraved cufflinks, maybe a gold chain—a present that spoke of the way she felt about him, but the perplexing start to their relationship had made her doubt herself. When Andre discreetly slipped a long, thin jewellery box, tied with a gold ribbon, into her hands, she was instantly embarrassed, regretful that she hadn't trusted her instincts. She tugged the ribbon off and opened the lid. Inside, on a satin bed, lay a white gold necklace with a round diamond pendant.

She sucked in her breath.

'Do you like it?' he whispered, watching her reaction intently.

'It's beautiful.' She touched the pendant with her fingertips, floored by it. Never had she received a more beautiful gift.

He covered the box with his hand and pressed it down, out of sight. 'We'll put it on you later, okay?' Clearing his throat, he moved away from her.

She closed the lid and dropped it into her lap, glancing around the room. Her gaze met with Uncle Benito's, standing by the fireplace staring at her, eyes narrowed, a perplexed look on his face. He'd seen the gift exchange, may have even noticed the white gold necklace and sparkling pendant inside, wondering why his son would give expensive jewellery to his sous chef. She could almost hear his thoughts turning over, clicking into place.

She quickly shifted her eyes away, unsettled by his apparent disapproval, and slipped the jewellery box into her pocket, feeling the weight of its beauty and its sin.

TWENTY-FOUR

The two weeks at the Tuscan farmhouse were over too soon, and everyone was back in Rome the day after Epiphany. Under cold, wintery skies, Rome sluggishly returned to life and Valentina's reopened for business.

With Avery still in Canada until the end of January and Riley returning to Leo's apartment after his vacation to the Alps, Belle had the apartment on Corsia Agonale to herself. This meant that when Andre walked her home of an evening, they no longer spent hours talking on the steps outside, rather they spent them in her bed, burrowed beneath the covers.

One night after work, they lay in bed beside each other, their breath steadying and their skin cooling. Andre traced his fingers along her bare shoulder and down to her breast where the white gold necklace and diamond pendant he'd given her for Christmas rested.

'I love that you wear my necklace,' he said. 'I never want you to take it off.' He kissed her neck, then her lips.

She let him fold her into his arms. Although it was late, they still had one more glorious hour before he reluctantly pulled his clothes on and walked home to the apartment he shared with Uncle Benito. They'd been desperate to steal a weekend away in Positano or Florence, but despite Rome still waking from its new year slumber, Valentina's had been busy, and Uncle Benito was declining staff leave requests.

'I'll always wear it,' Belle said, touching the necklace, pressing it close to her chest, to her heart. She pushed herself up onto one elbow to glance down at him. 'Can I talk to you about something?'

'Sure.' He propped himself onto one elbow too. Although it was winter, his skin was still golden and smooth, his arms taut, and she loved to lie in them.

'Your father saw you give this to me.'

He raised an eyebrow. 'The necklace?'

'Yes. On Christmas Day. I couldn't tell you while we were in Tuscany because we were never left alone, but yes, he saw. Has he said anything to you?'

Andre shook his head. 'No. Maybe you're mistaken.'

'I don't think so. He didn't look happy.'

'If Benito has something on his mind, he says it. We don't need to worry.'

'I think we should tell him.' she said, the words rushing out.

He glanced at her abruptly.

'I mean, isn't it time we stopped sneaking around like teenagers?' It had been six weeks since their first kiss on the steps outside and at times, it was hard to see their progress, stuck in a timelapse.

He dropped onto his back. 'Yes, we will tell him. I promise. I'm just waiting for the right moment.'

'Maybe there will never be a right moment. Maybe you just need to do it.'

'It's not that easy, Belle.'

'Why, because of Mary?'

He sighed. 'You know it's complicated.'

'Oh, I know. Riley's been hearing the same excuses for months.'

A flash of hurt crossed his face. 'This is not the same thing.'

'I'm failing to see the difference.'

'Okay, yes, it's taken longer than I thought, but you have to understand Mary and I were almost married. The date was set, the guests invited, the rings bought. And I broke it off. Two weeks before the wedding I ended things. Her parents were so gracious about it, so understanding, even when I caused their daughter pain and cost them a fortune in cancellation fees. They haven't pushed me because they think all I need is more time, which makes me feel even worse.'

'Then shouldn't you tell them the truth?'

'Yes, but how do you break someone's heart all over again?' he asked. He sounded tired—tired of her pushing, tired of the situation, tired of Mary's family holding a noose of guilt around his neck.

Andre was a decent person, a beautiful soul and he loathed to hurt anyone. It was what Belle loved most about him, but it still begged the question. Where did that leave *her*? In the shadow of an almost wedding? Unable to move forward because Mary and her parents and Uncle Benito were hoping, praying, that Andre would change his mind?

He exhaled slowly and took her hand, gently running his thumb over her knuckles. 'I understand this is frustrating for you. I hate it too, talking in whispers and kissing you in secret. Believe me, I'd like nothing more than to tell everyone about us. You don't know how crazy I am about you. But I also don't want to upset anyone, least of all my father.'

His eyes were full of conflict, and she bit down on her next complaint, reminded once again that he was caught between what he wanted and what was expected of him.

'I'm going to speak to him next week,' he said resolutely, 'and I'm sure he won't like what I have to say, but you're right. We can't keep living like this. And he will yell and scream, but that's just too bad.'

'I thought because I work in the kitchen with him, he'd be okay with the idea.'

Andre's eyes were full of sympathy. 'He adores you, Belle. Don't ever think otherwise. But this is about so much more than that. It's about culture and family and his friendship with Mary's parents.'

'I don't stand a chance, do I?'

'You do. And I'm going to make this right. I promise.'

She stared into his eyes and saw it there. Determination. All that she needed to hold on a little longer, to fight another day.

He slid closer to her, bridging the gap, and she tilted her head back, letting his lips graze her collarbone, her neck, then her mouth, hands roaming, until the grievances of earlier were forgotten. Belle closed her eyes as his body sought the places that made her weak, made her light-headed, made her run her hands hungrily through his thick hair and across the bunched muscles in his back, rolling him on top of her. It was a rhythm they were growing accustomed to, one that had bound them together that snowy Christmas Eve. And when he moved inside her, she felt the honesty of what they had—not a holiday fling or a casual romance, but love. Pure, exquisite, gut-wrenching love. The kind that had been simmering from the moment they met. The kind worth fighting for.

It was a long time before their hands unclenched and their bodies separated, their skin damp. Andre turned to her, dark, bottomless eyes drinking her in. His voice was husky and deep when he spoke. 'What does it feel like to fall in love?'

The question surprised her. 'Have you never been in love before?'

'No.'

She slid closer to him, their faces almost touching, as she whispered, 'It's the most terrifying and beautiful thing you will ever feel. You can't eat or breathe or sleep without that person being near you.'

'You mean it feels like *this*?' He held her gaze and she thought he could see straight into her soul, to a love that was breathtaking and blessed, that had been in some ways a slow burn, others devastatingly fast, but always so natural, so right.

'Yes, my love. It's exactly like this.'

AVERY RETURNED to Rome at the end of January, as the freezing weather released its grip. The sun began to emerge triumphant, as though it had woken from a deep winter sleep. With her presence in the apartment again, Belle and Andre's nights under the covers ended. No matter Andre's good intentions, he still hadn't had that conversation yet with his father, and their precious time together was played out once more on the steps of the apartment, where they huddled in the cool night and talked of a future that seemed further away to Belle than ever before.

'I'm going to tell him tomorrow,' Andre said one evening after work as they sat looking up at the sky.

'I hate to say it, but I've heard that before,' Belle replied.

Andre frowned. 'I know I've been putting it off. It's been hard to get him alone. The trattoria takes up so much of his time, and I don't want to just drop it on him. I want to take the time to tell him properly.'

'Maybe you're overthinking it. Maybe it needs to be done like a Band-Aid. Rip it straight off.'

He raised his eyebrow at her. 'There is no ripping the Band-Aid off when it comes to Benito.'

'At least let me tell Avery so we don't have to sit on these steps anymore.'

'I don't want to drag her into this and make her lie.'

Belle tried to keep the exasperation out of her voice. 'I'm just not used to all this tip-toeing around people. If you want something, you should be allowed to go for it.'

He pulled back, eyes narrowing slightly. 'You of all people should know what expectation feels like. You've lived half your adult life hiding your love for cooking because your father wanted you to study law instead. Is that not the same thing?'

Belle bit down on her lip, ashamed by her hypocrisy. Andre was right; she should know better than anyone what pressure and expectation from family felt like. It was exactly the same thing, just dressed in a different coat.

Andre shook his head, clearing the unease between them with a reassuring smile. 'Anyway, by tomorrow this will all be sorted out. I'm going to stay back in the kitchen and tell him. Because if I don't, there will never be a right time, so I might as well, as you said, rip the Band-Aid off.'

They were encouraging words, ones that she fell asleep to that night and woke to the next morning. Ones that put hope in her step as she strode across the piazza to Valentina's. They were words that sounded promising when previously, they had only ever sounded impossible, like a finish line never quite in reach.

The more a life with Andre dangled like the proverbial carrot, the more she knew with certainty that she'd move heaven and earth for it. She'd opened her heart to the possibility of love again, even if that love seemed at once a blessing and a curse.

Lunch service at Valentina's was busy that day, as the weather warmed, and tourists returned. Belle and Uncle Benito had trialled new dishes the previous week and, as they'd been a resounding success, they'd been added to the menu which was now with the printer for reprinting.

Belle hardly noticed anything but the inside of the kitchen. The service was frenetic and after the last customers left, she stepped out into the dining room for an espresso and a bite to eat with Andre. The break was fleeting though, and she returned to the kitchen thirty minutes later to begin prep for dinner.

Closer to eight pm, in the throes of the dinner shift, Andre burst through the kitchen doors, followed by Natalya, Josh and Chase. 'The officials are back,' he said soberly. 'Quick, out into the alleyway.'

Belle left the gnocchi she'd been plating, washed her hands and headed immediately for the back door with the others.

'Immigration?' Uncle Benito harrumphed. 'They were here just last week. Why are they back so soon? I already paid them.'

'Come speak to them, Papà,' Andre said. 'They have new agents with them.'

Uncle Benito scowled then scrubbed his hands at the

sink. As Belle stepped out into the alleyway, she turned and caught the image of him disappearing into the dining room.

Outside, the night had turned cool, nipping at her arms as she wrapped them around herself. Josh pulled up a crate to sit on and Chase lit a cigarette.

'I hope this will not take long,' Natalya complained. 'I just seated four tables and was about to take their orders. The delay is going to set me back all night.'

'The officials were here last week,' Belle said. 'Why are they back so soon?'

'Who knows,' Natalya said. 'There is no agenda with these guys. Not when money is passing hands.'

'Are we in trouble?' Belle asked. She'd never felt comfortable with the idea of working illegally, but she'd allowed herself to be lulled into a sense of security because nobody had ever seemed particularly concerned about it. She glanced at the three faces around her. Josh was checking his phone, Chase was dragging back on his cigarette and blowing smoke rings, and Natalya was leaning against the stone wall of Valentina's, rubbing lip balm over her lips. No one seemed worried, but no one had answered her question either.

Minutes passed like the pour of molasses before Andre burst through the back door. It flew open with a clang, almost knocking Josh off the crate. Andre's hands were laden with their backpacks. 'They're doing raids. Quick, take your bags and go!'

Chase jumped. His cigarette fell from his fingers, sizzling on the ground. 'What?'

'Take them. Now!' Andre shoved their bags into their arms.

'And go where?' Josh asked, eyes wide, taking his bag and flinging it onto his back.

'Back to your apartments. Gather up your things, but don't stay there long. Go to a friend's house or get out of Rome until we know what's going on. We're not sure if they have your names and addresses, but it might only be a matter of time before they raid your apartments. We can't take that chance.'

'What will happen if they catch us?' Belle asked. Her stomach roiled sickeningly and all the espressos she'd had that day threatened to come up.

Natalya's earlier nonchalance was replaced with the sound of fear. 'Prison or an immigration camp since we broke the law. Deportation eventually.' She shook her head emphatically. 'I will try France or Switzerland. I will not go back to Russia. No way.'

Belle glanced with panic at Andre as he pushed her backpack into her hands. 'Andre...'

He crushed his lips down onto hers as the others noisily cleared their throats. She heard Chase mutter goodbye to them, and Josh tell Natalya to be careful before their footsteps retreated towards the main street and they were gone.

When it was just the two of them left in the alleyway, Belle searched Andre's eyes. 'What should I do?'

He was breathing heavily, his countenance grave. 'Go straight to Avery's apartment. Pack your things in case we need to move you.'

'What about Riley?'

'Leo sent her a text. He told her to stay at his place and wait it out.'

'Maybe I should go there, too. Or up to the farmhouse. I don't want to be in Rome if they're raiding apartments.'

'We don't know what their intention is yet. Papà's talking to them, but it's getting heated. I need to get you away from here.' Andre ran an exasperated hand through his hair. 'I can't understand why they came back. They were here last week, and everything was fine. Yes, they have new agents but what reason could they have for coming back so soon?'

'I can handle being deported home, but I don't want to go to an immigration camp. Who knows how long I could end up there?'

'I don't want either to happen,' he said, his face falling. 'I can't lose you.'

She threw herself into his arms and he held her close. Tears threatened, but she fought to keep her wits.

'Go,' he said with reluctance, helping her pull her backpack onto her shoulders. 'Go to Avery's and don't stop until you get there.'

'Okay.'

'I'll come for you as soon as I can.'

She kissed him once more then ran down the alleyway, bursting out onto Via di Pasquino and racing across the piazza, not stopping until she was safely inside Avery's apartment.

TWENTY-FIVE

Belle locked the front door behind her and hurried into her room, flicking the lamp shade on, and snatching clothes from her wardrobe and drawers. She flung them into her suitcase, unsure if she needed to pack everything or just an overnight bag, if she was leaving for one night or forever.

She'd never been an illegal immigrant before, and her mind ran wild with the possible repercussions of it. Would she go to jail or a camp? Would she be sent home? Would they even find her here? Maybe all she needed to do was bunker down and ride it out for a few days. Uncle Benito would surely take care of it, for he always did.

But what if he couldn't? What if this time it was out of his hands?

She stopped throwing clothes into her suitcase and sat on the edge of the bed, clutching her chest, and forcing herself to breathe. *You're getting worked up. Calm down. Uncle Benito won't let anything happen to you.* She wondered where Natalya, Josh and Chase were, if they were madly hurling clothes into their suitcases like she was.

The silence was torturous, ringing in her ears, but she

didn't dare turn the TV on and the only light she afforded was from her small bedroom lamp, a glow that was visible to the back alleyway and not the front street. She tried to marshal her thoughts into order and steady her shaking hands, moving slower, still transferring items into her suitcase, but with a degree of forced control.

When she finished packing her belongings and the last few things that Riley had left behind, she retrieved her phone from her backpack and sat on the edge of the bed. She dialled Riley's number, but after a few rings, the call was answered by voicemail. She tried again but got the same result. Was she at Leo's apartment going out of her mind too? Or was she laughing this off?

Belle picked at dried flecks of dough on her chef's whites, noticing the sauce stain she'd never quite been able to bleach out, and the new slice to her thumb she'd acquired that evening while slicing the veal. Her heart clenched and time ticked towards nine pm, every distant police siren outside making her jump. She wanted to call Avery or Andre to find out what was happening but any kind of call to Valentina's could tempt fate. The worry in Andre's eyes flashed through her mind again. This hadn't been a routine check by immigration. This time was different, as though the old rules no longer applied. *They have new agents with them.*

She jolted at the sound of knocking on the door and jumped to her feet. Her first thought was to turn off the lamp and refrain from answering, but she heard Andre's low voice from the other side. 'Belle, it's me. Are you in there? Open up.'

She let out a trapped breath and hurried to the door. Unlocking it, she yanked it open, and Andre stepped inside, closing, and locking it behind him. She threw her arms around him, and he held her tight.

'Are you okay?' he asked.

'Yes. I'm fine. What's happening?'

He leaned back to look at her, his face flushed, eyes full of worry. 'They've closed our restaurant down. Just temporarily. There was a tip-off from a neighbouring trattoria. Apparently, they're sour because we've been enticing their business. They knew we had foreigners working for us and they lodged a formal complaint.'

'Can your father fix it?' Belle asked.

Andre shook his head. 'Money won't work this time. We have to get you out of here.'

It was as though someone had tipped an icy bucket of water over her, and she'd been jerked awake. 'Get me out of here? You mean I should leave Rome?'

'Not Rome,' he said with the saddest look in his eyes. 'Italy. They're investigating all foreigners, people who arrived but never left. Soon they'll come searching for you.'

He was still holding her, and she was still watching him with adrenalin coursing through her veins. 'Andre, I...'

'I know,' he said. 'I can't make sense of it either.'

'This is really happening.'

His shoulders slumped. 'Yes.'

She blinked several times, the room swaying around her. 'What about Valentina's? Is your father in trouble?'

'He'll be okay. He can talk his way out of anything.'

'But if I leave... the kitchen. How will he cope?'

'Don't worry, I'll help him.'

They fell silent again, holding each other against the rush of borrowed time, the clock marching agonisingly on with no way to stop it. Eventually, Andre kissed the top of her head. 'Come on, we should go. It will be worse if they find you here.'

Her body gave an involuntary shudder at the words, and she reluctantly let Andre go and walked woodenly into her bedroom. Her brain hadn't yet processed that she was leaving Rome. Leaving Avery, Uncle Benito, her Valentina's family. Leaving Andre. This was it, the moment she'd been dreading, a moment she'd never thought would come. She'd always thought the choice would be within her control, that together she and Andre would decide how the next days, months and years would play out. But Fate had grown impatient, insolent, taking matters into its own hands.

As she changed hastily into jeans and a warm jumper, throwing a scarf around her neck, and packing her chef's whites into her bag, she wondered where on earth Riley was. Making this journey alone was a frightening thought and while she couldn't reasonably expect Riley to join her, she needed to understand what her intention was.

If a goodbye was needed.

She zipped up her suitcase and grabbed the handle, a wave of fear and exhaustion washing over her. It was all too much, and she tried to hold back the tears as she tugged her suitcase out of the bedroom and back into the living room.

'Have you got everything?' Andre asked.

'I think so. But I can't reach Riley. And she hasn't called me either.'

'Leo told her to stay at his house and not make any calls. I guess she's going to ride this out.'

'A text would be nice, so we can say goodbye.'

'I'm sure she'll be in touch soon.'

Footsteps sounded in the stairwell of the apartment block, causing them both to jump. Avery burst through the door, tugged off her beanie and threw herself at Belle, wrapping her arms tightly around her. 'Jesus! Are you okay?'

Belle regained her balance after almost being thrown off her feet. 'Yes, I'm fine. What's happening?'

'I just got a text from Josh. They found Natalya and Chase and arrested them. They're raiding everyone's apartments.'

Belle's heart leapt wildly into her throat and Andre's face drained of colour. 'We have to get you out of here,' he said.

'Do they even know I live here?' Belle asked.

He collected her luggage and moved swiftly out the door, carrying it down the stairs. 'It takes one person to talk,' he said.

'Chase's landlady dobbed him in and they were waiting for Natalya when she got to her flat. Someone ratted her out,' Avery explained as they followed Andre down the stairs.

'The safest thing you can do now is to get out of Italy,' he said. 'If they catch you, they'll be rough. I don't want to risk you getting hurt.'

'But it's late,' Belle said as they pushed through the door downstairs and out onto the street. 'There won't be any flights to Sydney at this time of night.'

'Maybe a train over the border would be better,' Avery suggested.

'Go to Paris,' Andre said. 'Trains run all the time from Roma Termini. I'll meet you there in a couple of days.'

'Is it safe?' Belle asked. 'Can I cross the border into France, or will they stop me?'

'We are all in the EU, but every country has their own immigration policies. I don't think anyone will stop you.'

Belle hesitated. She had to move, for every tick of the

clock brought immigration closer to her, but she didn't want to take this journey alone. She didn't want to leave Andre or catch the train by herself, sleeping with one eye open every second of the way. She didn't want to navigate Paris or catch a flight back to Sydney. In the blink of an eye, it had all become too frightening and sudden and inexplicable, and she began to tremble.

Andre took her into his arms and stroked her hair soothingly. 'Come now, Belle, it will be all right. You just need to get on that train, and you'll be fine. I'll come with you in the taxi to Roma Termini.'

She shook her head. As comforting as that would be, if they were pulled over, Andre might be implicated. 'No, I'll go alone. I don't want you to get into trouble.'

'I don't care about that. I only care about you.'

She glanced up into his eyes as Avery whistled and wandered discreetly down the street. 'You'll come to Paris?' she asked.

His voice was hoarse. 'Yes, I'll meet you there. Stay in touch with me.'

'Because this can't be the end for us.'

He leant down and kissed her in a way that told her 'end' wasn't a word they knew. That no matter what happened, they would find each other. Still, she felt the first painful cracks of heartbreak tear at her chest.

There was so much she wanted to say to him, words she thought she could leave for another day. Now their time together was on notice, and she had no idea what the future held once she left him.

Walk away now, she told herself. *You're making it harder*.

'Someone's coming,' Avery whispered.

Belle and Andre glanced in the direction Avery was

pointing. Surely enough, a lone figure in the night was walking up Corsia Agonale towards them, tugging a suitcase.

Belle didn't need to wonder who it might be. She knew Riley's stride anywhere. 'What are you doing here?' she asked when Riley had almost reached them.

'Leo told me about the raids. I packed my bags and came as soon as I could.' She rested her suitcase upright. Dressed in dark blue jeans and a jumper, her long hair was pulled back in a sleek ponytail, and she had trainers on.

'I've been trying to call you,' Belle berated her. 'I was worried.'

'Sorry, I didn't want to use my phone just in case. What's the plan?' She looked to each of them expectantly.

It didn't matter that Belle was surprised to see her; she was just glad she was there. 'I'm going to try and get a train to Paris.'

'I'm coming with you.'

Belle eyed Riley's suitcase. 'What about Leo?'

Riley stiffened, as though she were trying to rein in a painful emotion. 'What *about* Leo?'

Belle knew in those words what Riley was saying that months of uncertainty, of confusion and rejection, no matter how unintentional on Leo's part, had worn her down. She was giving up. 'Have you told him?'

Riley nodded, then lifted her chin defiantly. 'What time's this train to Paris?'

'The last one from Roma Termini is around ten-thirty pm,' Andre said, pushing his sleeve back to glance at his watch. 'You've got forty minutes before it leaves.'

'We should go,' Riley said. She hugged Avery and Andre and started off towards the piazza. Avery followed her, leaving Belle and Andre alone.

'Are you sure I can't go to the farmhouse?' Belle asked, feeling the last of their time together trickle away. 'Just for a couple of weeks until it blows over.'

'But what if it doesn't and they find you? I'm not willing to take that risk.' His eyes held sadness but also determination. 'At least this way I know you won't end up in jail.'

'But I'll only be able stay in Paris a few days, then I'll have to leave for Sydney. What does that mean for us?'

He wrapped strong arms around her. His chest was warm, his body firm against hers, and she would have given anything for time to stand still, to wind back—a day, a week, a month.

He didn't answer her question. How could he when everything was so uncertain? Instead, silence filled the disquiet as they stood on the edge of the street holding each other.

From further up the corsia, Riley cleared her throat. 'Belle, we need to go.'

Belle reluctantly pulled away. She was certain she would never forget the moment Andre's arms dropped from hers, when the weight of them faded to nothing. Tears brimmed in her eyes as she grabbed the handle of her suitcase.

He leant down and kissed her one last time. 'Call me when you get to Paris.'

She nodded. Her reply felt like lead in her throat. 'I will.'

She forced her feet away from him, tugging her suitcase behind her. She passed Avery on the way, who engulfed her in such a fierce hug, Belle almost toppled over.

'Be careful. I'll see you in Paris,' she said.

Tears finally spilled over Belle's lashes. 'Thank you for

letting us stay with you. For being the best kind of friend. We'll always be in each other's lives, okay?'

Avery screwed up her face, as though the words were too upsetting to hear. Her bottom lip quivered, and tears dripped onto her cheeks. She swiped at them, nodding emphatically. 'I'll come to visit you in Australia. We can travel through the Outback and wrestle crocodiles.'

Belle gave a watery smile. 'I wouldn't wrestle a crocodile with anyone else.'

Avery choked back a sob then walked away, returning to Andre's side to watch them leave. He threw an arm around her shoulders as she spluttered noisy tears.

Belle reached for Riley's hand and together they headed towards the piazza. From the other side of the square, they would catch a taxi to Roma Termini ten minutes away. There they would board a train bound for Paris, in the hope that no one would stop them, and they could make it over the border into France.

As they rounded the corner into the piazza, Belle glanced back once, her eyes locking with Andre's. In that single beat of the butterfly's wing, everything had changed. What was next for them she didn't know, but one thing was certain, without him, a part of her would cease to exist.

TWENTY-SIX

They reached Roma Termini and boarded the train without interruption. The station was quiet at that late hour, the travel rush over, as a few stray passengers caught the last train to Paris.

Belle had held her breath the entire way, from the taxi ride over to the purchase of their tickets and checking in of luggage, to approaching the customs area. Her heart had thumped against her ribcage so painfully that she thought it would burst its way out of her chest. Riley, too, had looked wan as they'd moved towards tired and bored customs officials to have their passports stamped, to finally take their seats on the train. And when the carriages pulled away from the platform and Belle released a proper breath, she caught one final look at Rome's lights.

She wished she'd had the chance to say goodbye to her properly, to her gleaming church spires and ancient bell towers, to her charming, cobbled lanes and crumbling stone facades, to her vibrancy and beauty, her rawness and vulnerability. To her unwavering friendship.

'You brought me back to life,' she whispered to the city

lights shrinking beyond the window. 'And for that, I will always love you.'

Riley touched her arm gently. 'You okay, kid?'

Belle glanced at her sadly, then nodded. 'Yeah. How about you?'

'I've been better.'

'It all happened so quickly. I just... I can't.' Belle's bottom lip quivered. It was too much to reconcile and she couldn't construct the words needed. Only hours earlier she'd been cooking in Uncle Benito's kitchen, Andre on the cusp of telling him about their relationship, and now she was fleeing Italy.

'You'll see him again,' Riley said. 'Andre, I mean.'

Belle drew her knees up to her chest and wrapped her arms around them. 'Everything's changed. I don't know what happens from here.' She met Riley's eyes. 'Why did you come? What about Leo?'

Riley rested her head against the headrest and closed her eyes. It was a long time before she opened them again. 'What was the point of staying? I think we all knew how it was going to end up.'

'Did you get to say goodbye?'

'Over the phone.'

'Ri...' Belle reached for her friend's hand. 'You should have stayed.'

'There was nothing to stay for.'

'But you love each other.'

'Sometimes that's not enough,' Riley said sagely.

Belle thought about Andre. Was love enough for them to see this through, wherever it might lead? Across a border into France or an ocean to Australia? Mary flittered through her mind, the ex who would always be there, able to live her life in Rome, a convenient and reliable choice for Andre.

Her heart broke all over again over the way things had turned out.

Riley drifted to sleep somewhere near Bologna, but Belle tossed and turned, unable to shut off her thoughts completely. It was unrealistic to believe she could stay in Paris or anywhere in Europe long term in the hope that her relationship with Andre could continue. London was an option, but how long could they maintain it? He was busy at Valentina's and wouldn't be able to get away often. And now that she'd broken the law in Italy, it would be years before she'd be allowed to return. So at what point did they let go?

Then she berated herself for throwing in the towel this early. Wasn't love worth fighting for? But she had fought twenty years for Ben's love and what had it amounted to?

Sleep finally took hold, troubled and broken, as they climbed north towards the Swiss border and the city lights of Milan shone through the train window.

DAWN BROKE over the Swiss Alps as the train wended its way through Zurich and Basel, then finally over the border into France. Belle had managed an hour's sleep before opening her eyes to grey skies on their approach into Dijon. From there, it was an uninterrupted journey to Paris.

Riley had been silent for most of the trip. Her phone had beeped several times and she'd replied to those texts, presumably from Leo, for her eyes held a depth of sadness Belle had never seen before. She reached for her phone too, texting Andre and Avery to let them know they were safely over the border, to which their relieved responses came instantly.

I'll see you tomorrow. I can't wait, Andre replied.

At eleven am, the train pulled into Paris Gare de Lyon and Belle and Riley dragged their exhausted bodies onto the platform and to the baggage collection area. Once they had their suitcases, they found the taxi rank outside the station.

'Andre's coming to Paris tomorrow,' Belle said. 'Did Leo say if he was coming with him?'

Riley glanced up at steely skies, rain threatening to blanket the city in a last surge of winter stubbornness. 'I didn't ask him. It's better if he doesn't.'

'Are you sure?' Belle prodded gently.

'What's the point of dragging out the inevitable?'

Belle dropped the subject as a taxi swung in. 'Let's find a hotel. We can shower and eat, then work out what to do next.'

They climbed into the taxi and after enquiring with the driver about places to stay, he suggested the Hotel Barriere Le Fouquet's Paris and promptly drove them there. Situated close by the Champs Elysees and Arc de Triomphe, the façade alone told Belle it was more than she'd hoped to pay for a hotel, but Riley reasoned that it would be a long time before they returned so why not splurge?

They checked into their room, dropped their luggage, and showered. Belle pushed through her exhaustion, slipping into comfortable clothes and trainers, and packing her backpack, intent on hitting the streets. She could dwell on the events of the past twelve hours, or she could make the most of where they'd landed. It seemed Riley had the same intention.

Before they left, Belle called her mother and explained all that had happened.

'I'm not going to say I told you so,' Grace chided. 'You don't need to hear that. I'm just glad you're both okay.'

'We're fine. Just disappointed that we had to leave Rome.' She'd confided in her mother about Andre during previous conversations and she knew Grace understood the meaning in her words.

'I know you're going to miss him, but I'm sure he can visit you in Sydney, or you can meet each other halfway.'

Belle had thought of similar options on the train ride from Rome, but a visit here and a few weeks there was not how she'd envisioned a life with Andre, nor was it practical to expect that he'd be able to get away from Valentina's for weeks at a time. She wasn't even sure what her life back in Sydney would look like. Would she go to culinary school? Would she appease her father and study law? Could she slot back into her old life as though Rome had never happened, as though she'd never become a completely different person?

Then, of course, there was Ben. While it had been months since she'd thought about him, returning to streets that were haunted by her former relationship made her stomach flip unpleasantly. The tug of home was always strongest when she spoke to her mother, but there were also many reasons why home didn't feel like the answer.

'Let me know what time your flight is coming in and we'll pick you up from the airport,' Grace said. 'I'll reserve us a table somewhere for dinner. If you're not too tired, we can celebrate your homecoming.'

Her mother's attempt to make it more bearable made her smile. 'Okay.'

'And when you get back, you can move in here with us until you figure out your next move.'

Given that she'd be homeless and had few other alternatives at her disposal, she wasn't going to complain about living with her father again. 'Thank you.'

There was no talk of how he would react to the news. They skirted the topic as they had grown accustomed to doing and ended the call with Belle promising to send through her flight details as soon as she knew them.

Next, she called Andre who was dressing for work. 'Is Valentina's open again?' she asked.

'Yes. But we're four people down. It's going to be crazy until we hire new staff.'

'Will you still be able to come to Paris?' She held her breath, preparing for bad news.

'I'm coming, and so is Avery, but we'll only be able to stay a couple of days.'

'I guess a trip to Sydney is out of the question then.' She couldn't keep the disappointment from her voice. The end for them was drawing nearer and she could feel it in every fibre of her body.

He sighed deeply. 'I'm afraid not. Not for a while.'

She nodded resolutely. 'I miss you. Just come to Paris and we can figure out the rest later.'

'Riley can keep Avery company. I don't plan on leaving your side.'

Or her bed, she hoped. Belle wanted to reach across the distance and wrap her arms around him. 'We're staying at the Hotel Barriere Le Fouquet's Paris, room four-two-four. Call me when you arrive.'

Belle and Riley spent the rest of the day exploring, which suited her perfectly, for it provided enough distraction from all that she couldn't change. They strolled along the Avenue Montaigne, drank *café au lait*, and stopped to gaze in the windows of expensive *haute couture* shops. They wandered down to the River Seine, the cloud-leaden sky finally giving way to a gentle sun that warmed their skin. The first hint of spring was in the air and Belle realised that it had been spring when she'd first arrived in Europe all those months ago, making it a year since she'd been abroad.

'What's the plan?' Riley asked.

They'd found a seat by the river and were unwrapping chicken and mayonnaise baguettes they'd bought from a café nearby. Belle was ravenous. It was the first decent meal she'd eaten in over twenty-four hours.

'Andre and Avery will be here tomorrow. We can spend a couple of days with them before they head back. Then I guess we go home.' Belle bit into her baguette.

'Are you ready for home?' Riley asked.

'Not really,' she replied. 'I'm not ready for any of this.'

Riley nodded and bit into her baguette too, chewing silently.

Boat-homes and old barges lined the river's edge as tourist-packed river cruises and maritime vessels sailed past. The tourists waved and Belle waved back.

'I'm not going back to Sydney,' Riley said.

Belle abruptly stopped waving. 'What?'

Riley stared out at the river. 'There's nothing for me there anymore. No family or job or place to live.'

'But...' Belle forced the chunk of baguette she'd been chewing down. It sat like lead in her stomach. 'Where will you go?'

'Western Australia. I'll spend some time with my dad. He's going to fly in from the mines and meet me in Perth. I'm thinking of staying there for a while. I'll look for work and a place to stay.'

Belle set aside her baguette, her appetite vanishing. If she'd thought the future looked grim, it was even bleaker now. There would be no Andre or Riley, and nothing to anchor her to Sydney except her mother. In her late thirties, moving back in with her parents as a homeless, unemployed nomad was not what she'd envisaged. Her best friend would be hundreds of miles away, on the other side of the country, and the one who'd stolen her heart even further.

Once again, she'd almost had it. Happiness. That elusive thing she'd wrapped her hands around briefly after Ben, lulling her into a false sense of hope before it was wrenched from her. Now she would start all over again, more alone than ever.

———

THE NEXT MORNING, they woke early and booked their flights home, Belle calling her mother afterwards to relay the details. Then, with an entire day to fill before Andre and Avery arrived, they headed out.

Despite weeks of uncertainty ahead of her, there was a lightness in Belle's step when they left the hotel, stopping for croissants and crêpes in a café on Rue Vernet. She'd slept well in the knowledge that Andre would be with her by that evening, and they'd have two glorious days in Paris to fill before they'd have to say goodbye.

After breakfast, they returned to the Seine, boarding a river boat, and travelling down the river like the tourists they'd seen the day before, sun gleaming off the water as the propellers trudged up sediment from the murky riverbed. Afterwards, they queued for the Louvre and spent two hours walking the halls, then ate a late lunch in the Tuileries.

Back at the hotel in the afternoon, Belle collapsed onto the sofa. 'I wouldn't mind a quick nap before Andre and Avery arrive.'

Riley glanced at her watch. 'We've still got a few hours

before they land. I might head back out and get my dad a gift.'

'What did you have in mind?'

'Something from Rue Saint Honoré. Maybe a Hermès scarf or a wallet.'

'So he can parade it around on the mine site?' Belle said, chuckling at the thought.

Riley snorted with laughter. 'Exactly. I'm trying to jazz him up a bit. Help him find a lady.' She gathered up her backpack and headed for the door. 'While I'm out, I'll stop by the Palais-Royal Theatre and get those tickets we talked about.'

During their expeditions that morning, they'd come across *Aladdin*, a show that Belle and Riley had both been wanting to see. They were going to surprise Andre and Avery with dinner and tickets to the theatre.

'Thank you. Do you mind if I stay? I'm not sure my feet could carry me,' Belle said. She wanted to conserve her energy for Andre.

'Stay and nap. I won't be long.' Riley slung her bag over her shoulder and left the room.

Belle kicked her shoes off and stretched out on the sofa, tucking a pillow beneath her head. Her mind drifted to him, already anticipating the weight of his arms around her and the playful kisses he would drop onto her lips. They would fill the next two days with each other, build enough of a reservoir to get them through the weeks and months ahead. And they'd have to talk, an inevitable decision to be made about how they moved forward.

So much thinking, so much walking that day, and Belle's eyes grew heavy. She rolled onto her side and curled into a ball, tucking her hands under her chin. She didn't expect sleep to come as swiftly as it did, until she was hovering on the cusp of it, dreaming of Andre and Valentina's and Aladdin soaring through the air on a flying carpet.

IT FELT like only minutes later when her mind became aware of distant knocking. She peeled her eyes open, then closed them again, hoping it would go away. But it didn't. It seemed to grow louder, more insistent, until she realised it was someone at the door.

Belle groaned. She had no idea what time it was or how long she'd slept for. She thought it had only been minutes, but the shadows in the room had changed and she realised she must have been out for longer.

There was another knock and Belle finally dragged herself into a sitting position, wondering who it could be. Not Riley. She had her own access card and could let herself in. And it was too early for Andre and Avery to arrive. Maybe it was hotel services, although she hadn't asked for anything to be sent up.

She climbed to her feet and trudged to the door, reaching for the handle. When she swung it open, the person standing there was not who she expected to see.

TWENTY-SEVEN

'Ben!'

He stood there, in the corridor, like an image she couldn't comprehend. She closed her eyes, wondering if she'd fallen asleep again, but when she opened them, he was still there, in the flesh, exactly how she remembered him. Soft brown hair. Deep blue eyes the colour of the ocean.

'Surprise!' he announced. He wore a Ralph Lauren polo shirt, the collar turned up at the neck, and dark blue jeans. He looked travel-worn, but still perfectly put together in all the ways Ben could, no matter how long ago he'd showered and dressed. Beside him rested his suitcase.

Belle shook her head, still trying to process that Ben—her Ben—was standing outside her hotel room. In Paris. 'I'm sorry. I don't know what to say.' She stumbled over the words.

'I know. Crazy, right?' he said, as if he too, couldn't quite grasp that he was standing there. He looked beyond her into the room. 'Can I come in?'

'Uh.' She hesitated. 'Okay, sure.' She motioned for him to step inside, and he wheeled his suitcase through the doorway and parked it in a corner. She breathed him in as he walked past her and she was hit with the dizzying familiarity of his scent—the smell of his clothes, his hair and skin... the decades they'd spent together. She had to force the thoughts away before they overwhelmed her.

Ben glanced around the room, then his eyes settled on her. 'Wow. You look amazing. Beautiful. Europe agrees with you.'

She gestured for him to sit down. 'Sorry. I'm still trying to process that you're *here*, in Paris.'

He took a seat on the sofa while she remained standing, watching him.

'I wanted to see you. I spoke to your father yesterday. He said you'd left Rome. He's been keeping me informed of everything you've been doing.'

'My father?' She crossed her arms and stared down at him. 'What has he been telling you?'

'Just about your life in Rome. He said you brought an ailing trattoria back to life with your cooking.'

She rolled her eyes. 'That's a bit of a stretch.'

'He said you worked as a sous chef. He actually sounded, well, proud.'

'*Proud*? We're talking about the same person, aren't we?' she asked with a sniff.

Ben smiled at her. 'I know you and your father haven't always seen eye to eye, but during the conversations I've had with him, all I saw was pride. In fact, I'm the one who's been the disappointment.' His gaze dropped to his hands as though he could no longer meet her eyes.

Belle was aware of how highly Ben regarded her father and that to utter such a phrase must have cut deeply. She relaxed her stance, still a little awed that Ben had used *her father* and *proud* in the same sentence about her. 'Is that why you're in Paris? Did my father send you?'

He shook his head. 'No. I came when I heard you were here. I jumped straight on a flight.'

'Why?'

He met her stare directly. 'Because I need to talk to you, Belle.'

She was still trying to fit the pieces together and her confusion must have been obvious, for Ben shuffled over on the sofa and patted the spot beside him. 'Here, sit down.'

She relented and sat beside him.

He reached for her hand and held it firmly in his. 'Belle, I treated you badly a year ago.' He let out a ragged breath, as though the idea of it was thoroughly shameful. 'It was appalling behaviour and I'm sorry for that.'

'You came all this way to tell me you're sorry?'

'Yes. I mean no.' He ran his free hand through his hair. 'I came to tell you I made a mistake.'

Belle gulped. She had waited a long time for those words and hearing them brought back the pain of everything he'd put her through. Everything he *should* feel sorry for. She shook her head, trying to clear the confusion. 'Wait, I still don't know exactly why you're here. To apologise? To tell me you made a mistake? What difference does any of it make now? I've moved on.'

'It makes the world of difference,' he said with urgency in his tone.

'Where's Olivia?'

He chewed his lip. 'She's back home.'

'You came here on your own?'

'We've been having some... issues.'

Finally, the pieces fell into place, and it dawned on her why Ben had travelled thousands of miles at the drop of a hat to see her. Things were rocky with Olivia. She tried not to scoff so obviously.

'I know,' he said. 'I get it. You don't want to hear it. I was awful to you, I cheated on you and now here I am, begging for your forgiveness. I've got a hide, right?'

'Yes, you do,' she said brusquely.

'The thing is Belle, for the past year I've missed you. Nothing's been the same since we ended things.'

'Since *you* ended things.'

'Yes, okay, since I ended things.'

She studied him closely, a man who had once been so thoroughly entwined in her life that it had been impossible to tell where he'd ended, and she'd begun. She knew everything about him—the way his cow lick couldn't be tamed, and that laugh lines crept around his eyes when he smiled. She was attuned to every mood and quirk, to the way he made love and the songs he sang in the shower. There wasn't another soul on the planet she knew better than Ben. And he knew her. Unconsciously, her heart stirred with the memory of him, and she had to remind herself that he'd hurt her in ways she'd never thought possible.

He watched her carefully now, his eyes shadowed, his shoulders slumped, not the formidable Ben she was used to seeing. Just as she was contemplating what on earth to do with him, an access card clicked in the door and Riley stepped into the room. She stopped as she processed the scene, her eyes widening and her mouth gaping open.

Belle snatched her hand away from Ben's and tucked it guiltily into her lap. But Riley's eyes followed, and Belle knew the intimate moment had not gone unnoticed.

'Well,' Riley said, letting the door swing closed behind her, 'I was *not* expecting to find this.'

Belle jumped to her feet. 'Ben's here, in Paris, from

Sydney.' She was stating the bleeding obvious, but she couldn't hide the way her cheeks flamed, as though she'd orchestrated it.

'I can see that,' Riley said, crossing her arms.

'Hi, Riley,' Ben said, wiping his palms down the front of his jeans and rising to his feet.

Riley harrumphed, ignoring him. She turned to Belle. 'Can I talk to you for a minute?' Without waiting for an answer, she grabbed Belle's elbow and steered her into the bedroom. Once they were behind the closed door, Riley wheeled on her. 'What is *he* doing here?'

'I didn't invite him if that's what you're thinking,' Belle said. 'It's as much as a surprise to me as it is to you.'

'He just showed up here?'

'Yes. While you were out. I was asleep on the sofa.' Belle put a hand to her chest and took her first proper breath since he'd arrived.

'What does he want?' Riley asked.

Belle frowned. 'What do you think?'

Riley's eyes narrowed. 'No. After what he did to you? He has some nerve.'

'I know.'

'What about Olivia?'

'They separated, apparently. I don't have all the details. Right now, I just need to figure out what I'm going to do with him.'

'What do you mean? He can go back where he came from.'

'He turned up with his luggage, straight from the plane. I'm guessing he doesn't have a place to stay yet.'

'Well, he's not staying here,' Riley said sharply. 'He's a grown man. He can find his own way. The days of you being responsible for him are over.'

'I'm aware of that.' Belle's tone rose defensively. 'I'm not suggesting he stay here. But I think I need to hear him out, then he can go back to Sydney.'

'Hear him out?' Riley let out an incredulous breath and shook her head. 'What's there to hear? The guy cheated on you.'

'Again, I'm aware of that,' Belle said, trying to force patience into her voice. 'But we weren't just a fling. We had twenty years together. I can't turn him away.'

Riley's cheeks puffed. 'Well, then you have a problem on your hands. I just ran into Andre and Avery downstairs, checking in.'

'Already?' Belle glanced at her watch. 'They're not due for another two hours.'

'They were able to get an earlier flight. He wanted to surprise you.' Riley stared at her. 'What are you going to do?'

Belle wasn't sure. She searched deep within herself for the kind of spite and retribution that would see her kicking Ben out with a slap to the face, but no matter what he had done or how hard she searched, she couldn't find the resentment she needed. Perhaps she was too lenient, too kind. But hate always weighed heavier than forgiveness. She owed herself an hour with him, to listen, to say goodbye and to close that chapter of her life forever.

'I'm going to deal with Ben first. I'll need an hour at the most,' she said. 'Then I'll be ready for dinner and the theatre.'

'God,' Riley muttered. 'You're playing with fire, kid.'

'I just need an hour,' she pleaded. 'But I can't keep Ben here. We're going to have to go out. I don't want Andre coming up and the two of them running into each other.' It would be her worst nightmare for Andre to think Ben was back in her life.

'One hour,' Riley said sternly. 'I'll buy you some time. I'll tell them you went out to grab something. After that, you're on your own.'

Belle threw her arms around her friend. 'Thank you!'

'I can't even begin to understand why you're giving him the time of day,' Riley said, 'but you're welcome.'

Back in the living room, Ben met Belle's eyes with apology as Riley strode past them and out the door. As soon as it swung closed and they were alone again, he asked, 'Is everything all right? I didn't cause an argument, did I?'

'No, it's fine. But I don't have long to spend with you,' she said firmly. 'An hour at most. I have plans for this evening.'

'Oh.' He looked disappointed. 'Sure.'

'I thought we could go for a walk, talk a little, then you can find a place to stay.'

'Right.' He didn't seem enthused with the suggestion, probably hoping for more. 'Shall I take my bag?'

'Yes.' She glanced at him as he reached for the handle of his suitcase. He looked forlorn and suddenly very small in her hotel room. Her heart ached with remembered love for him, which was both complex and confusing, but she didn't have time to dwell. Andre was downstairs and the clock was against her.

TWENTY-EIGHT

It seemed that all of Paris had emerged from the grips of winter. The air was balmy, streets full of lilting music, and the air rippled gently through the trees. Lovers smoked cigarettes and kissed in cobbled lanes, and the smell of bread and coffee lingered on the breeze.

Belle strolled alongside Ben, the mood mellow after the tension in the hotel room. There was small talk of his flight from Sydney and the changing season back home, and when they didn't talk, it was filled with companionable silence, borne of their years spent together.

They wandered down Avenue George V, and Belle pointed out the Papilles Café, a place she'd passed frequently in the last two days and had been wanting to try. It was bustling with an early dinner service already. Diners were sitting outside in the alfresco, surrounded by a wall of hedges, tables draped in white tablecloths beneath strings of lights. The smell of food emanated from inside and Ben sniffed the air eagerly.

'Just one drink,' Belle reminded him. 'I have to get back.'

He held up his hands in concession. 'Okay. One drink.'

A waiter arrived and seated them outside in the alfresco, resting Ben's suitcase against the hedge wall. Belle ordered a coffee and Ben a scotch. When their drinks had arrived on the table, there was a shift in conversational pace as Ben looked at her apologetically.

'I really am sorry, you know,' he said, swirling the ice in his drink as cubes clinked together. 'For turning up like that. I didn't mean for you and Riley to argue.'

'We didn't argue. You just caught us by surprise.'

'Maybe I should have called first.'

Belle sat back in her chair and crossed her arms. 'What are you really doing here? And what's going on with Olivia?'

He sighed, his shoulders seeming to sag under the weight of the question. Belle noticed him properly for the first time beneath the strings of café lights. Flecks of grey sprinkled his temples that hadn't existed a year ago and his eyes were more lined than she remembered, shadows that spoke of exhaustion and stress.

'Olivia and I are over,' he said soberly.

'Oh.' She winced, feeling neither hope nor joy at the news. 'I'm sorry. I'd heard you were engaged.'

'Yeah, well.' He raised his eyebrows, then stared into his drink. 'Things went downhill after you left, and she moved in.'

'In what way?'

'She was intent on changing everything. She wanted to paint over the walls and rip up the carpet. She wanted to decimate your kitchen.'

'It's not my kitchen.'

'You know what I mean,' he said. 'She became obsessed with ridding the house of the memory of you. It was childish and insecure of her, but it was my fault. I made her feel that way. Without realising it, I was comparing every little thing she did to you.' He sighed with regret. 'The truth is, I missed you. And Olivia was sick of living in your shadow. I asked her to marry me, but in the end, we both knew that wasn't going to fix it.'

Ben drained his scotch and quickly signalled the waiter for another. 'Nothing has made sense since you left. And Olivia isn't you; she never could be. I was a fool to think I could love anyone else.'

Fool or not, he'd made his choice and he'd broken her heart in the process. 'Where's Olivia now?'

'She's moving out of the terrace. By the time we get back there, she'll be gone.'

By the time we get back there? There was an undercurrent of assumption in his words, as though they'd be returning to the terrace together.

'Belle, I didn't come here expecting instant forgiveness or for things to go straight back to the way they were,' he said as a waiter set down a fresh glass of scotch. 'I just wanted to see you, to explain and say sorry for being an idiot. And to see what you thought about it all. I mean, us. What you thought about us.'

'You didn't have to come all the way to Paris,' she said. 'I would have been home in two days. You could have spoken to me then.'

He shrugged, and his face softened into a boyish grin. 'I was kind of hoping that, after tonight, you'd want to spend a week here with me before we went back.'

Belle looked across the table at the man she'd once loved. A man whom she'd laid next to countless times, felt his skin on hers, his breath in her ear, his lips on her body. A man she'd shared her dreams and her laughter with, had wanted children with; a man she'd once loved so desperately that she'd thought it would consume her.

But this man had hurt her terribly, and after all the tears and heartache she'd come out on the other side happier, stronger, with a definite sense of who she was. Now he was asking her to go back. Part of her wanted to say yes, to return to a remembered love that was easy and familiar, and yet part of her realised that was all it was—easy and familiar.

She shook her head empathically. 'I'm sorry if you came here expecting more, but I can't stay here with you.'

He swallowed audibly, then stared down at his scotch. 'You won't even consider it?'

'You hurt me, Ben,' she said, her voice rising more than she'd intended it to. 'You broke me. And now you're here telling me you're sorry, that it was all a mistake.'

'I know how it sounds.'

'How it sounds? How it feels!' She closed her eyes, anger bubbling under the surface. She would love Ben until the day she died. They had spent years together and those years couldn't be so easily erased, but she wasn't *in love* with him. Her heart didn't ache for him as it ached for another.

'Who's Andre?' he asked.

Her eyes flew open, startled. 'What did you say?'

'Andre. Who is he?'

She faltered, wrongfooted by the question.

'It's okay,' Ben said. 'You don't have to tell me. It's just that I heard you and Riley talking about him. I didn't mean to eavesdrop. Riley was talking pretty loudly.'

'Andre is someone I met in Rome,' she answered truthfully. 'Someone I grew close to. We want to be together but it's complicated.' She didn't want to regale Ben with details of her relationship with Andre, nor did she have the time. She was conscious that Andre would be wondering where she was, and she was desperate to get back to the hotel and see him.

She fetched her phone out of her bag to check the time and was dismayed to see that an hour had flown by. Riley had sent two texts asking where she was, and that they were heading out for dinner; to meet them as soon as she was done. The night was fast becoming a disaster, as Ben knocked back his second scotch and grinned lopsidedly at her. Lack of food, jetlag and two drinks in quick succession had left him drunk.

'I really have to go,' Belle said, pushing her half-finished coffee aside. 'And we need to find you a place to stay.' Before he became too intoxicated.

He reached across the table and wrapped his fingers around hers. 'Are you sure I can't change your mind about us? There's too much history to throw away, Belle. We've been glued to each other since we were sixteen. You're my first love, my only love.'

She shook her head sadly at him. 'I'm sure.'

He sighed audibly. 'Well, just so you know when we get back home, I'm going to keep trying.' He winked. 'The terrace is there for you to move back into whenever you're ready. Just say the word.'

'I'm moving back in with my parents.'

'Ouch.' He removed his hand from hers and clutched his heart. 'If you're choosing your parents over the terrace, we must be over.'

It was impossible to stifle a chuckle. 'I'm sorry.' She gathered up her purse and phone and signalled for the bill. 'Come on, we have to go.'

While she waited for the bill to arrive, she typed a reply

to Riley. *I'm going to help Ben find a hotel, then I'll be on my way*. She sent it, then compiled a text to Andre. *I got held up. I miss you. I'll be there soon!*

But before she could hit send on his, three jolting bangs from down the avenue split the air. They echoed against the buildings, causing birds to scatter from trees and the diners in the Papilles alfresco to cease talking and glance around.

Belle straightened with alarm; her finger frozen above the send button on her phone. 'Goodness, what was that?'

Ben was playing with the ice in his glass, and he set it down on the table, his brow furrowing. 'I have no idea, but it was loud.' He rose slightly to peer over the hedge wall. Several more bangs cracked the night, followed by shouting. Belle turned in her chair to look over the hedge too. People were hurrying along the street, past the Papilles, their faces tight, eyes round with fear.

Ben was on his feet now. 'Something's happening down there.'

'An arrest?'

'I don't think so.'

Belle glanced around her. The other patrons in the café looked confused too, talking amongst themselves, dinner paused, the air static.

A shrill scream reverberated down the avenue, and a woman yelled, '*Pistolet. Pistolet!*'

'Something's not right,' Ben said. He flicked his head towards the door. 'We should go.'

His face held grave worry, and Belle quickly climbed to her feet, dropping her phone into her bag, her eyes scanning the alfresco. They were boxed in by the hedges. Whatever was happening, whatever those frightened souls were running from, Ben, Belle, and everyone else in the alfresco were trapped. Their only options were to climb over the hedge wall, which was four feet at least, onto the street, or exit back through the main part of the café.

'Should we take your suitcase?' she asked.

Ben glanced at his luggage still propped against the wall. 'Yeah.'

More pops cracked through the air like a whip and there was no denying that terrifying sound. It was gunfire and it was moving closer, up the avenue towards them.

'Forget it,' he murmured and snatched up her hand instead, dragging her towards the alfresco door. Frantic diners, noticing Ben's haste to leave, climbed to their feet, gathered up their belongings and clambered around the entranceway too, until it became a bottleneck. Belle's heart pounded wildly as she squeezed Ben's hand and he squeezed it back.

'Try not to panic. We're okay.' His voice shook as he held her close, and they were pushed and shoved by other diners trying to force their way through.

A series of gunshots rang out, so loud that they amplified throughout the Papilles Café, and Belle felt her insides liquify. A man in a heavy dark coat with a thick beard appeared at the front door of the café, his gun aimed, his finger on the trigger, shooting at everyone inside.

Belle froze, her blood pulsing in her ears as she watched the scene unfold in the main dining room of the café. The people trying to squeeze through the alfresco door turned and ran, terrified, back into the outdoor area, tripping over tables and chairs. Ben grabbed Belle and dragged her as she forced her legs to work, but they were like concrete, heavy, and unwilling. He led her to the hedge wall, positioned a chair, and told her to climb over, onto the street, but as she climbed up, a second gunman appeared on the other side, his weapon raised over the hedge, peppering bullets into the alfresco.

She tumbled off the chair, hitting the concrete with a thud. Screams pierced the warm air, bullets shattering crockery and glasses. Ben hauled her up and away from the wall, his hand folded tightly around hers, never letting her go, whispering to her, 'I've got you, Belle. We're okay, we're okay,' until a shot rang out in her ears. She ducked her head and Ben was no longer whispering, his hand no longer in hers.

TWENTY-NINE

Belle was flung forward, and she hit the ground, covering her head protectively with her hands as bullets ripped past her ears. Diners trod on her, seeking refuge where they could, and some fell beside her, drawing their last breath as they did.

She curled into a tight ball, her mind blank, her lungs barely working. The smell of gunfire was acrid, clogging her throat, and the sound of firing bullets rang in her ears. Time slowed, a massacre playing out above her. When sirens finally wailed in the night, the gunfire halted, and the sound of the gunmen's footsteps retreated down the street.

Belle wasn't sure how long she'd remained curled up, but when all fell quiet, when there was little more than the whimpers of the injured, she dared to let go of her head and peer around. People were everywhere, barely moving or not at all. Someone wailed and a plate toppled from its precarious position on the edge of a table and smashed.

Belle waited for the pain to come, a bullet wound or a broken bone from falling, but aside from a stinging pain in her arm, she could move her limbs without difficulty. She began to crawl on her elbows along the concrete, searching for Ben, for she dared not rise to her feet. She encountered bodies and broken pieces of plates, the café lights hanging in shreds and draping along the floor. The alfresco, only minutes earlier filled with food and people and laughter, was a scene of carnage.

'Ben,' she whispered, then with slightly more courage, 'Ben.'

She needed to hold his hand, to feel him beside her—to reassure her again that they would be okay. But there were so many bodies, so much destruction and smoke in the air that it was almost impossible to see anything.

Then her eyes fell on him, lying motionless on the floor beside a chair. Belle crawled to him, her body sliding over jagged edges of broken dinner plates, noticing first the stillness of him, then the blood pooled around his head. There was a wound near his right temple. Large, round and perfectly fatal.

Belle's ears filled with the sound of her screams. She dragged him to her, holding his head in her lap, rocking back and forth as shock seized her muscles. She became distantly aware of movement in the alfresco, as the living grieved over the dead and the injured bled out, with sirens, closer now, piercing the Paris night.

Ben's body was warm, as though life still flowed through his veins, and she cradled him, her hands covered in his blood. It drenched her clothing, seeped through to her skin, the metallic scent of it, like rust, filling her nostrils. A guttural, heart-wrenching howl burst from her lungs, mingled with the wails of the others.

Please, God, let me wake from this nightmare. Please.

Everything halted—the sirens, the screams for help, the cries from the survivors. It was just her and Ben, a man she'd once loved with all her soul, who she would always be connected to, in this life and the next. She would hold him. She would hold him forever, and she would never let him go.

WHEN BELLE OPENED her eyes again, someone was feeling her neck for a pulse, then shaking her gently. Sounds in the alfresco enticed her back—voices of authority and pieces of crockery crunching underfoot. Red and blue lights flooded the night, bouncing off buildings.

Belle wasn't sure how long she'd been lying there. Long enough, she deduced, for first responders to appear and start making sense of the tragedy. Ben was still in her arms, his lifeless body growing rigid, the exit wound at the back of his head a gaping mess.

'Madame?' A hand on her shoulder. 'Madame.'

She attempted a few syllables, but her throat was painfully dry. The lights hurt her eyes and she closed them, hoping to drift away again to a moment not so long ago when Ben was alive and making silly declarations about wooing her back.

Ben and his bravado had always made her laugh.

But the person crouching beside her would not let her sink into that place of comforting euphoria, the hand shaking her more urgently now. She wrestled her eyes open, and the alfresco crashed into focus once more.

'Madame. *Venez avec moi, s'il vous plait.*'

She looked at the stranger talking to her. It was a French police officer, and he was saying something to her that she couldn't understand.

'Madame. *Venez avec moi, s'il vous plait,*' he said again.

She shook her head at him, her body beginning to tremble all over. 'I don't know what you're saying.'

He spoke more fervently, and she pulled Ben closer. 'You can't take him.'

The office reached for Ben's body, trying to pry him from her, but she swiped at him furiously and he backed away. Tightening her arms around Ben, time slipped. She tilted with it and blacked out.

———

BELLE AWOKE AGAIN to another officer, this time a female, who'd dropped to her knees and was resting a hand on Belle's shoulder.

'Madame,' she said softly. '*Parlez-vous français?*'

Belle shook her head. 'I don't speak French.'

The officer nodded. Her face was kind. 'Okay, no problem. We must move you from the area. Are you injured?'

'My friend is hurt.'

The officer glanced at Ben and her mouth set in a grim line.

'What's happening?' Belle whispered. Her teeth chattered as cold wrapped itself around her bones.

'Paris is under attack. Can you walk?' The officer gripped Belle's elbow and tried gently to lift her.

Belle jerked away from her grasp. 'No! I'm not leaving him.'

'Madame, you have to. We must clear the area. I need to take you to the ambulance. Your arm is cut.'

Belle looked down at her arm. She hadn't noticed she was bleeding.

'Come, Madame.'

'I'm not leaving him!' She held Ben closer. They would

have to forcibly remove her. *I won't let you go, Ben. We're okay. We're okay.*

The officer pursed her lips. 'Please, I understand, but we can't let you stay here. You're going into shock. We must leave. And I'll make sure that your friend is looked after.'

Belle shook her head, tears streaming down her face. 'I can't leave him.'

'There's nothing you can do for him now. We have to go.'

Belle ran her fingers along Ben's pale face, across the blue of his lips and through his blood-matted hair. Her body shook with silent sobs, and while she quietly willed him to wake, to draw another breath, to beat another heartbeat, she knew he was gone.

She gently rested his body on the ground and allowed the female officer to help her to her feet. Sifting through debris, she located her bag and Ben's suitcase beneath an overturned table, where they'd been flung during the attack. She collected them both, then allowed herself to be guided across the alfresco and towards the side door that led back into the café.

Inside the Papilles, she averted her gaze from the blanketed bodies, shock and grief rising up her throat, until she was safely outside, where lights flashed brightly in her eyes and the monotonous drone of choppers hovered overhead. The female officer was still beside her, her presence like a pillar, as she guided her towards triage and a bank of waiting ambulances. Belle was thankful for that officer, for were it not for her reassuring hand, her legs would have buckled beneath her.

She turned to glance back at the café, at the outdoor alfresco, with its pretty string lights hanging in tatters, and tried not to think of Ben's lifeless body lying behind the hedge wall.

BELLE SPENT thirty minutes in the triage tent erected on the street. The entire block had been sealed off as multiple stretchers were loaded into ambulances and driven away. She'd refused similar transport to a hospital, opting instead for a bandage on her arm and a blanket to settle her shock. When colour returned to her cheeks and her pulse slowed to an acceptable level, the critical care specialist was happy for her to vacate the overrun triage, and she stepped back out onto the street.

The female officer, who was returning from the café, flagged her down. 'How are you feeling?'

Belle was still too numb to feel anything. She shrugged woodenly.

'Shouldn't you go to the hospital?' the woman asked.

'They said I could leave. They have far worse cases than me to deal with.'

The officer nodded soberly and plucked a card from her jacket pocket. 'My name is Albane. I'm an officer with the *Préfecture de Police de Paris*. This is my card.'

Belle accepted it and placed it into her bag.

'What's your name?'

'Belle Hamilton.'

Albane gave her an encouraging smile. 'Call me in the morning, Belle. I'll give you details about where your friend was transported. I'll also need to take a statement from you. But we can take care of that tomorrow.'

Belle swallowed thickly. Her throat was like sandpaper,

for triage had refused to give her a drink while she'd recovered from shock.

'Where are you from, Belle?'

'Um.' Belle wiped at her blood-stained face, her thoughts disconnected. 'Sydney. I'm from Sydney.'

'Okay.' Albane touched her shoulder. 'You need to get back to your accommodation and stay there, where it's safe. Would you like someone to drive you?'

Belle shook her head. 'No. It's just up the road.'

'Don't go wandering the streets. Go straight to your accommodation and call your family and embassy. Tell them you're safe because you see up there?' She pointed to the choppers hovering in the air. 'That's the media. Australia will wake to the news soon.'

Belle felt a dizzying wave of nausea grip her. 'Will they take care of him?'

Albane nodded, laying her hand on Belle's arm. 'Yes. They'll take good care of him.' She began walking back towards the Papilles Café but turned around again. 'Belle, what was your friend's name?'

Belle's eyes welled, her grief resurging like a tidal wave. 'His name was Ben.'

THIRTY

Although Albane had instructed her to return immediately to the hotel, Belle sat on a bench near triage and watched the recovery mission unfold around the café. She knew she shouldn't be there, that someone would eventually tell her to move on, but she wasn't sure she could leave Ben yet. Leaving his body alone on the concrete floor of a Parisian café while she'd walked away had felt unnatural and cruel, as though he were crying out for her. *He's gone*, she told herself, *he doesn't know anything anymore*, although she could have repeated it a thousand times and it still wouldn't have made leaving him easier.

With trembling fingers, she retrieved her phone from her bag and dialled Riley's number, but the call dropped before it rang. It was likely the cell service in Paris was jammed. Riley, Andre, and Avery would be in the theatre by now, and they wouldn't have a clue as to what had happened. They'd think she hadn't bothered to show.

The night air had turned cool, the faint stars above Paris bleeding together. First responders and the injured walked past her and the triage tent loomed, the activity within it frenetic. Everything looked surreal against the backdrop of ambulance lights and media crew. It was hard to imagine that she and Ben had been making small talk only hours earlier as they'd walked along this avenue.

Belle stared down at her hands stained red with blood, seeped deep into her cuticles, jeans sticky, the colour of rust. She was at a loss as to what to do, frightened, with the distant pops of gunfire still making her jump. Something was happening to Paris. Those men were still out there. *Paris is under attack.*

She tried Riley's phone again, then Andre's and Avery's. Her attempts to reach them remained futile and when two police officers noticed she was loitering and began walking her way, she forced herself to her feet, deciding she'd better move on.

Outside the exclusion zone, the rest of George Avenue V was eerily silent and bereft of its magic. The pavements were deserted, cafés and restaurants closed, and the window shutters of apartments above were securely shut. It all looked barren and apocalyptic. *Paris is under attack.*

Belle concentrated on placing one foot in front of the other, tugging Ben's luggage behind her, struggling to recall the way back to the hotel, even though she'd walked that avenue several times in the past two days. Eventually, she found the Hotel Barriere Le Fouquet's Paris although she wasn't entirely sure how she got there.

Back in her hotel room, adrenalin began to course through her body, her pulse rushing in her ears. She leaned Ben's suitcase upright against the wall, paced a few laps around the room, then sat on the edge of the sofa and stared at it.

It was a Lacoste bag. Navy blue. She'd bought it for him for Christmas two years ago and he'd loved it. He'd taken it everywhere and had purchased the backpack and toiletry bag to match.

Oh, Ben...

Minutes slid by and she was unable to calm her thoughts or quell the tremor in her legs, her feet tapping the carpet with unspent energy. She was suddenly overcome with everything that she hadn't had the chance to tell him, that she would always cherish his friendship, that she'd forgiven him for what he'd done. That she wanted him in her life. She couldn't even remember the last thing she'd said to him.

The room was disarmingly quiet, the walls closing in on her and she needed sound. She turned the television on while she waited for the cell network to decongest so she could call Riley. The BBC channel filled the screen with images from the Papilles Café. Belle watched as the operation unfolded to retrieve the dead. The police had set up large tarpaulins to conceal the view of the deceased from the media. The reporter told of twelve killed and thirty-six wounded as three gunmen had embarked on a shooting rampage down Avenue George V and into the Papilles Café, where diners were trapped like sitting ducks.

'An act of terrorism,' declared the news reporter.

Plucking her phone out of her bag, she tried Riley's number again, then attempted to reach Andre and Avery. When every call frustratingly refused to connect, she called her mother. It was seven in the morning in Sydney, and she got through without a problem.

Her father answered on the second ring. 'Belle? Oh, thank goodness. Your mother just saw what happened on the news. Are you okay?' He called out to her mother in the background. 'Grace, I have Belle.'

'I'm okay, Dad.'

'She was just about to call you. We've been worried sick.'

She couldn't remember a time when she'd ever heard her father sound so panicked for her safety and she desperately wanted to see him, to hug him.

'I was at the café, Dad. The one that was attacked.' Her voice shook and broke.

'Good grief,' he said. 'Are you injured? Where are you now? Wait, I'll put your mother on.'

Even in times of crisis, her father, the formidable Edward Hamilton, still looked to her mother for direction. When Grace's voice filled Belle's ear, she sank to the sofa, her legs unable to hold her up.

'Belle, sweetheart. Are you safe?'

'Mum, I...' She couldn't even say the words. They lodged somewhere at the back of her throat. 'We were there. Ben and me. The café was being shot at. We couldn't get out.'

'Oh, sweetheart. Oh, dear lord. Are you still there now? Are you safe? Where's Ben? What was he doing there?'

It was a flood of questions, Belle trying to consolidate them. 'Ben came here to see me. He wanted to talk. We went to the café for a drink, and we were there when it was attacked.'

'Oh, Belle.'

'I'm back at the hotel now. But, Ben, he... he...' The room spun and she clutched the edge of the sofa as panic threatened to seize her again.

'Ben what? What happened to Ben, honey?'

Somehow, Belle found the words to explain how she and Ben were at the Papilles Café, of the gunshots they'd heard, the frantic people, the bodies, how they quickly became trapped within the hedge walls of the alfresco. She told of bullets raining down on them and the fatal one Ben had sustained to the head.

Her mother was crying when Belle finished. Grace would hang up shortly and inform Edward of the news, and Belle could only guess as to the full weight of the grief that would bear down upon him. It was her grief too, intermingled with the guilt of knowing that Ben had been there to see her. He had been at the Papilles Café because of *her*. If he'd been safely back at home, he would still be alive.

'Mum, can you call Ben's parents? I don't think... I just couldn't...'

'Of course.' Her mother's voice shook.

'Can you also call the Australian Embassy?'

'Yes, we'll take care of it,' Grace said. 'Now will you please come home?'

'I can't get in touch with Riley.'

'She's not with you?'

'She went to the theatre with Andre and Avery, and I can't get a hold of them. It might just be the phone service, but I've been trying for a while now.'

'We'll try to call her father.'

'Thanks, Mum.'

'Do you want us to come there? There's still time to catch a flight out today.'

Belle shook her head. 'No. Don't come all the way here. It's ten pm now in Paris. I'll call you when I know more.'

She hung up the phone and stared around the room. She couldn't sit and wait for Riley and the others to return. She couldn't be alone with her anguish and her palpating heart. She needed to do something, to move, to feel less idle, so she left Riley a note in case she came back, gathered up her bag and headed out the door.

Downstairs in the lobby, people stared at her. Realising

with dismay that she was still covered in blood, she hastily swiped at her hands and face.

When she approached reception, the man behind the desk gasped.

'I'd like a taxi, please,' she said, trying to control the quiver in her voice.

'Madame!' he exclaimed. 'So much blood. Are you hurt?'

'I'm not hurt. I just need a taxi.'

'Would you like to go to the hospital?' he asked kindly. He had grey hair and vivid blue eyes that searched her face with grandfatherly concern.

'I'd like to go to the Palais-Royal Theatre.'

His eyes widened. 'Madame, the Theatre du Palais-Royal was just attacked. A car bomb. Is there any reason why you'd want to go there?'

Belle felt her legs buckle beneath her and she hit the floor. Deft hands collected her under the armpits and pulled her to her feet. She was led to a chair where she was placed gently down, and someone put a glass of water in her hand.

The elderly man from reception knelt beside her. His name badge read Edgar, and he had the kindest eyes. 'Madame?'

'A car bomb?'

'*Oui*. Just outside the theatre.'

'Were there any fatalities?'

He looked grim. 'Six people were killed, I believe. Several more injured.'

'I have friends who were at the theatre,' she cried. 'I can't get a hold of them.'

'The cell service might be jammed. I'm sure if you keep trying—'

She shook her head quickly. 'I just called my parents and was able to connect. I don't think it's a jammed service. I need to get over there.'

Edgar touched her shoulder. 'I doubt very much you'll get close to the area. It's blocked off. And it's not a good idea to wander the streets now. You're safer at the hotel.'

Belle began to tremble violently, her hands shaking as she held the glass, water sloshing over the rim. She didn't know what to do, where to go, how to reach Riley, Andre and Avery. She didn't even want to think what that might mean.

'Madame, please, let us take you upstairs again. You're in shock. We'll make some calls for you and see what we can find out.'

Belle allowed Edgar to assist her to her feet. He guided her to the lift and up to her room.

———

BACK INSIDE THOSE silent walls again, she avoided the sight of Ben's luggage in the corner and sat down, her foot recommencing its relentless tapping. The television was still on, news of the theatre now flashing across the screen, relaying it as Edgar had, a car bomb detonating by the front entrance.

Reports were coming in of a third bomb too, detonated at a busy evening marketplace in the Goutte d'Or area of the eighteenth arrondissement. Seven people had been killed there; numerous others injured. The BBC news flicked between the Papilles Café, the Palais-Royal Theatre, and the marketplace. Three locations. Three coordinated attacks.

Paris was under siege.

By midnight, Belle still hadn't heard from Riley. Edgar visited her once to relay that he'd called the hospitals for her, but they'd been overwhelmed with the injured and were unable to confirm if her friends were among the casualties. Belle was left to pace the room again, checking her phone constantly and jumping at the sound of gunfire that still rumbled in the distance. The police were raiding properties in Paris, the BBC reports said. They were searching for the people involved—the bomb-maker, the gunmen, anyone else who'd been involved in the attacks.

By one in the morning, Belle was so wired she thought her head might explode. Dread lurked on her shoulder like the Grim Reaper. Not knowing the fate of her friends was hardest of all. Were they hurt? Had they been detained somewhere? Were they even alive? The bomb at the theatre had exploded four hours ago, so if they weren't injured or worse, then where were they?

With little left to do but wait, she took a shower. Ben's blood was stiff and cracking on her skin. She peeled the clothes from her body, stained a rusty red, and bagged them to throw away in the morning. Hot water ran over her skin, dark red rivers washing down her legs and into the drain. She scrubbed her hair and fingernails and gingerly removed the bandage from her arm, her own injury an afterthought. She must have been cut by flying crockery or the side of the hedge when she'd fallen. Maybe she'd sliced her arm open on the ground. It hadn't required stitches, but the water stung it and it was almost a consolation to feel something other than the infuriating seesaw of despair and adrenalin.

When she'd dressed into clean pyjamas, she trekked back to the lounge. Just as she was preparing to call Uncle Benito, an access card clicked in the corridor, and she looked up as Riley walked in.

Belle ran to her. 'Riley!'

'Belle!'

They held each other, and Belle caught a glimpse of Edgar in the doorway looking immensely relieved. He smiled before pulling the door shut and leaving them.

'Are you okay?' She took Riley's arm and led her to the sofa.

Riley nodded. 'I'm okay. That nice man walked me up.' Her bewildered eyes darted around the room.

'Where have you been?' She tried not to chastise, but her nerves were frayed, and it caused her voice to sound shrill. 'I've been trying to call your phones. All of you.'

'There was an explosion at the theatre. I don't know where our phones are, probably destroyed,' Riley said. Her clothes were bloodied, her face streaked with mascara.

Belle assessed her. 'Where did all this blood come from? Were you hurt?'

'It's not mine.'

Belle's stomach roiled. 'Whose is it?'

'Andre's,' Riley said. 'He's in the hospital. We were standing outside when it happened. He was thrown by the blast and has internal bleeding and a head injury. I've been at the hospital with him; I didn't want to leave him there alone. My bag and everything in it was lost. And my mind went blank earlier... I just... I couldn't remember your number, otherwise, I would have called you.'

Belle walked quickly to the bathroom, filled a glass of water from the tap, then returned. Riley took hold of it with trembling hands.

'They rushed him straight into surgery,' she said, taking an unsteady gulp. 'He's out now and in an induced coma. I didn't know what else I could do for him, so I left the hospital. A police officer drove me here.'

'But you're sure he's okay? Will he be okay, Ri?' Belle searched her face with desperation.

'Yes, I think so.'

Belle sat on the sofa, her heart in her throat. 'We need to ring his father.'

'I gave the hospital the name of the trattoria. They've already called him. He's catching the first flight in the morning.'

Belle dropped her head into her hands. Thank God Andre was okay. He was injured, he had internal bleeding, but he'd survived. She glanced up suddenly. 'Where's Avery?'

Riley shook her head as tears spilt onto her cheeks.

Alarm shot up Belle's spine, her skin flooding with goosebumps. 'Where's Avery? Is she at the hospital?'

At first, Riley didn't speak. Her voice seemed to seize, and she cried.

'For God's sake, where is she, Ri?'

'She's gone,' Riley said, in a voice so tiny that Belle almost missed it.

'Gone? What do you mean, *gone*?'

'She didn't make it.' Riley sank to the sofa beside Belle. 'She was on the phone to a friend. She'd walked ahead of Andre and me, to the entrance of the theatre, standing by a parked car.' She squeezed her eyes shut, then opened them again, eyelashes drenched in tears. 'Then there was an explosion. I've never felt anything like it, like the ground had blown apart. I couldn't find Avery after that. I saw what was left of the car she was near, but I couldn't find *her*. It happened so quickly.' She cried great heaving sobs that she seemed to have no control over.

Belle felt the floor slide away from beneath her.

'I promise I tried. But my ears were ringing,' Riley said

through her sobbing, 'and there was so much smoke. I couldn't find Andre. I couldn't even get close to the car to look for Avery.'

Riley's entire body was trembling, and Belle knew she needed a blanket or a jacket, but she couldn't move. She was frozen, her entire world teetering on the brink of some inexplicable horror.

'I finally found Andre, but he was unconscious. He'd been thrown by the blast. I remember being loaded into an ambulance with him and I was trying to tell the police that Avery was still out there. They said anyone in the vicinity of the car wouldn't have stood a chance.'

It was the final straw. Belle rose and went into the bedroom to fetch Riley a blanket, but when she got there, she couldn't hold back the tears. They racked her body as she held a pillow to her mouth and sobbed.

Her heart was broken for a girl who'd opened her home to Belle, a girl who'd been a terrible cook and a dreadful house cleaner but who'd made Belle laugh with her eye rolls and wild spirit. A girl with swinging plaits and freckles on her nose. A girl Belle had loved like a younger sister.

Her heart broke for Ben, a love she'd known like no other, and for Andre; the thought of losing him too much to fathom. And her heart broke for Paris, as sirens jarred the night, and a city came to terms with unspeakable tragedy. As it lay exposed and frightened, changed forever.

A city in mourning.

THIRTY-ONE

Dawn broke and the sun lit the sky like fire.

Riley was in the shower, washing the night's atrocities from her skin and Belle finished a call with her mother. She walked into the bedroom as Riley was pulling pyjamas over her head, her eyes puffy from crying.

Belle threw the covers back from her bed and they both climbed in, lying side by side, staring up at the ceiling. It was then that Belle told Riley about the Papilles Café, about the gunmen who'd stormed the eatery, and how they'd been trapped there, of Ben being shot and killed.

Riley blinked, fresh tears leaking from her eyes and sliding down her cheeks.

'He was trying to get us both out of there,' Belle said, squeezing Riley's hand. 'They were shooting people down in the café. One of them came around the alfresco. We couldn't get out.'

Riley drew a ragged breath. 'Is this really happening?'

Belle shook her head because she didn't know. Shock still seized her, causing her to think and move as though she were underwater.

'I can't believe Ben's gone,' Riley said. 'I mean, I stood here only hours earlier and said those awful things about him.'

'You weren't to know this would happen, Ri.'

'I just didn't want him to pull you back. You've become so strong... and you have Andre too.' She closed her eyes, then opened them again. 'As much as Ben infuriated me, I never wished him harm. I never wanted anything bad to happen to him.'

'I know.'

Riley sniffed and turned towards Belle, curling herself into a ball. 'I'm just glad you're okay. Because if anything happened to you, I don't know what I would do.'

They fell silent, holding each other's hands, but neither of them slept.

LATER THAT MORNING, Albane called as promised, and Belle spent twenty minutes giving her a statement. She explained the events of the evening, of what little she could remember, given how rapidly everything had unfolded. Albane informed her the police were still searching for the gunmen and bombmaker. Every hour that slipped by their grasp loosened on them, until eventually, they would melt through their fingers altogether.

'It's happened before,' she said soberly. 'They'll go to ground quickly, like cockroaches.'

Albane then relayed details of where they'd transported Ben, to the morgue at the Hôpital Saint-Louis on the Avenue Claude Vellefaux. After their call, Belle showered quietly and leaving Riley to rest, she slipped out the door. Ben's family were arriving the following day and she would accompany them to the hospital to view him, but right now, she needed to be by Andre's side.

She purchased a bouquet of blue lilies from the hotel florist and, with a stomach tense with knots, she caught a taxi to a different hospital. The Hôpital Cochin.

She stared in silence out the window as the driver navigated over the Seine, around the university and onto the rue du Faubourg-Saint-Jacques in the Latin Quarter. The sun was shining brightly, the sky blue and endless, which seemed like an insult given the tragedies of the previous night.

On most streets, Paris had returned to normal. The taxi driver told her of heightened security at airports and train stations, but as they drove, she saw cafés and shops open and streets bustling with cars.

'They won't take away our freedom,' the French president had declared on the news that morning. Paris was defiant.

She arrived at the hospital and went immediately to the service desk, enquiring about Andre. A harassed-looking receptionist who was juggling a flashing switchboard and a crowd of concerned loved ones directed her to ICU. Belle set off, a labyrinth of walkways carrying her deep into the belly of the hospital, as she tried to comprehend French signage. Eventually, she found Uncle Benito hunched over in a chair in the quiet ICU corridor.

He noticed her arrival and climbed wearily to his feet. He seemed to have aged a hundred years, lines of despair etched deep into his face. 'Bella,' he said, embracing her. He sniffed back tears, then pulled away to study her. 'Are you okay? What is this on your arm?'

'I'm fine, Uncle Benito. It's just a cut. How's Andre?'

His exhausted eyes indicated the room behind them.

Through the open door, Belle could see Andre lying still and blanketed in a bed. The room was dark, the curtains drawn, the air quiet and undisturbed. His face was concealed, for someone was sitting beside him, blocking Belle's view—a female who looked familiar, with dark hair, her back to the door.

'He's stable and in a coma. They'll wake him tonight. They say the swelling in the brain has gone down and they've stopped the internal bleeding.' He did a quick sign of the cross on his chest and kissed upward towards the heavens. 'Mary is with him.'

Belle felt her heart plummet as she sank onto a plastic chair. *Mary?*

'She came with me this morning on the plane,' he said, sitting heavily on the seat beside her. 'She'll help me take Andre home and care for him in *Roma*. She's good for my Andre, you know. He'd be happy with her. I just wish he could see that.' He seemed dismayed at the prospect that Andre would never love Mary quite like she loved him.

'I'm sorry about Avery.'

He hung his head in sorrow. 'God bless her soul. And my poor sister. She and her husband are on their way here. They left Vancouver a few hours ago. Parents should never have to bury their children.' He paused to wipe his eyes. 'I failed my sister. I failed her husband, and I failed my niece. She should have been safe with me. She should have been in *Roma* where I could keep my eye on her. Why did I let her come here?'

Belle was unsure if this was directed at her. If, in some way, he was laying the blame at her feet. He wouldn't have been unfair in doing so.

They were in Paris for you.

All of them.

'Uncle Benito, is there anything I can do? I could stay here with Andre while you and Mary get some rest.'

Uncle Benito reached for her hand and patted it gently. 'Child, I know you love him. Anybody can see that. But it can never be. Go home to your parents.' Although his tone was kind, his meaning was clear. 'You've been away from home a long time. And now this. They must be worried. They need to see you, to know you're safe.'

'What about Andre?'

'Mary is here for Andre.'

The notion cut deep, and Belle was certain she'd visibly flinched. She'd spent countless hours working alongside Uncle Benito in the kitchen and they had a mutual respect and admiration for each other. Among all else, he was fair, but this was Andre they were talking about, his only son, lying comatose in an intensive care bed because he'd been in Paris visiting Belle.

A girl like Mary presented minimal complications. She was a devout Catholic, lived in Rome and there was no risk of Andre flying to another part of the world to be with her. Andre would be safe with a girl like Mary. Could Belle blame Uncle Benito for wanting predictability over uncertainty for his child? For wanting Belle to discreetly disappear and leave them be?

She stared at the lilies in her lap, her throat tight with emotion. She'd once been so sure that she and Andre had a future together, even if culture and expectation would test them. Now, they were the ultimate defeat.

She glanced at Uncle Benito. 'Is it okay if I say goodbye to him?'

He nodded and rose to his feet. 'Only one person is allowed in at a time. And you must be quiet.' Standing in the doorway of Andre's room, he beckoned to the girl in Italian. 'Mary. *Vieni.*'

She glanced up in surprise, then bent to stroke Andre's hand tenderly before emerging from the room, eyes glazed and red-rimmed. Her dark hair was pulled into a ponytail, her young face lined with worry. She was pretty, in a way that was neither plain nor striking. *Safe.* Clutched tightly in her hands were a string of gold rosary beads, and Belle suspected she might have been willing Andre to convalescence through prayer.

Mary fixed her eyes upon Belle as she walked past her and took a seat in the corridor with Uncle Benito. There was no jealousy found there, nor resentment, just an innate curiosity, as though she were intrigued by the girl who'd won Andre's heart. Belle fought off the pummelling in her stomach, clutched her lilies and walked into the dark room.

Beneath a crisp hospital blanket, Andre's body was still. His eyes were closed, and his skin was marked with shrapnel wounds and small burns and grazes. His head was swathed in a bandage, treating the head injury he'd sustained, and he had a bandage on his right arm. A tube for oxygen aided his breath; the gentle rise and fall of his chest. A drip fed into a cannula attached to his hand and he was surrounded by intermittently beeping machines.

Pale and broken.

Something inside Belle constricted and she searched for a vase to distract herself. This was what devastation did. It stripped away the noise, the things that had once seemed so significant and it left behind a trail of pieces. Why hadn't she fought harder for that visa? For Andre? Why had she left everything to chance? And why had she allowed him and Avery to follow her to Paris?

The questions circled her brain like trapped birds until

she stifled a sob. The guilt of it would plague her forever, the missed opportunities, and she took several anguished breaths to calm herself. She couldn't fall apart here, not now. Her hand closed around a vase, and she retrieved it, filling it with water from the tap and arranging the lilies inside.

Finally, she turned and walked to the seat vacated by Mary, lowering herself into it and reaching for Andre's hand. It felt warm but lifeless, owing to his deep sleep. She stroked his arm, her hands tracing the outline of his bandage, then up to his face, the strong, angular curve of his jaw. She brought his fingers to her lips, held them there and kissed them gently, and she didn't care if Mary was watching, although she had little doubt that she was.

She told Andre that she was leaving, and that she wanted him to be happy, that he should be with Mary, if he wanted to be. She didn't want him to wait for her, to sacrifice for her, to leave Rome or be in a relationship that would challenge them, even though she wanted all those things.

While she spoke, a part of her hoped he would open his eyes and smile at her. The same smile that lit up his eyes, deepened his dimples and spoke of everything he felt for her. When she uttered the word goodbye, something inside her broke.

They say that people in comas can often hear. That somewhere, deep in their unconsciousness, they can still process the words of a loved one. Belle wasn't sure if it was her imagination because she so desperately wanted to feel his response, but she thought she felt the faintest flicker of movement beneath her grasp. As though through his touch, Andre wanted her to know that he was there. That he could hear her.

That he didn't want her to go.

THIRTY-TWO

Saying goodbye to Andre, then walking out the hospital doors, was one of the most difficult things Belle had ever done. Like a thief in the night, she'd stolen away, leaving him to wake to the news of her departure. It had taken every ounce of her willpower to let his fingers slip through hers, to touch one last kiss to his forehead, to say farewell through silent tears. She'd left his bedside, embracing Uncle Benito for a final time before forcing herself away from ICU with Mary's gratified gaze coaxing her out.

Maybe it was best this way, for if Andre had been awake, he would have begged her to stay and she wouldn't have been able to say no, despite Uncle Benito's wishes. It didn't hurt any less though; it hurt more than she thought possible. Never would she see Andre's smile again, the one that seemed only for her, or hear the calm gravel of his voice. Never would her days be filled with him, drinking espresso, and talking about a future together, even if it had always been complex ground to cover. At least back then it had been a possibility, but time had not done the work she'd hoped it would. On the contrary, time had given up on them.

She leaned her head against the window of the taxi, clutching the diamond pendant at the base of her throat that Andre had given her for Christmas, the only thing she had left of him. The driver accepted defeat early on when his attempts at conversation were met with stark silence, and he fell blessedly quiet.

Belle closed her eyes, sore and swollen from tears and exhaustion, her stomach hollow but unable to bear food. Her mind failed to sequence cohesive thoughts. The last few days had been a terrifying rollercoaster, and she had felt every frightening loop and turn.

Back at the hotel, she found Riley on the sofa, transfixed by the television. The BBC news was on with its rolling coverage of the attacks.

'They found the gunmen from your café,' she said, as Belle closed the door behind her and set her bag down on the table. Riley looked wired. Her eyes were wide, as though she'd drunk several cups of strong coffee in succession, and her hands had the unmistakable tremble of post-traumatic shock.

Belle sat beside her on the sofa. 'Have you eaten something today?'

Riley shook her head, her eyes locked on the broadcast.

'You need to eat. I probably do too.'

'I'm not hungry.'

Belle's gaze fell upon Ben's luggage, where it remained untouched in the corner of the room. She still hadn't moved it, the handle bearing faint red marks from the blood on her hands as she'd tugged it back to the hotel the night before. The memory of it washed over her and she quickly averted her gaze.

'They raided an apartment in Brussels,' Riley said, referring to the news. 'They found weapons and parts to make bombs. They also found the gunmen from the Papilles inside. They took them into custody.' She gnawed on a fingernail, the skin around it raw. 'The bomber escaped. He's on the run in Belgium and they can't find him. They'll never find him. He's melted into the population.'

'They'll find him,' Belle said, with more conviction than she felt, trying not to think of Albane's words. *They'll go to ground quickly, like cockroaches.*

'He'll hide, bide his time, then attack some other place,' Riley said, fortifying her thoughts. 'I've been watching the news reports, how they flee to the mountains, back to their terror cells, to plan the next attack. All the while we're just living out our lives, then boom, they attack out of nowhere. How are we supposed to function, not knowing where or when we're going to get hit? Like Avery. Like Ben!' Her voice rose shrilly, her eyes wide.

Belle reached for the remote and turned the television off. 'Enough of the news for now. Have you spoken to your father?'

She sniffed and blinked, as though the trance were lifting and in its place was infinite sadness. 'Yes. I called him from the room phone while you were out.'

'And Leo?' she coaxed gently.

Riley shook her head.

'He must know by now what's happened. He's probably going out of his mind with worry.'

'I don't have my phone anymore,' she said, as if that were the preventing reason. 'I lost it last night.'

'You could use mine,' Belle countered. 'Or the room phone.'

She sighed deeply. 'The best thing for Leo to do is forget about us and move on with his life.'

'You don't have to do this alone.'

Riley smiled sorrowfully. 'I'm always alone, Belle. I was a fool to think it could be any different.'

Belle reached for her friend's hand, and they sat in silence, surrounded by the echoes of a horror they never thought they'd see in their lifetime. 'Come on, we need to get out of this room.' She climbed to her feet. 'We could do with some air. And maybe a new phone.'

BEN'S PARENTS, Robert and Penelope Turner, arrived in Paris the next morning, accompanied by Ben's older brother Matthew and his wife Claire. Through Grace, they'd arranged to collect Belle from her hotel for the ride to Hôpital Saint-Louis.

Belle opened her door to four faces of immeasurable grief. Ben's father looked unbearably worn but it was Ben's mother's expression of utter devastation that would haunt her forever, the eyes that told of a trauma so great that one day it might break her.

They rode in silence to the address that Albane had provided, twenty minutes across the city. Penelope sat in the back of the taxi with Belle, Richard in the front, and Matthew and Claire took a separate taxi. Penelope held firmly to Belle's hand and there was no judgement or accusation in her eyes, the silence interspersed only when Penelope said things like, 'He never stopped loving you' or 'Olivia was a mistake' as she stared vacantly out the window.

At the hospital, they were led down to the morgue by an

attendant. Belle sat in a stiff, plastic chair in a sterile waiting room as Ben's family took the steps no parent should have to take, into a private room to identify him.

The sharp smell of disinfectant stung her nostrils. She tried to concentrate on something other than the thought of Ben's lifeless body on the stainless-steel tray, ice-cold from the chamber, lips blue and skin grey. When she heard Penelope howl in incomprehensible grief through the thick walls of the morgue, she stared down at the worn linoleum floor and tried to absent herself from the nightmare.

After the viewing, Penelope and Claire departed for their hotel to lie down, and Robert and Matthew accompanied Belle to her room to collect Ben's luggage. With trembling hands, she passed the suitcase to Robert, his eyes spilling over and his shoulders quaking as he took the handle and rubbed his thumb over it, pain contorting his features. He looked so like Ben that Belle's heart almost folded in on itself.

After they left, she stared at the empty corner where the bag once stood, despair rising in her throat again, for everything that had happened, for the clock that couldn't be wound back, and for the guilt that sat on her shoulders like a wicked beast.

They were here for you.

Later that night, Belle and Riley accompanied the Turners to the Papilles Café for a memorial that had been organised by the Council of Paris. The air was warm, the breeze whispering reluctantly through the trees on Avenue George V. Belle wasn't sure she could return there so soon, to witness the place that had stamped horror into her mind, never to be erased, but she owed it to Ben's family to show them where he'd spoken his last words, where he'd taken his last breath. No matter how hard it was for her, they needed it more.

Memorials and tributes had been set up across the city. Flowers and candles lined the front of the Theatre du Palais-Royal and the Papilles Café. People gathered at the marketplace. Churches overflowed with the city's need to be embraced by its faith.

When they arrived, Belle was stunned by the vibrant sea of flowers that coloured the avenue. The heady scent of blooms tickled the air. Bouquets of flowers extended from the café all the way up the avenue, for the murderous rampage had started long before the Papilles. People stood in silent vigil, holding candles. Some were singing softly, others holding loved ones close. The café was closed, and the police tape wrapped around the hedges of the alfresco told of the grave atrocity that had taken place there.

Belle tried not to look at the wretched hedge walls that had blocked them in, at the precise spot the gunman had stood while he'd peppered them with his fury and hate. Instead, she concentrated on placing her bouquet on count-less others, to ensure that the folded note with her words of goodbye to Ben were tucked away securely in the petals.

Standing between Penelope and Riley, with a sea of people around them, she felt the moment Penelope's brave façade cracked for the millionth time. She reached for her hand, closing her fingers around it, as the mournful tune of 'Ava Maria' rang out somewhere on a distant balcony and the whispers of the grieving clung to the air.

THIRTY-THREE

Belle was nestled in a chair beside the hotel room window, staring out. She'd been sitting by that window for most of the morning, a mug of tea in her lap, her hands folded around it. Beyond the glass, thick clouds gathered in the sky as though the weather had finally caught up with the tragedies of the past week. Somewhere in the city, church bells tolled, signalling eleven o'clock.

It had been five days since that fateful night when hatred had spilt onto the streets of Paris, when lives had been lost, a country left bereft and confused, asking questions that might never be answered, because who knew what motivated such hatred? She'd turned this question over and over in her head until it ached. She would never pretend to understand why people did the things they did, whether it was an eye for an eye or just plain evil. Maybe only the likes of God would ever know why the world turned on itself.

Avery's remains had been found, but there was little left. The explosion had been so great she'd had to be identified through dental records. Her parents had left Paris two days before, their entire world torn apart. Ben's family had left too, their son's body making its journey home to Australia, where he would be laid to rest.

Uncle Benito had sent Belle a message the previous week to let her know Andre had woken from his coma. He was still in hospital recovering from his injuries and asking for her. But the message had been mere courtesy, absent of an invitation to visit the hospital again, so she'd respectively kept her distance. When he was well enough, Uncle Benito and Mary would take him home to Rome.

Riley shifted on the sofa; her long legs tucked beneath her. 'We should probably decide what we're going to do next.' She spoke softly, as though careful not to disrupt the delicate equilibrium in the room.

Belle turned away from the window to face her. 'Yes. Are you still planning to go to Perth?'

Riley nodded. 'I'll fly to Sydney first to keep you company, then on to Perth.'

Belle placed her mug of tea on the windowsill and drew her knees to her chest. 'I was thinking I'd like to go to Vancouver. Avery's funeral is next week. I want to say goodbye.'

Riley smiled softly. 'I'd like that too.'

'Then home to Sydney for Ben's.' The words caught in her throat.

'I'll arrange the flights.'

Belle wrapped her arms around her knees, leaning her head against the window. 'Will I ever be able to close my eyes and not see that café?'

Riley shook her head sadly. 'I don't know.'

'We haven't slept all week.'

'We may never sleep again.'

Belle picked up her tea, closed her hands around it and stared out the window.

———————

SEVERAL DAYS LATER, they boarded their flight, bound for Vancouver. Passengers shuffled idly up the aisle, locating seats, and pushing luggage into overhead compartments.

Belle fastened her seatbelt and rested her head back against the seat. Since the attack, she'd felt as if she'd been taking tiny gulps of air without ever satisfying her lungs. Her heart rate sped up of its own accord and she'd been locked in a battle with tormented sleep. There was never rest, never comfort, only nightmares and perpetual exhaustion.

Her gaze slid across to Riley, who looked equally as wretched, her friend staring out the window at planes parked at terminals, the first spots of rain dripping down the glass.

Belle's phone rang in her jacket pocket, and she retrieved it, an unknown number on the screen. 'Hello?'

The voice on the other end was both startling and familiar, a voice she knew like her own. 'Belle?'

'Andre.'

A flight attendant hurried by with a disapproving purse of her lips. 'Network devices on flight mode, please. We're preparing for take-off,' she said, before marching down the aisle to take care of other pre-flight business.

Belle sank lower into her seat, dropping her voice to a whisper. 'Andre, are you okay?'

'I've been better. How are you?'

Where did she start? There was so much to tell him and

yet, with the plane about to leave, so little time. How did she explain about Ben and the Papilles, about her heartbreak for Avery, or how much she loved him and had wanted to stay by his bedside? All she could offer was an unconvincing, 'I'm okay.'

'I woke last week, and I've been asking for you. My father told me you visited the hospital.'

'I did.'

'And you never came back?' He sounded hurt.

Belle swallowed past a lump of regret in her throat. She willed herself not to cry in front of the other passengers. 'I don't think... I mean... us. It can't work.'

There was a long pause, then, 'Why would you say that?'

'Your father was clear about it. You should be with Mary.' Her words held little conviction, but she forced them out anyway.

'I don't want Mary,' he said. 'Come back to the hospital, please.'

'I can't. I'm on a plane. We're about to take off.'

'You're leaving Paris?'

'We're going to Vancouver to say goodbye to Avery.'

'And you weren't going to say goodbye to me?'

'I did,' she said, her voice quivering. *I held your hand and cried tears onto your bed and told you that I loved you. Then I walked out of your room, and it ripped my heart out.* She forced strength into her voice. 'Will you be at Avery's funeral?'

'No,' he replied soberly. 'I want to be, but I won't be discharged from here in time.'

She'd hoped he would be there, that the universe would relent and throw them into each other's paths again. 'I'm sorry I won't see you.'

'Don't leave,' he said urgently. 'Stay. Come back to me.'

She shook her head. 'I can't.'

'I know I didn't make things easy for us. I will always regret the decisions I made where I didn't put us first. I was stupid, so stupid, Belle. I thought I had time to do right by everyone.'

Yet here they were, and their time was up. Distance and clashes of culture and obligations had become too insurmountable to overcome.

'I don't want it to end like this,' he said, desperation in his voice. 'What can I do? Tell me what to do.'

'Don't you think if there was something that could be done, I'd have done it?'

'Then I'll come to you.'

She pressed the phone closer against her ear. 'What are you saying?'

'That I don't care what people expect of us.'

'Andre, your father—'

'I won't lose you again,' he said. 'Once I've healed, once I'm out of this damn bed, I'm coming straight to Sydney.'

Her heart stopped. 'Sydney? But what about the trattoria? You can't leave for that long.'

'I can and I will. If you'll have me.'

Belle stared out the window, the Parisian sun briefly illuminating a dark and brooding sky. She understood what he was saying. He wanted her to take a leap of faith with him, to be fearless, to dive in headfirst because who knew what the next day would bring? Ben and Avery were gone; they thought they'd had time, time for love and experiences and to enjoy the fruits of a life well-lived. In the blink of an eye, their chance had been extinguished.

The old proverb *life's too short* sounded in her head. She and Andre had wasted so much time already, trying to keep everyone happy. And she had cheated death—they both had, so was it fair to ask that they be cheated of love too? It would mean defying Uncle Benito's wishes, a man she greatly respected, which she was loathed to do.

What she did know was that she couldn't live without Andre. That days and nights without him hurt too deeply to fathom. And perhaps, once she cleared all the noise, it was as simple as that. *I can't live without you.*

'Belle?' Andre's voice pushed through her debate. 'What do you say?'

She smiled through her tears as the plane pulled away from the terminal and rolled out onto the runway. 'I'll see you in Sydney.'

ACKNOWLEDGMENTS

When I first began my writing career, I produced a little-known debut called *Interwoven*, book one in the Belle series. The story was a culmination of all the writing knowledge I'd acquired at the time, which was only minimal. There were several stops and starts, with plenty of learning along the way, and after a year, I reached the finish line and published it.

I went on to write two more books in the Belle series, which I'm extremely proud of, for they signify a journey that was full of first steps and courage. I've since written several other stories too, dappling in historical fiction, which I have a deep fondness for.

To some degree, I've learnt now how to craft a tale. I've learnt how to build it from a few threads of an idea into something polished and (hopefully) worth reading, so I felt it was only fitting that Belle, the character who had held my hand during that first terrifying year of writing and publishing *Interwoven*, should get a polish too. Several years later, we have *The Summer of Everything*, a rewritten, rebranded version of *Interwoven*.

Of course, none of this would ever have been possible without the support of my most favourite people in the world. Brett, Eve, and Connor, you make this journey possible. Thank you for all the love and patience, for the cooking and the cookies and for not being too disappointed when I have to stay in and write.

It's hard to know who to thank next when there are so many who help to make it all happen. As always, Jo Libreri, Liz Butler, Natasha Booth, Bianca Nash, and Erika Slaby, like the four seasons, you are a constant in my life, always supporting, always unwavering. Thank you for being *you* and for putting up with me.

Thank you to my parents and in-laws, Carmen Montebello, Joe and Michelle Montebello, Rhonda and Joanie Flynn, Roger Campbell, and Paula Jeff. I love talking books with you. It's a miracle you aren't bored by me yet!

My deepest gratitude to my editors, Lynne Stringer and Marcia Batton, who take my novels from their early drafts and mould them into something publishable. I've worked with you both a long time now and you are not only an integral part of my writing, but dear friends.

To my cover designer, Kris Dallas, people are drawn to my books first and foremost because of your stunning covers. Thank you for all the designs and for the long hours spent poring over ideas.

Love to my wonder gal, Tanya Nellestein, early-reader, and long-luncher. You are a superstar! Thanks for lending your ear and just being generally awesome. And to Helen Sibbritt, Craig and Phil from HappyValley BooksRead, and the broader literary community, you are always on the sidelines cheering writers on. Your enthusiasm knows no bounds. Thanks for the love and support.

Last but by no means least, to my readers, you make every day bright with your kind words and encouragement. Thank you for reading *The Summer of Everything*, especially if you have already read *Interwoven*. I couldn't ask for more enthusiastic and loyal readers. You are everything about this journey and more. Thank you.

ALSO BY MICHELLE MONTEBELLO

www.michellemontebello.com.au

Seasons of Belle

The Summer of Everything

To Autumn, With Love

The Colour of Winter

The Spring Farewell

———

The Quarantine Station

The Lost Letters of Playfair Street

The Forever Place

Beautiful, Fragile

To Autumn, With Love

MICHELLE MONTEBELLO

TO AUTUMN, WITH LOVE

SEASONS OF BELLE: BOOK 2

A year on from Paris and Belle Hamilton is still searching for solace after everyone she's lost.

When her father falls gravely ill, an astonishing truth is revealed, causing her to question all that she knew about herself.

Searching for answers, she travels to Scotland with her friend, Riley, and her partner, Andre, determined to discover her lost past.

Amidst the raw beauty of the Highlands and the stunning Scottish coastlines, Belle pursues a man that holds the key to everything. But finding him is not easy as he eludes her, leaving a trail of questions behind.

Will Scotland reveal what Belle desperately seeks, or has the past been lost forever to the seasons?

ABOUT THE AUTHOR

Michelle Montebello is a writer from Sydney, Australia where she lives with her family. She is the internationally bestselling author of *The Quarantine Station*, *The Forever Place* and *The Lost Letters of Playfair Street*.

Her books have won several awards. *The Quarantine Station* was a finalist in the 2021 International Book Awards for Best Historical Fiction. *The Lost Letters of Playfair Street* won the 2020 ARRA Awards for Favourite Contemporary Romance and Favourite Australian-Set Romance.

Michelle has twice been shortlisted for ARRA Australian Author of the Year.

If you would like to subscribe to her newsletter, visit www.michellemontebello.com.au.